A TALENT FOR KILLING

Also by Ralph Dennis

The War Heist

The Hardman Series

Atlanta Deathwatch
The Charleston Knife is Back in Town
The Golden Girl And All
Pimp For The Dead
Down Among The Jocks
Murder Is Not An Odd Job
Working For The Man
The Deadly Cotton Heart
The One Dollar Rip-Off
Hump's First Case
The Last Of The Armageddon Wars
The Buy Back Blues

A TALENT FOR KILLING

RALPH DENNIS

BRASH BOOKS

ISBN: 1-7324226-3-X
ISBN-13: 978-1-7324226-3-6

Published by
Brash Books, LLC
12120 State Line #253
Leawood, Kansas 66209
www.brash-books.com

PUBLISHER'S NOTE

A *Talent for Killing* combines and interweaves two Ralph Dennis manuscripts — the novel *Deadman's Game,* which was published in paperback in 1976, and *Kane #2,* the unpublished, long-lost sequel. Both manuscripts were significantly revised to create this new, standalone novel.

CHAPTER ONE

Kane waited. Waiting was a part of a hardfist job. The light was dim, his eyes were watering from the cold, and he knew that he might have to identify Pepper Franklin by the square shape of his shoulders and his swagger-walk when he came.

If he came.

It was almost three A.M. and Kane was in his sheltered position, coat collar up, hands flexing in his pockets, bending his knees now and then so they wouldn't lock up on him. He was so deep in the shadow cast by the porch of the old mansion that he was part of the darkness.

At exactly midnight, he'd watched the light go out in the front, bedroom window. That meant Pepper Franklin's wife Esther had given up the waiting and gone to bed. A few minutes later, at a distance in the windy silence, Kane heard the back door close. The cook and the chauffeur — man and wife — scurried down the back steps and did their middle-aged sprint for the servants' cottage a hundred yards behind the mansion house. It was a routine Kane had noted over the last three nights.

Pepper Franklin was the unpredictable factor. He wouldn't return until the last drink was out of the bottle and the last bounce out of the bed. It was his way.

The spot where Kane stood now, near the high, white columns and the slave-made bricks, had once been the exact center of the old Mack Foster estate. Back in the 1920s and 1930s, the Foster mansion and the lands around it had been the showplace of Aiken and the whole South. The Foster Cup had been run the second Sunday of each May on the track near the southeast boundary line. There were polo matches in the field in the center of the track. And in the fall, wealthy men from all over the world hunted dove in Mack Foster's private preserve while they murmured about wheat and steel and copper.

But Mack Foster was long dead and his only son, Virgil, had died with a bottle clamped between his knees on a highway outside of Charlotte. Esther, the old man's daughter, was the last of the family and there wasn't much of her father in her. Only the hungers and the appetites. She liked young men and she liked to marry them and that and her other follies had brought the estate down to 200 acres and the last fifteen million dollars.

Esther was a vain woman in her late forties, pale and slender, her hair the color of soot. Her clothes were too young and her makeup was suited for a girl in her twenties. She was a woman who would not let herself grow old. She fought the clock and the years from the time she got up in the morning until she went to bed at night. If she was careful, Kane thought, there would be time enough and money enough for two or three more husbands.

This time, there would be no large financial settlement for Pepper Franklin. No half a million tax-paid gift. This time she would be free and clear.

A car came. When the headlights swept across the porch, Kane didn't move. He was so much a part of the shadow that the lights didn't touch him. But he closed his eyes and held them that way until he felt the headlights' brightness and heat fade. Seconds later, eyes open now, Kane watched Pepper Franklin slam the door to the blue Continental and stagger toward the porch steps.

Franklin was a big man, six-five or so and nearly two-hundred and forty pounds. Even drunk, he carried himself with the swagger of the athlete he'd been a few years back. He'd been a forward on a couple of good North Carolina teams back in the mid-sixties and he'd gone on to play pro ball before he'd met and married Emily. He'd been a man with a kind of heavy grace, a soft touch from fifteen feet in, and stone elbows when the rebounding began.

Now he was thirty and drunk and bed-tired and there was a beginning sag to his stomach and a puffiness arounds his jowls. He played tennis and handball and spent hours in the steam bath but the mark was on him. Not even the club sunlamp could cover it.

At the foot of the brick steps, level with Kane, he stopped and fumbled in his pocket for his keys. He'd separated the keys from the thick wad of bills when Kane stepped out of the center of the shadow.

"Hold still," Kane said.

"What?" Franklin blinked at Kane. "A mugging? I'm being mugged right on my front steps?" He laughed and held out the wad of money toward Kane. "Take it. Leave me alone."

Kane took the money. He held it in his left hand without looking at it.

"May Lovell," he said.

"What? What did you say?" Franklin's eyes narrowed and for a brief moment, he almost seemed sober.

"May Lovell," Kane said again.

"Yeah? What about her?"

Kane shot him twice in the chest.

The Woodsman Sport .22 made its noise but it might have been limbs breaking off in the high wind. It might have been car doors slamming in the distance.

Franklin fell back across the brick steps. Kane leaned over him and held the Woodsman Sport about a foot away from him and shot him four more times. All four struck him in the face. Two slugs hit bone and remained in the skull. The other two passed through soft tissue and splattered against the bricks.

By sunrise Kane had left Aiken behind him. Driving well below the speed limit, he crossed the line into Georgia and headed for Atlanta.

CHAPTER TWO

Jackson Carter. Certified Public Accountant, that was in raised brass lettering on the door, and there was a fulltime secretary, a Miss Sarah Timmers, who sat behind an almost empty desk in the reception room and answered the phone. In the two years she'd worked for Carter, she'd done no billing and she'd written no letters. The late model IBM Selectric on the typewriter wing of the desk had not had its ribbon changed since its purchase from the Peachtree Business Company. What Miss Timmers did not know was that she'd been hired on the basis of the single call when she'd phoned for an interview. Her interview. Her voice had a flat, unpleasant, nasal quality. Carter, hearing it for the first time, drew a child's version of a five-pointed star beside her name.

Sarah Timmers had one real duty. She answered the phone. If the caller asked for an appointment so that he could discuss with Mr. Carter some tax work or consultation over his company's books, her answer was always the same: "Mr. Carter is not taking any new accounts this year." The caller, without being able to place it exactly, would always turn away from his phone with the definite sense that he'd been insulted.

The reception room where Miss Timmers spent her lonely mornings and afternoons might have been created by a film designer on instructions from a producer: "No ostentation, a feeling of bedrock honesty and reliability." The walls were cream colored with a slightly darker molding. The carpet was dark green and the desk heavy and traditional. And finally, there was Miss Timmers: plump and appetizing as a wax grape.

4

Jackson Carter's office was quite different. There was a large window spread across the rear of the office so that during the day, when the drapes were open, no artificial light was needed. Light poured across the desk and illuminated a huge painting on the wall facing the desk. It was an abstract, about four feet by four feet, a massive brawl of a painting in which the muddy reds and blacks struggled with the slant of the sun.

The desk was oak, shaped like a diseased kidney. It had a dull natural finish without a gleam to it. Like props on a stage set, there were usually a few file folders on the blotter. From time -to-time, those folders were dusted and moved about. Along one whole wall, to Jackson's left when he sat behind his desk, was a floor-to-ceiling bookcase filled to capacity with a collection of books on business, on Federal and state tax laws, and accounting procedures.

To his right, there was an antique cabinet. The top three shelves were lined with decanters of whiskey, brandy and gin. The bottom shelf was shared by an ice bucket and a set of Swedish crystal.

There was a door beside the cabinet. The door led into a bathroom and it was never left open. Near this door, on the desk side of the doorway, a mirror with a discolored pewter frame was embedded in the wall. The mirror seemed a bit out of place. Occasionally, Carter paused before the mirror to brush his thin hair back or straighten his tie. To any guest in the office when he did this, it seemed to hint at some secret vanity in him.

It was eight thirty at night. The drape covered the window. The painting was only a blob and a shadow. A wreath of indirect light defined Carter and the woman who sat across the desk from him. She was an attractive woman, a woman just past forty. The mink coat she wore into the office had been thrown carelessly over the back of the chair, which matched the one she sat in. Her dress was black wool, with long sleeves and a hemline that barely reached her knees. They were plump knees and Carter stared at them with a bland, undisguised interest. Her face, while sagging a bit, still had some good years left, her ash blonde hair had each strand in place, and her makeup was the proper blend of taste and recent fashion.

Jackson Carter was forty-three, a game rooster of a little man with more than a touch of the dandy in him. He was five-six in his tailored lift shoes and his suits were made for him, six a year, from the patterns kept in the J. Press shop in New Haven. His face was lined and grooved and his eyes bulged, as if the top lids were deformed or the result of some comic operation. His face was as composed as that of an undertaker.

"I think," Carter said, "that you will find this of some interest." He leaned forward and placed the folded newspaper on the front edge of the desk. The paper was the Blue Streak edition of the *Atlanta Journal,* opened to page 6A.

The woman hesitated for a count of four to five, vanity struggling with the truth of age. In the end, she opened her purse and brought out a pair of gold-rimmed reading glasses.

Kane watched them through the two-way mirror. The room where he sat, beyond the pewter framed mirror, was little more than an enlarged closet. The molded plastic chair was comfortable enough and the air flow from the ventilator kept him warm in the winter and cool enough in the muggy Atlanta summers. A brass ashtray and a plastic glass of water were on the low shelf in front of him. A cigarette burned in the ashtray notch, forgotten by him, as he watched Jackson Carter and the woman begin the terminal interview.

From the sparse details in the newspaper article, it was obvious that the news had reached the paper too late for much to be made of the killing.

Robbery-Murder Of Aiken Sportsman

The woman read the two-paragraph news story once and, without looking up from the paper, read it a second time. When she lowered the newspaper and placed it on the desk, she said, "I don't know how I'm supposed to feel."

"Relieved, perhaps, Mrs. Lovell. Or satisfied."

"I suppose I am." She'd forgotten to remove her glasses and now she blinked behind them. And then, in a small voice, she added. "It was justice, wasn't it?"

"For me, there is no doubt at all," Carter said. He unlocked the center desk drawer and lifted out a file folder. He placed the file on top of me newspaper. "This is the full report. It is fully documented. You may read it here in this office or not at all. As soon as you have read it, it will be burned."

"I understand." She picked up the folder and held it in both hands. "I would like to meet Mr. Kane and thank him."

"That isn't possible." Carter pushed back his chair and stood up. "Mr. Kane is out of town."

"I'm sorry."

Jackson Carter rounded the desk and stopped beside her. His eyes rubbed across her knees while he said, "At any rate, I believe you can understand why that would not be good business."

She opened the file and began to read the first page.

"I'll be in the outer office," Carter said, "if you have any questions." He stopped, half turned away. "And, of course, there is the matter of the final half of the payment."

Kane stubbed out the cigarette when the smoke began to irritate his eyes. That done, he leaned forward and watched Mrs. Lovell read the report he'd written, night by night, over the last two weeks. There were no gaps and no blanks in his investigation.

Mrs. Lovell was reading the deposition of the abortionist when Kane stood up and walked to the door. Hand on the knob, he pivoted and looked at her once more. He burned the image of her into the secret places of his inner eye. She was crying now, hardly aware that she was, as she read the old doctor's admission of the bungling he'd committed on the body of seventeen-year-old May Lovell. How May Lovell had died on the table in his office that night because Pepper Franklin would not let him, when the massive bleeding began, take the girl to the hospital. How he and Pepper Franklin had taken the dead girl, nude and without identification, from the office and left her on a trash dump.

Kane left his little room before she finished reading the report and went down a flight of stairs to the parking lot.

At a bar far out Peachtree Road, Kane ordered Bisquit and a cup of black coffee. While he sipped the cognac and followed it with gulps of coffee, a young girl down the bar watched him.

She wasn't a hooker, just a girl who hadn't found herself that right man since she moved to Atlanta from Charlotte a year ago. What she saw was an athletic-looking man in his mid-thirties. A man in an expensive, hard-finish gray tweed jacket and dark slacks. Black hair worn shorter than most of the young men she knew wore theirs. Slate-gray eyes and a thin mouth that she knew, with a brush of chill, had the promise of some kind of cruelty behind it. And though the man interested her, though she knew how empty her bed was, she decided against smiling at him. She left most of a drink and walked out, heading for another bar down the road, a place where all the young men were liars and talked over their heads about this deal and that one and told dirty jokes that she didn't think were that funny. And usually, even before the first hour had passed, they made their play. It was the bitterness of reality: long-term things like love would have to wait.

Kane saw the girl. He read the strong interest in her face and he felt the stirring in himself. Still there after she passed, the soft traces of perfume circled him long after the door closed behind her.

He told himself that it didn't matter. But the honest part of himself knew that it did. Sourness and ashes were in him. And he knew that somehow she'd read that part of him. He tossed back the last of the Bisquit and shook his head at the bartender as he moved toward him.

He left the bar and drove home. A sadness in him like a single flute note.

It would be a few days before he'd be ready for people.

CHAPTER THREE

The room was dark. On one wall, the hands of a lighted clock placed the time at five after ten. It could have been morning or night. There were no windows in the room, no way for the light or the darkness to give their clues.

When the buzzer sounded, the man with his head down on the desk stretched out his right hand and pressed two buttons on the metal strip that ran down the right side of the desk.

"Yes?"

By the time he spoke, the band of lights above him had lost their flutter and he'd pushed himself upright. His name was Whistler. He was a blocky man in his early fifties. His hair was light brown, tending toward red. It was thinning and in time he'd have to consider a hairpiece. He was five-ten. Not a tall man by many standards but tall enough so that he didn't have to struggle against the small man's pride and acrid temper.

"It's Burden, sir."

"Come on in," Whistler said.

The last button on the strip was larger than the others, about the size of a quarter. Whistler pressed that button and held it down until the door opened and Fred Burden entered.

Even in his Brooks Brothers suit, Burden carried himself in a way that told anyone who was interested that he'd been a paratrooper before he'd been recruited by the Agency. He walked as if he still wore the heavy jump boots and there was a hint of a swagger in the way he moved his shoulders.

Whistler made a mental note to himself. Burden had been with the Agency for a full two years. That was enough time to lose all the military trappings. Unless Burden dramatized himself. Unless Burden was hopeless. The mental note he made: some kind of walking lessons for Burden. If such lessons existed. If not, they'd have to be created.

Burden stood with his back to the desk until he was certain that the door had closed and the lock was set. When he turned to face the desk, Whistler saw that he carried a thin folder in one hand. The way he carried it, it might have been a swagger stick.

Whistler cleared his throat. "What's it about?"

Burden placed the folder on the desk. "It's Cain."

"What about him?"

"He's killed again."

"Where?"

"Aiken, South Carolina," Burden said.

Whistler inserted a finger in the folder and flipped it open. There was a single sheet of paper in the file. Exactly centered on the paper, held there by Scotch tape, was a clipping from a newspaper.

Athlete-Sportsman Victim of Robbery & Murder

Whistler read the first paragraph and closed the folder. He placed a relaxed hand on top of it. "How do you know it was Cain?"

"The small caliber weapon. The way it was handled."

"The weapon?"

"Police think it was a .22." Burden shrugged. "Of course, you know what happens to a .22 when it hits bone? It splatters, fragments."

"Any other reason to believe it was Cain?"

"After I clipped this, I made a call to Atlanta."

"To the Blue Mole?" Whistler said.

"The Mole confirmed."

Whistler leaned back, settling into his chair. "It wasn't political, was it?"

"Domestic," Burden said. "A revenge contract."

Burden looked at Whistler and remembered the talk he'd heard around the Shop. Whistler was a widower now and he had a young daughter, Peggy, in her second year at Smith. The word was that he loved that daughter very much and he spent at least one weekend a month with her, no matter what kind of hell was breaking out all over the world, no matter how much the Agency needed him.

"A young girl killed by a crude abortion," Burden said. "Her mother took out the contract. Not sure why they didn't use one of the hospitals that do safe abortions, unless the man was afraid the mother might find out about it. At any rate, Cain traced the man responsible. A young man married to an older woman with money." Burden's eyes were level with Whistler's. "It was the kind of contract you or I might have carried out. Without pay."

"How many is that now?"

"Five this year," Burden said. "He seems to select the jobs with some degree of care, only the ones that interest him for some reason."

"Any mistakes?"

"Sir, Cain doesn't make mistakes." And though he tried to fight the urge, there was a chance to flatter a superior and his junior officer's sensibilities overcame him. "You trained Cain, didn't you sir?"

"And recruited him as well," Whistler said.

"A natural, huh?"

"Read his file," Whistler said.

"I was told not to, sir."

"That was last month."

"Yes, sir." Before Burden backed away from the desk there was almost a hint of a heel click and a jerk of his shoulders as if he'd fought back a reflex that would have led to a salute. Whistler touched the large button and watched Burden march out. Damn that walk anyway. Even a four-year-old child knew what it meant. It would have to be corrected before Burden went into the field again.

After the door closed and locked, Whistler looked down at the file. He yawned and rubbed sleep from his eyes.

Cain. That had been so long ago, so very long ago. That time, the growing friendship. In Cain he'd thought he'd found the son that Martha had never given him. And he remembered watching Cain with Peggy then, when Peggy had been all bony arms and legs, when Cain had been a mirror for the frightened teen-aged girl, when he'd shown her the beautiful things he saw in her. Helping her through the bad times until the woman in her appeared. And at times he'd believed that Cain might move from being the son he never had to the son-in-law he could love and respect.

A good man on a hunt. Lightness and grace on the surface and under all that the strength and the courage of a man who didn't have to prove his balls every day.

Wasted now. Lost now.

If he'd been a softer man, a man who couldn't accept the cards as they came to him, Whistler might have broken down the middle.

Wasted now. Lost now. And in his mind Whistler turned the cards and dropped them in the center of the table.

CHAPTER FOUR

I t wasn't gradual. Nothing like that. One second Kane was deep under, snoring slightly, and the next second he was alert, head clear, a flywheel spinning quietly but not engaged. Not a rigid muscle showed. Not a quiver revealed that he was anything more than he seemed. A man in a deep sleep.

Head down in the pillow. He remained that way until all his senses told him that he was alone in the bedroom. Only then did he turn and stare out of the window. The gray winter light back-lighted a grim still life beyond the open curtains. Tall pines in the distance and closer up a pecan tree that threw its stunted fruit on his roof during the fall. The high winds harvested the pecans and some nights the rattle against his roof awoke him. And he'd listen, knowing what the sound was, but trying to identify the noise in some half-remembered, elusive dream.

Alert again. He could feel movement. It was somewhere in another part of the house. He rolled to the side of the bed and swung his legs over the edge. His feet hit the floor without a sound. His thigh-length robe was over the back of a chair. He slipped it on with one smooth turn of his body. Belting it, he leaned across the bed. He bypassed the rumpled pillow and shoved his hand under the unused one. His hand came out with his fingers curled around the butt of a Woodsman Sport, a twin to the one he'd used in Aiken some thirty-odd hours before.

At the bedroom door, he hesitated just long enough to be sure there was a shell in the chamber and that the safety was off. That done, he opened the bedroom door a foot or so and stepped sideways through that space and into the living room. The Woodsman Sport was up and swinging for a target. His eyes read the details of the room. Halfway through the sweep the Sport dropped to his side. There in the center of the carpet was the vacuum cleaner canister, the top open, ready for a new dust bag. Kane whirled, the safety clicking on, and leaned back into the bedroom. He tossed the Sport onto the bed and pulled the door closed.

"Reba?" The tension peeled away like a damp shirt. "Is that you, Reba?"

"It's Wednesday, ain't it?"

A black woman appeared in the narrow doorway that led to the dining room. She was a huge woman, in her fifties now though there wasn't a gray hair showing on her head. He weight might have been on the heavy side of a hundred and eighty but there was the spring and energy in her walk of a woman half her age and weight.

"I forgot," Kane said.

"Don't remember much, do you, Mr. Callan?" Nearing the vacuum canister, her hands working to open the plastic bag, she turned her face and looked at him. Strong disapproval traced across her face. "Mr. Callan, I might not be much more than a poor widow and some people might backbite me about some of my morals, but that ain't no reason for you to stand there in front of me almost buck naked."

Kane grinned at her and reached behind him to locate the doorknob and twist it. He backed into the bedroom. Even before he closed the door behind him, he heard the full, rich dark laughter. It was a put-on. She'd won another round.

And he laughed with her, back at her, as he scooped up the Sport and locked it away in the night table drawer beside the bed.

At eleven, Fred Burden left his office and marched down the long hallway to RECORDS. He'd had only about five hours sleep the night before and he could feel the grit under his eyelids. It was like that after a duty night.

Bull Racklin sat behind a green metal desk beyond the check-out counter, ramrod stiff, always on parade. A short, thin whippet of a man. Tough and deadly, according to the word around the Shop. A kind of legend from his days in the field before he'd been shifted to desk work. About fifty now but he looked forty or forty-five. Once, on a dull day, Burden had read his file. Bull had used that blue Dan Wesson .357 he wore in the scarred holster, butt forward, on his left side.

"The Kane file," Burden said.

"Is that K-a-n-e or C-a-i-n?"

"Both or either," Burden said.

Racklin nodded and stood up. He moved out of sight down the corridor that ran between the high file cabinets. He was gone a minute and a half by the clock at the end of the counter. When he returned he stopped behind his desk. "This one is red flagged, Mr. Burden."

"Call Whistler."

Bull lifted the phone and placed it squarely on top of the file folder. He dialed a three digit number. The conversation was short and to the point, without a wasted word. At the end, Racklin broke the circuit without saying either good-bye or thank you and brought the file to the counter. He was relaxed now and he placed the folder in front of Burden while he bent over and lifted a clipboard from beneath the counter. Racklin noted the file number, the date and the time out before he spun the clipboard toward Burden, who signed his name in a slow careful script. Unlike his check signature, it could be read.

Back at his office, with the chill of Bull Racklin pushed far away, Burden placed the file folder on the center of his desk blotter and lit a cigarette. Seated, with the curve of his back fitted into the frame of the captain's chair, he flipped the file open.

CODE NAME: Cain

BORN: Edward Forrest Starke. *PLACE OF BIRTH:* Richmond, Virginia. *DATE OF BIRTH:* 12/28/1939. *PARENTS:* Emily Cross Starke and Alvin Forrest Starke, both deceased. *EDUCATION:* 3 years U. Va., 1957–1960. Liberal arts. No membership in clubs or honorary societies. *MILITARY SERVICE:* None, exempt because of football knee injury, suffered in high school in 1956. (PAGE 2)

RECRUITED: subject first noticed by Whistler, 12/12/1961 at Pine Lodge, North Carolina. Subject worked in gun shop at Lodge. Hunted a number of times with Whistler. Whistler noted reflexes, instincts with firearms.

PREFERENCE TESTING: subject approached in New York bar 1/4/1962 by agent, code name Cullman. Cullman engaged subject in conversation about sports. After short, friendly talk Cullman made homosexual advance. Subject showed restraint. No anger or sign of agitation. Subject said, "That is your problem, not mine, but finish your drink before you leave." (TAPE FILE # T 345221) 1/11/62 subject approached in New York hotel lobby by agent, code name Rosemarie. Request for street directions led to conversation and dinner invitation from subject. Culminated in hours of lovemaking in agent's apartment. Rosemarie found subject virile and uncomplicated in sexual tastes. When offered anal intercourse showed no morbid interest. (FILM FILE # F 345221) Rosemarie noted that, if properly motivated, subject might be employed in entrapment of alien females. (PAGE 3)

INTERVIEW: subject believed his interview with Whistler was for possible position as arms salesman with WORLDARMCO.

EXTERNALS: subject at ease, relaxed and comfortable. Obviously has some affection for Whistler but at all times courteous and respectful.

RESULTS: in answer to question about his attitude toward covert activity, subject said if it was called for he would not hesitate to engage in it. In answer to question about defending himself if rival faction sought to block arms sales by force, subject said he knew no strangers whose lives he valued more than his own. That he would kill to protect himself.

INTERVIEWER'S APPRAISAL: Whistler believes, if the G series psychological testing reveals no prejudicial flaws, job offer to be made. Subject to be trained for covert work, specializing in cancellations. Suggests one year training term at Valley Farm.

(PAGE 4)

PSYCHOLOGICAL TESTING: G series. Subject showed major, though not debilitating, dysfunction. Has fatalistic sense of all life, including his own. Has a strong belief in self. Loves and hates at the far ends of the poles. Blacks and whites, no gray areas. PART 3d suggests that subject would kill with minimal remorse and psychological damage. PART 4d leads analysis-comp to conclude that subject may already have killed at least once, though nothing in background investigation confirms this.

CONCLUSION: blue chip prospect

(PAGE 4a)

ADDENDUM: further background check supports finding in G series, PART 4d. Subject, while freshman at U. Va., during Christmas vacation 12/21/1957, abused and threatened by two drunk on-leave paratroopers, subject killed Cpl. Thomas Brewster with single upward blow to nose which drove bone fragments into brain. Other paratrooper, Sgt. Alvin York Tarrs, left fight with broken ribs and severe concussion. Tarrs, contacted at present base assignment in Berlin, confirmed account. Admitted concocting story about attack by several sailors after argument in bar to cover death of Cpl. Brewster.

(HAND WRITTEN NOTE AT BOTTOM OF PAGE) No prejudice here. On the contrary. Subject is not being recruited to teach Sunday School or lead a scout troop. *Whistler*

(PAGE 5)

RECRUITED: subject offered job in Agency 4/6/62. Subject showed no surprise that Worldarmco had been cover for Agency interviews and testing. *ASSIGNED: to* Valley Farm, Maine. One year term.

CHAPTER FIVE

Under the shower, the whine of the vacuum cleaner buried under the water's roar, Kane counted his scars once again. Not that he really had them numbered. But his fingers, as he moved the soap and the cloth over his body, knew and found each of them. The scar high in his left shoulder. A gray pucker. A small point of entry in back, the larger flesh flower in front. On his right side, hip to above the second rib. A new one that hadn't faded yet. A scalded red look to it. That was from the terrorist bomb when he worked for A.I.D. in Saigon. The other scars too: a dot here and a bird track there, all from the flying bits of steel. Like leaf shadows all over his hips. And when the count was right, Kane ducked his head under the needle points of water and watched the soap run down his legs and out the drain.

He dressed in gray double knit slacks and a soft wool shirt. He crossed the living room and passed through the dining room. He found Reba standing over a skillet in the kitchen. On the table behind her there was a single place setting.

Kane stood in the doorway and smiled. "Reba, I don't pay you to cook my breakfast too."

"That's easy enough."

"What?"

"Pay me five dollars more a week and stop fussing."

He picked up the glass of juice from the table and sipped it as he leaned over her shoulder. Six eggs frying over easy in the skillet. On the counter next to the stove about half a pound of bacon crisped and draining on paper towels.

"Reba, I can't eat that much."

Laughing at him, turning her head so that he saw the two gold crowns off the top right of her mouth. "I thought you'd never ask me, Mr. Callan. Hard as I work for you I can always use myself a second breakfast and call it lunch."

"Of course you're invited," Kane said.

Kane got down another plate and placed a napkin and silverware beside it. By the time he'd poured her a glass of juice, she'd scooped three eggs into each plate and placed the bacon platter in the center of the table.

Sighing as she sat down across the table from him, Reba said, "Poor widow woman like me can't be sleeping all day and eating breakfast at eleven thirty in the morning."

Kane used his fork to divide the bacon into two almost equal portions.

"Mr. Bill from next door's been dropping by some. Acted like he was worried about you."

"It was a longer trip than I thought it would be," Kane said.

Her eyes levelled with his, intent. "Some of the time I don't believe you. All this talk about business."

"Huh?"

"I got this feeling some woman keeps drawing you out of town."

"Not me." He shook his head. "I don't know any women."

"And I'm a dark fox with the mange," Reba said.

Burden leaned back and rubbed his eyes. He lit another cigarette from the pack at his elbow without thinking about it. It tasted like three o'clock in the morning, or as he'd heard a paratrooper say once, somebody's dirty foot. He stubbed the smoke out and tossed the package into a drawer and slammed it shut.

Back to the file. He skimmed over pages six, seven and eight. He noted only the scoring and evaluation in armed and unarmed combat. High marks and an unusual degree of aggressiveness.

(PAGE 9)

DISPOSITION: subject ready for assignment and transferred to Agency under Whistler.

(PAGE 10)

CANCELLATION # 1

Bulgarian cultural attaché, Egor C. Had entrapped Mary Ellen J., Pentagon code clerk. Hardfist called for and agreed upon. Cain assigned. Locale: Rockville, Maryland.

8/4/1963. Egor C. with history of weekend chasing and drinking. Kill made with Woodsman Sport at close range in Bulls and Bears Tavern parking lot at midnight plus ten. Clean operation, no trash. Signs of tampering with locks and windows of Egor C.'s car led local police to believe Egor C. surprised thief in act.

Apology by State Dept. 8/5/63.

Articles and editorials, prepared week ahead of time, planted by Agency in local papers. Decried state of crime in Washington-Maryland area.

8/11/63. Our agent, Cedar, killed in hit and run in Sofia.

Burden buzzed for his secretary. He sent her down the hall to the wardroom for a cup of coffee. By the time she'd returned he'd skimmed pages eleven through nineteen. His fingernail drew a snail's track under a sentence in the account of CANCELLATION # 8. *Wound in left shoulder after successful Berlin Hardfist, clean wound, no complications.*

He allowed himself a bitter half-smile over the entry on page nineteen. It detailed the use of Cain in the entrapment of Emilia R., a minor secretary in the Italian Embassy in Paris.

Operation successful: a top-secret position paper on Italian waffling on NATO received.

Then a notation at the bottom of the page, in Whistler's distinctive handwriting, was bone blunt. *Not suited for this kind of pimp's work.*

(PAGE 20)
CANCELLATION # 10 Aborted.
Objective South Viet. national, Marshal Duc. Believed to be dealing both sides of street. (see LOTUS TOAD file) Action agreement reached Paris, 8/12/69. Hardfist set for Sept. same year. Cain inserted Saigon 8/23/69. Cover as A.I.D. advisor on one month tour of pacification area. Passport issued to John M. Kane, Rockville Center, N.Y.

Cain object of take-out attempt 9/6/1969. Bomb explosion at Saigon restaurant. 41 dead, 57 injured. Among dead, pro-regime agent, Clerice. Eyewitness account she blew apart in front of Cain's eyes. Secret police report points to love interest between Cain and Clerice.

Marshal Duc deep-watered same day. Showed up one month later in Zurich. Duc no longer factor, cancellation called off. Operation aborted.

(PAGE 20a)
ADDENDUM
Report spread that Clerice real object of take-out explosion. Had function in LOTUS TOAD operation given as cause. Cain said innocent bystander.

To Cain and Clerice love interest: Clerice applied
for American visa and Cain influence used. Clerice
booked flight leaving Saigon 9/28/69, same day
and flight as planned exit for Cain.

The next few pages weren't the kind of reading Burden liked.
In diagram and medical terms, all of Cain's wounds were noted
and the treatment prescribed. A skin graft for the wound on
his right side. Notations made of the weight of metal fragments
taken from Cain's thighs and hips. Burden moved through these
rapidly. He had his own wounds and scars and they had their
own kind of pain memory that giving their correct anatomical
designations didn't relieve.

He slowed down only when he reached the psychiatrists'
reports. But he found the neatly typed pages a kind of bog, style
and language the swamp that hid the meaning. Frustrated, curs-
ing under his breath, he skipped through the pages until he
found the section headed *Prognosis.*

The severity of the concussion, coupled with
the horror of his last memory, the virtual disin-
tegration of the young Vietnamese girl, suggest
a degree of death trauma that could be beyond
any known treatment. Alone, the concussion
might respond in time. Memory and a sense of
his past might be restored. Statistics show better
than a 64.5 percent recovery in tissue trauma
circumstances.

Death trauma, on the other hand, especially
the death of someone the subject deeply loved,
may have forced him to construct a dense and
impenetrable shield. This shield hides his own
sense of guilt, the prototype of the assassin's
guilt. As Van Arsdale writes in *Death, Guilt and*

Man, (page 301, paragraph 4) "The paid assassin has *I Kill* engraved on his forehead. As soon as he is aware that such an inscription exists, he becomes responsible for all deaths that occur near him. The assassin, Hartke, illuminates this concept. When his three-year-old daughter died of a respiratory disease, friends and family were unable to convince him that he had not killed the child himself. His subsequent suicide illustrates the depth of the depression, the remorse and dark fantasy that the assassin is capable of after he has embraced the *I Kill* mental aberration as a part of the ordinary."

In line with this concept, it is probable that the subject, at the moment of the death of the young girl, created the shield so that he would not remember that he said or thought *I have killed her, I am responsible.* He insulated himself against the certainty that he would remember his guilt.

For the above reason, it is our contention that the subject is an acceptable risk for utilization in the Queens' Butcher-Baker Plan.

The report was signed by three psychiatrists.

At the bottom of the final page, headlined by what seemed to be a touch of flippancy, was the *Minority Report.* It was signed by Dr. Malcolm Dranke.

The risk is not an acceptable one. The Van Arsdale concept is flaccid and questionable. The patient-subject is a man accustomed to dealing in death, to violence as a part of his day-to-day life-style. The prognosis reached by the majority is predicated upon death trauma as the central cause of the memory loss. To argue death trauma, as yet unproven, is the same. as arguing about unicorns.

It is the minority opinion that the single factor blocking the patient-subject's memory is a physiological one, the concussion and the resulting cranial and tissue trauma. Time and the generation of new tissue will result, I feel, in full or partial recovery of past senses and/or memory.

The sensitive nature of the Queens' Butcher-Baker Plan makes the patient-subject a high risk factor.

CHAPTER SIX

The noise of the dishwasher tagged Kane out the front door and into the winter-spoiled front yard. Even with the door closed, he could feel the low vibrating whine rubbing his nerve ends raw.

It was a typical Atlanta winter day. Cold and gray with the barest hint of warmth in the sun patches. But in-the deep shadows there was the cutting scent of ice. Below the front steps, at the sidewalk, he stopped under a dogwood tree. Before him, across the street, stretched the gash-like narrowness of Jenner Park. It was one of the neighborhood parks, about half a block wide and two city blocks long. Now, in the wind and the chill, the swings and the slides were empty.

In the spring and summer, he liked to sit in the swing-glider on the far side of the park, shaded by the single magnolia that grew there, and close his eyes and feel the breeze and listen to the children playing, the thin reedy voices that seemed to come out of his own past, out of a past he'd almost forgotten.

But there were no voices today and when he felt the chill he turned up the driveway. He stepped over the low wall that separated his house from the one on his right. By the time he'd reached the back steps, Bill Gordon had seen him and swung the door open.

"Come in, boy. You just get back?"

"Yesterday," Kane said.

Bill was spare and lean, his gray hair cropped close. He was seventy-two and he admitted it proudly. His pale blue eyes were clear and steady. And the last time Kane hunted with him, his hand was as steady as his eye. They'd been after quail and Bill had bagged his limit in the first hour while Kane had his troubles.

"Coffee?" Bill waved Kane into the kitchen. He was dressed as he always was, in tan whipcord trousers, a faded denim shirt and heavy work shoes.

Kane shook his head. "I've had two cups of what Reba calls coffee."

"Awful, wasn't it? I made the same mistake myself once. Now I have a lie ready in case it's offered again."

"But she's got a good heart," Kane said.

"The best." Bill nodded toward the ceramic teapot in the center of the small kitchen table.

Kane touched the side of the teapot. It was scalding hot. "What flavor this time?"

"Darjeeling."

Kane sat at the table while Bill brought out two heavy mugs. He didn't bother to offer cream or sugar. Neither took anything with their tea.

"I saw you coming," Bill said.

"Glad you did."

"Good trip this time?"

"Fair," Kane said. He watched Bill pour. He drew his mug toward him and leaned his face down into the warm cloud of steam that arose from it. He pulled in the aroma and smiled. When he opened his eyes, he saw Bill grinning at him and nodding, like they shared some secret that no one else understood.

"Tell me about the hunting," Kane said.

Fred Burden gave up. The urge for a cigarette was just too strong for him. He reached into the drawer and drew out the pack. He shook out a single cigarette and lit it. Drawing the smoke into his lungs he decided, after the cup of coffee, it didn't taste as bad.

❧   ❧   ❧

(PAGE 29)

EXTRACTED FROM THE FRIDAY MEETING,
12/8/1969

PRYOR: And now to the matter of Cain.

WHISTLER: I assume all of us have read the medical report and the psychiatrists' evaluations. I guess it would be my tendency to go along with the consensus position.

DUNDEE: Dr. Dranke's attitude worries me a bit.

PRYOR: What's Dranke's reputation?

WHISTLER: A bit of a troublemaker. A brilliant man but one who won't pull with the other horses.

DUNDEE: Even allowing for that, Dranke is the top man in the field, the whole area of trauma and memory. Ask any expert and you'll get three names. Dranke's will be one of the three.

PRYOR: I have a feeling we have a stand-off here. What are the options?

DUNDEE: Elimination. It's the only clear choice left to us. In fact, the choices are so limited they aren't choices anymore.

PRYOR: That's extreme for one of our own.

DUNDEE: I understand your feeling about that. But Cain's part in the Marshal Duc cancellation try, if it got out, could be an embarrassment in the light of our present priorities.

PRYOR: If the cat got out of the bag.

DUNDEE: Exactly. It's too big a risk. It's a risk the Agency can't afford.

PRYOR: Whistler?

WHISTLER: I can't go along with Dundee. Nothing in Cain's past history, the work he's done for the Agency, would lead me to believe that he represents any danger to us. His loyalty is red-lined, at the top. Jesus Christ, you know where this kind of thinking could take us if we follow it to the absurd? Ten people, maybe twelve, know about the Marshal Duc plan. Why don't we make sure that nobody ever reveals it? All we have to do is eliminate those ten or twelve people. That includes you and you and me.

DUNDEE: Of course, we don't have to take it to the absurd.

WHISTLER: My option involves the Queens' Butcher-Baker Plan.

PRYOR: And the New Identity File?

WHISTLER: Yes, that too.

DUNDEE: I don't know who came up with this proposal, but I want to go on record...

PRYOR: (laughing) Say it loud and clear.

DUNDEE: It won't fly.

WHISTLER. That's what the physics professor out in the midwest was saying five years after the Wright Brothers flew at Kitty Hawk.

PRYOR: If I understand the Queens' Butcher-Baker Plan and the New Identity File, the way it would work, it is an experiment, and in all experiments there is a high degree of risk.

WHISTLER: That's true enough. But it is a risk that three out of the four consulting psychiatrists think feasible.

DUNDEE: It is not their risk. The Agency takes the risk.

PRYOR: Run it past me one more time, Whistler. I'm not sure I understand

WHISTLER: Think of it as a pilot program. Here we have Cain and he has no memory and no past. It's like he was born about three months ago. So we create a new identity for him and we spoon-feed it to him. We give him a past that reaches back to the womb and up to now. What is important about this past is that we leave the Agency out of it. We don't exist for him. He never worked for us.

PRYOR: Is that possible?

WHISTLER: Our experts think so. Now, as soon as this New Identity File is implanted, we put Cain on a long rope and watch him. No matter where he goes we furnish him friends, agents who have one purpose, the reinforcement of his false past. If and when he shows signs that he has recovered his true memory, then it will be time to consider Dundee's solution.

DUNDEE: It might be too late then. I'm telling you that any revelation of the Agency's part in the Marshal Duc plot could be more devastating than a Watergate or a Teapot Dome.

PRYOR: You talk about it being a pilot program, Whistler, I don't see any application....

WHISTLER: Dr. Smathers at the Link Foundation has been, for the last five years, working on a covered grant, doing research on drug-induced memory dispersal. The latest report from him, dated late in October, suggests that he may be approaching a solution. Of course, until now, he had been working with animals. There are limitations to this kind of experimentation.

PRYOR: Animals?

WHISTLER: He's mainly worked with rats.

DUNDEE: It's all crap.

WHISTLER: Smathers does some of the classic kind of work with rats. Teaches them to run mazes and performs certain tasks that produce food for them. Then, when the rats have mastered these skills, he injects them with Kartin-23. You'd be amazed. I've seen this. Here they are, trained rats that only minutes before had a number of learned skills. Now, after the injection, they're lost. They have to start over. They can't produce food for themselves and they can't run even the simplest of the mazes.

PRYOR: I'm still a little in the dark about how this kind of experimentation could be of any value to the Agency.

DUNDEE: Exactly.

WHISTLER: It's simple enough. Say we have a defector. Someone from the Soviet bloc. As usual we spend as much time as we need to pump him out, flush him of everything he knows. All the standard techniques until we know there's nothing left. At that point we bring in Dr. Smathers. He induces memory dispersal on our defector with Kartin-23. From then on, our man is a blank tablet we write on. We give him a new identity, a past and a present. We turn him into a butcher or a baker and we set him up in Queens. Some place like that. It could be Charlotte. Chicago. New Haven. Once he's set up, he's no longer a problem for us or for the government. He lives out the rest of his life as Joseph L. Smith, American blue-collar worker. And even if the unlikely happens, if agents from his former country find him, what can he tell them? He won't remember his former life and the Agency doesn't exist in the new past we've created for him.

DUNDEE: Do we need that many butchers and bakers?

WHISTLER: Think of it as a metaphor.

PRYOR: Blue-collar covers a wide range.

WHISTLER: Everything from cab driver to construction worker.

PRYOR: Of course, I can see where there are some gaps, details that have to be worked out, but it has possibilities.

WHISTLER: You mean the money angle?

PRYOR: That, yes. Cover and money are the big problems. And there's always the chance that the defector will regret his decision and decide to be repatriated. That can be an embarrassment.

WHISTLER: I don't have the latest figures with me. The last ones I saw, just in money terms, put the cost per defector at about forty or fifty thousand dollars a year. And if the bargain has been struck ahead of time, before the defection, it can be a lot more than that.

PRYOR: If we keep the bargain.

WHISTLER: Of course.

DUNDEE: I've tried to be patient with this science fiction. It won't work and it's not a solution. Cain is a threat and the only way to deal with a threat is to eliminate it... once and for all.

PRYOR: I don't think you're looking at the long run benefits of the proposal. Whistler has...

DUNDEE: I don't like saying this. It goes against my grain a bit. But Whistler has let his emotions blind him to the real issue. I assume you know that Whistler recruited Cain. That he and Cain were close friends?

WHISTLER: In this room, where the interests of the Agency are concerned, I have no friends. Not Cain, not you, not anybody else.

PRYOR: Green.

WHISTLER: Green.

DUNDEE: Red.

PRYOR: Two to one. You've got a green signal, Whistler. I'll send you a memo in the next two days about some of the problems I see with the Plan. Now, unless there is some new business ...

(FMT 12/8/69)

(PAGE 35)

NEW IDENTITY FILE

John Marshal Kane.

Born Richmond, Virginia. Parents deceased. No family ties with either side of family.

Graduated U. Va. with degree in English, 1961. Recruited by DuPont for advertising and marketing internship. Retained with company after completion of program. Drafted by Army in 1965. Trained for construction battalion. Served one year of two-year tour in Vietnam. Received shoulder wound in Mekong operation/Honorable discharge in 1967. Worked one year with Delta Construction Company in New York City. One year with Maryland Highway Department. Returned to Vietnam as A.I.D. advisor in 1969. Victim of terrorist bomb 9/6/69. Returned to states for treatment of wounds. After discharge from A.I.D. used family money (budget allotment # 18675) to open sporting goods stores in New York City.

Personal Profile: a loner. Strong sex drive but no marriages. Engaged to Ellen Carson prior to Army drafting. Received Dear John while in Vietnam. Ellen Carson now married and living in Bay area. Available female agent if Kane travels to San Fran. *Close friends in New York:* Bart Klinger

(Ross), Ed Faison (Sensor), Jim Stark (Reed), and Betsy Steinman (Star). Klinger has cover as U. Va. college friend; Faison as Army buddy; Stark as co-worker in A.I.D.; Steinman as old girlfriend from 1967–68. *Group name:* Long Rope.
ALL DOCUMENTATION FOR ABOVE FURNISHED.

The next thirty pages were routine weekly reports from the Long Rope group. What Kane said to Faison over lunch at O. Henry's in the Village. A N.Y. Ranger game with Klinger. An evening of drinks and girl chasing with Stark. Each report short and to the point and each ending with *No evidence of recall.* And weekends spent with Betsy Steinman in Maine. *Subject seems to accept his past and present without question.*

Burden skimmed these pages in a matter of minutes. He'd read his share of dull and ordinary reports, enough to last him a lifetime. And he'd written his share as well. Lulled into a kind of boredom, he was halfway through page 65 before a phrase caught his interest and he moved back to the beginning of the report and read it through slowly.

(PAGE 65)
QUEENS' BUTCHER-BAKER REPORT # 31 Source: N.Y.P.D. reports and agent follow-up 10/5/1972. Subject in bar in East Village. Subject alone. Bar: The Villa. 2350 hours four young toughs take over bar. Owner and bartender, attempting to eject, badly beaten. (Report is argument began with non-payment of tab.) Kane is one of ten in bar. Drinking cognac at bar, watches, does nothing. Young girl abused. Two of young men decide to manhandle Kane. One holds knife on Kane while other cuffs him. Goes too far and Kane, using bottle and chair, kills those two and batters other

pair. Eyewitness states violence lasted no longer than a minute.

Kane left before police arrived.

Search for Kane flagged down by Whistler. National security reason given. NYPD put case in inactive file.

(PAGE 66)

QUEENS' BUTCHER-BAKER REPORT # 32

Source: Sensor.

10/10/1972. Kane depressed. Confides that he is thinking of leaving New York.

(PAGE 67)

QUEENS' BUTCHER-BAKER REPORT # 33

Source: Star.

10/12/1972. In pillow talk, Kane says he has decided to move to Atlanta. That he will leave sporting goods store with broker for sale. Will leave at end of month.

(PAGE 68)

QUEENS' BUTCHER-BAKER REPORT # 34 Action: by Whistler.

Alert Blue Mole in Atlanta. 10/13/1972.

Reply from Blue Mole 10/14/1972. No longer willing to do 9 to 5 for Agency, but will undertake holiday work. Agreement reached 10/15/1972. Payroll handled through National Insurance Co. $200/month and bonus.

(PAGE 68)

QUEENS' BUTCHER-BAKER REPORT # 35 Source: Sampler.

11/3/1972. Same flight with Kane. Subject stayed at Hyatt House until 11/7/1972. Moved into apartment Briarcliff Road.

Blue Mole alerted.

11/11/1972. Witnessed contact between Blue Mole and Kane. 1234 hours in Reed Sporting Goods, Broad Street. Blue Mole made it appear accidental. Sampler recalled.

CHAPTER SEVEN

The phone rang in Bill Gordon's living room. Kane was at the back door, hand on the knob, when Bill called him.

"It's for you, John."

"For me ... here?"

"Reba must have referred the call," Bill said.

When Kane took the receiver from him, Bill moved away, until he stood in the doorway to the dining room.

"Yes?"

"Kane?"

He knew the voice. "Yes." He could feel the chill. It was early for another call. One job hardly done and the bitterness from that one not digested yet.

"I think it's one that will interest you," Carter said.

"When?"

"Primary interview Monday night, eight o'clock."

"I'll be there." Kane broke the call without saying good-bye.

Bill Gordon waited in the doorway. Concern made deep wrinkles around his eyes. "Trouble?"

"No," Kane said, "just business."

Whoever the Blue Mole was, now retired, now out of the business, he'd probably been a good man in his time, Burden thought.

Starting with Report # 36 the Blue Mole was the single source. Each week a page for the file. The prose honed, thinned down to the bone. *1/8/73 Lunch with Kane at 1776 Restaurant, Luckie Street. Large check from N. Y. broker. Sale of Sports Goods Store. 1/22/73 Closing on house 758 Harvard Street, near Jenner Park. $42,500. Bank account down. 1/29/73 thru 2/2/73 Job hunting. Two job offers made. Not interested.*

Burden pushed back his chair and stretched. Still standing, he flipped through another month of reports. Routine, nothing out of the ordinary.

It changed with Report # 52.

Unusual Request. Approached by Jackson Carter. Carter running Murder-for-Hire operation out of Atlanta under cover of C.P.A. business. Had lost hardfist operative in unsuccessful contract. Carter requests permission to recruit Kane as replacement.

TRANSCRIPTION PHONE CONVER. BETWEEN MOLE AND WHISTLER 3/14/73

WHISTLER: This Jackson Carter, what do you know of him?

BLUE MOLE: A bit. He's really a C.P.A. He could make a good living out of that. Doesn't want to for some reason.

WHISTLER: What's his background?

BLUE MOLE: Out of a mob family. Father a low soldier with Gambetti in New Orleans. Carter made his bones at 18. Might have gone that route but it was noticed that he had a talent with figures. Educated by Gambetti with the idea of going into the organization as their in-house C.P.A. He didn't. Somehow got the education without having to pay the organization back. Might have slipped by during the transition after death of Old Carlo.

WHISTLER: How long in his present business?

BLUE MOLE: About five years. That's an estimate.

WHISTLER: How many contracts?

BLUE MOLE: Again this is an estimate. About five or six a year.

WHISTLER: Good planning?

BLUE MOLE: One mistake. Not his fault. His hard-fist got careless.

WHISTLER : I need your best answer on this one. What do you think about Carter's request?

BLUE MOLE: That puts me on the hotplate.

WHISTLER: Just your best answer.

BLUE MOLE: It's what he does best. Him in a book-store or selling insurance, that would be like making a race horse pull a plow.

WHISTLER: That's a sad comment on a man.

BLUE MOLE: Nobody said it had to be happy all the time.

EXTRACTED FROM THE FRIDAY MEETING, 3/16/73

PRYOR: That's enough argument. It's time for a vote.

DUNDEE: Green.

WHISTLER: Red.

PRYOR: Green. The greens have it. Whistler, I think you'd better pass the word down to Blue Mole.

WHISTLER: As soon as the meeting breaks up. (FMT 3/16/73)

He'd read enough. There was still about an inch of material left. That could wait for another day, some morning when it was slow. He's read the keys, the important decisions.

On his way to RECORDS to return the file, Burden glanced at his watch. It was twelve ten. Time to think about lunch.

CHAPTER EIGHT

It rained that Monday. It fell in thick sheets when Kane crossed the parking lot and climbed the back stairs. Now in the small room beyond the two-way mirror, he could feel the damp leather on his feet. He reached down and unbuckled his shoes and kicked them off. Wet socks. The heat from his body would dry them in time. There wasn't anything he could do about the socks. He'd have to suffer the discomfort until he could return to his home and change them.

On the shelf in front of him, there was the usual ashtray and the plastic glass of water. And one thing more: this time there was a brown file folder anchored by the weight of the ashtray. He moved the ashtray aside and opened the folder.

In the other room, Jackson Carter leaned forward and planted an elbow solidly on the desktop. The blonde young man facing him flinched and leaned away, as if he thought he might be struck. His name, according to the file in front of Kane, was George Webb. Kane judged the young man's age in the nineteen or twenty range. He was broad in the shoulders and narrow in the hips, an all-American boy from the 1940s, before the beats and the hippies. He had his hair cut short and he wore a dark blazer with some kind of crest over the breast pocket. Webb was sweating now and he'd developed a twitch below his right eye since he'd sat down across from Carter about five minutes ago.

Carter said, "All businesses have rules and ours is a special kind of service. For that reason the rules we have are ironclad ones."

"Yes, sir."

"If your contract is taken by us, or if for some reason we refuse this contract, it is the same to us. You will never talk about how you contacted me or what we talked about or the location of this office. You will never, even if you've had a few drinks, tell a funny story about how you took out a contract once or almost took out one. Nothing like that. Drink is not a valid excuse. And when you're married, you will never confess this to your wife. Or to your psychiatrist or your family doctor."

"I understand." In the wreath of light that surrounded the desk, the oily sweat glowed on Webb's forehead.

"I hope you do. Any breach of this agreement and you could find yourself in grave trouble."

"Grave?" The young man forced a laugh. "Is that a pun?"

"No," Carter said, "it is not a pun and it is not a joke either."

George Webb closed his mouth. He tried to hold it in a tight line, but his lower lip trembled.

Carter lifted his elbow and leaned away. "That understood, tell me about it, Mr. Webb."

The first item in the file was a newspaper clipping. A notation in the margin stated that it was from the *Atlanta Journal* with a date about a month before.

Gangland Death In Ansonville

This Georgia resort town was shocked by the latest apparent gangland death in the past year. A car belonging to Barton Riker, bloodstained and riddled with bullets, was discovered on a deserted side street. Though no body has been found, Ansonville police believe that Riker was killed in another flare-up in the year-long struggle between factions for control of this usually peaceful town. In the last year, there have been three execution style murders. So far none of the crimes has been solved.

ROB

BENN, A F

87257

December 18

1060007036204   A talent for killing / Ra

Police Chief Rance Mattingly said that he expects an early arrest and...

In the office George Webb said, "I thought you knew all about it. I told Mr. Hogan ..."

"I need to hear it again. What was Barton Riker to you?"

"My brother."

Carter let out a breath. His eyes flicked for a brief second toward the pewter framed mirror. "But the names ...?"

"It was his way ... of not hurting the family." Webb had been staring down at the backs of his hands. Now he lifted his eyes. "Maybe he was all those things the police said about him. A member of the Dixie Mafia, a gangster, a gambler." There was a shake and a tremble in the young man's voice and he hesitated, until he'd controlled it. "But he was always a good brother to me and I don't think he deserved to die like that."

"You knew he was in the rackets?"

"I guessed it. The last time I saw him ... that was in late August before I left to start college ...."

"What college?"

"Harvard."

"Go on," Carter said.

"Well, he called me. He said he wanted to see me. So I borrowed a car and drove down."

"From where?"

"Here in Atlanta. We live here."

"Who's the *we*?"

"My mother and my sister."

Carter lifted a hand and rubbed the side of his nose. "Webb's an old name in Atlanta. Your father was ...?"

"Judge Martin Webb," the young man said.

Carter nodded and dropped the hand palm down on the desk top. "I thought so."

"You knew him?"

"Go on with the story."

"I drove to Ansonville and met Barton at the club."

"What club?"

"The one he managed. It's called the Nineties Club."

Kane unclipped a pen from his shirt pocket and, on the inside cover of the file, wrote *managed club ... who owned?*

"What happened?"

"Nothing at first," Webb said. "We had dinner in the dining room with a girl who worked at the club. Karen Fisk. And we had a few drinks and Barton said he'd already sent off a check to cover the first year's tuition and expenses. And then we left Karen and I went back to his office with him. He said he wanted to be sure I had enough spending money. He opened a wall safe and took out two envelopes. One envelope was sealed and the other wasn't. He opened the unsealed one and showed me a couple of books of traveler's checks. All I noticed at the time was that they were fifties and hundreds. Later, when I did count them, they added up to ten thousand dollars."

"And you thought that was odd?"

"Not at the time," Webb said. "Barton said they were better than checks any day."

"You don't sound so sure now."

"That came later. I heard somebody talking. One of the guys who lived down the hall from me. He said traveler's checks were a way of hiding unreported income."

"But you spent it?"

It wasn't really a question. The young man nodded and a few drops of perspiration scatter-sprayed his knees. "I needed it."

"But it made you wonder about your brother?"

"Yes." Webb dug a handkerchief from the side pocket of his blazer and dabbed at his forehead. "But I wasn't sure until I opened the sealed envelope."

"Tell me about that."

"When he gave it to me that night, he said I wasn't to open that one unless something happened to him."

"You took that sealed envelope to Cambridge with you?"

"Yes."

"And you didn't open it until …?"

"Until Mama called me. Until I was on the plane flying back to Atlanta."

"And?"

"It was a typed letter authorizing me to take charge of the effects stored at a storage warehouse in northwest Atlanta. And there was a key taped to the bottom of the page."

"Nothing else?"

Webb shook his head. "Just that. No letter to me."

"And when you went to the storage warehouse?"

"It was a locked box, like a safety deposit box in a bank. There was a package inside, wrapped in newspaper. I waited until I got home before I opened it."

"Money?"

Webb nodded. "A hundred thousand in hundreds."

"And that tied it up for you. Then you knew." There was an odd, dry quality to Carter's voice now.

"Yes. The police said he was a known gambler. And they said they thought he was a gangster. How else would he have that kind of money?"

"Exactly," Carter said. "What do you want of us?"

"I want them killed. I want whoever killed him killed."

"Why?"

"The police don't seem to care. It's like … like they decided he deserved what happened to him. And then they forgot about it. Maybe Barton wasn't much, but …"

Carter leaned into the full blaze of light. The movement was abrupt, a shock, and the grin on his face was the full measure of the contempt he felt. "Do you believe that? Don't put that puke and crap on my rug."

The silence lasted a minute and then another. Kane watched the young man. Webb didn't move and his eyes were closed. Still staring at him, Kane fumbled with the pack in his shirt pocket and drew out a single cigarette. He lit it and smoke curled upward, blinding him in his right eye, but he didn't blink.

"No," George Webb said, "it wasn't like that at all."

"How was it?" Carter said. Suddenly, without any warning, he'd shifted gears. Now his voice was warm, with a kind of understanding in it.

"You couldn't know how it was after Daddy died. There wasn't much money. Bad investments, the lawyers said. And it was Barton who held the family together. Even then I knew he couldn't make that much money just managing a nightclub. The first of every month the check would arrive. It would come through a lawyer here in town and it would be enough to keep Mama in the social position she was used to and it was enough to keep my sister, Emily, and me."

"Where?"

"Where we were. In high school. And then in college."

"The good son," Carter said.

"Maybe this won't make any sense, maybe I can't say it right. Even when he was alive I had the feeling that Barton was wasting himself. You didn't know him. He could have been anything he wanted to. But he needed money for us and I guess crime was the quickest way to make it."

"Wasting?"

"It was like he gave up on his own life, what he could have done with it."

Kane took the cigarette from his mouth and stubbed it out in the ash tray. Beyond the two-way mirror George Webb talked on and on. It was a hymn of almost tearful praise for his dead brother, but there wasn't a solid bit of information in it all.

⚜　⚜　⚜

Carter returned from seeing George Webb out. He leaned across the desk and picked up the stack of hundred dollar bills. He faced the mirror and pinched them at one end, ruffling through them like a deck of cards. Smiling, he stuffed them into the inside pocket of his jacket.

"Twenty thousand," he said. "That leaves eighty thousand to support the family until Buster there finishes Harvard and starts mailing home money orders every Christmas."

"It ought to be enough," Kane said, even though he knew that Carter couldn't hear him. It was a one-way system that fed the sound from the office into the small room beyond the mirror.

"You'll leave for Ansonville in the next day or two."

"Tomorrow or Wednesday," Kane said.

"The sooner the better. It's a month old and the tracks are getting rained on.

Kane closed the folder and stood up. He placed the ashtray on top of the folder. He pushed his feet into the damp shoes.

"The corpse hasn't been found yet," Carter said, "but that doesn't mean anything. It's probably in one of those clay pits out there. The blood type in the car matches. The G.B.I. lab established that."

Kane buckled one shoe and then the other. Right away he could feel the dampness drawn into the almost dry socks. He turned and walked toward the outside door. Behind him, Carter said, "It's all a blank. You have nothing to start with, nothing except the Nineties Club. Maybe you can make an impression on them. Maybe somebody at the club will offer you a job."

Kane stepped through the doorway and pulled the door shut behind him.

By morning, the rain had stopped.

Kane sat in the kitchen with a fresh Chemex of coffee on a mat in front of him. It was still gray and dark outside. The crust of a toasted English muffin was on a dish off to one side.

He placed his wallet on the table and while he sipped the dark, French roast coffee he emptied all the compartments. This done he replaced the money. The other articles he'd taken from the wallet, all the proof that he was John Callan, he scooped into a neat stack before he stored them in a brown envelope. Another sip of coffee and he sealed the envelope with tape and pushed it aside.

There was another envelope in the pocket of his robe. JOHN CASSIDY was written on it in heavy print. He tapped the envelope on the table several times before he tore the end away. He poured the contents onto the table and spread them.

A social security card in the name John Cassidy. *Too new looking.* He dipped a finger into his coffee cup and wet a finger. He made a blotch near the lower right-hand corner. He blotted it with his napkin and, still not satisfied, he lifted a slipper and rubbed the card, back and front, on the sole until he'd given it about twenty years of wear. He inserted the card in one part of the plastic card folder and picked up the driver's license. It had been issued in North Carolina. The color photo was full face, not profile. The sideburns were even shorter and there was a hint of graying around the temples. He'd have to do something about the graying and the sideburns before he left town. The license was authentic. It had cost him two hundred dollars through a source in Raleigh. And it was an identity he hadn't used yet.

After that, he inspected the other aspects of his new life. A Master Charge. American Express. Gulf charge card. A handful of scraps of aged paper with first names and phone numbers. And in one stack, held together by a rubber band, a couple of dozen business cards.

John R. Cassidy
Dealer in Antiques
2212 Campbell Road
Charlotte, North Carolina
(704) 962-3047

Before Kane left the house around noon he wrote a note for Reba and left a check for her on the kitchen table. Afterwards, he drove to Hartsfield International and parked in the lot. Inside the terminal, he placed his parking lot ticket in an already addressed and stamped envelope and dropped the envelope in a mail slot. The ticket would wait for him in a rental box at the Peachtree Center postal substation.

At the Economy Car Rental booth in the concourse, he rented a blue Plymouth Duster, just like the one he had at home, using the Master Charge in the name of John Cassidy.

Five hours later, he drove into Ansonville.

CHAPTER NINE

Twenty years before, Ansonville was nearly a ghost town and Lake Tarver, on the outskirts, was fished out and polluted. Main street was a shell of empty storefronts, except for a general store and a hardware shop.

That's not what Hardy Winston saw when he returned from the Korean War and looked at the town. He had a vision of the future. He saw two or three blocks of craft shops, antique stores, a couple of auction houses, and maybe a butcher making home-cured hams and bacon. He saw an eighteen-hole championship golf course and Lake Tarver filled with trout.

It took him nearly two decades, but Winston succeeded. Main Street was now five blocks long. Most of the craft shops and stores were the renovated one-and two-story original buildings. And midway through the town, taking up most of the central block, the Town Square Hotel, all glass and steel and glitter.

Kane moved with the slow, cruising traffic. Even in the chilled wind, the dampness, the streets were full. At one corner, caught by the red light, he turned and looked into the Whitley Gallery. Inside, beyond the steamed up windows, the early auction was in progress. As the door opened up to let some people inside, he could hear the garbled rant of the auctioneer.

And in all directions, he saw the lighted windows of the craft shops. Here a potter at his wheel, there a glassblower at work, here four old women worked at a patchwork quilt, there an old mountain man weaved a basket. There was an audience outside each window, as if watching a TV screen.

In the center of town, were the respectable people. Money and the middle class at play. But as Kane followed the flow of traffic and took a right off Main Street, he found himself in a different kind of city. Two blocks west and he was in the neon sputter and the sound of live bands. And on these darker streets, there wasn't the slow pace of Main Street. The flow was spastic, jerky, the cadence of drink and women, the rush from one bar to another.

There were motels here, flanked by bars, and with their own bars nestled under their wings. Kane drove on.

It was fifteen minutes before Kane found what he wanted. An old motel in the belt between the bars and clubs and the rooming houses and apartment buildings. The Restaway Motel. It looked like it might have been the first motel built in town or it had been built out of cheap materials and had begun to crumble the day it was completed.

Kane registered in the small office under the interested eyes of a thin, faded blonde woman. He told her he thought he might be staying a week. She stood in the doorway and watched him as he drove from the office and parked in front of unit ten.

After a shower, and a change of clothes, he unpacked both suitcases. In the bottom of the second suitcase, wrapped in plastic, was a Woodsman Sport. Holding it, he made a slow circuit of the room, then used a dime to unscrew the back from the battered black and white TV set. He tucked the Sport into a space next to the chassis and replaced the back.

A few minutes, later he parked in the lot in front of the Nineties Club.

It wasn't a big night. From the doorway, before he moved to the bar, he could see about ten people in the bar. Four seated at the bar and the others at tables. And through a doorway off to his right, the dining room showed the same kind of slack time. Only four or five tables were being used and the waiters clustered together, bored and probably wishing the kitchen would close.

Kane stopped at the near end of the bar. The bartender, a young man with a thick neck and the arms of a weight-lifter, saw him and drifted over. Kane ordered Bisquit and a coffee.

"No coffee at the bar," the bartender said.

Kane shook his head and backed away from the bar. He hadn't eaten since breakfast and now he passed through the dining room doorway and sat at a small table off to the side. He ordered the London broil rare and after he'd finished, he asked for the check and a refill on his coffee. He paid the bill and added a good tip and, while the waiter stared at him, he carried his coffee through the doorway and up to the bar.

The seat at the end of the bar was still empty. He sat down and placed the coffee in front of him. The bartender put a hip against the bar and looked at the coffee cup. He didn't say anything.

"Now I'll have the Bisquit," Kane said.

He was on his second cognac and down to the dregs of the coffee, when he saw the girl. She entered from a door in the back of the bar, one marked OFFICE. She ducked through the opening at the other end of the bar. In one hand, she carried a zippered bank change bag. While she stood at the open register, putting rolls of change into the back trays, he watched her. Five-nine or so. A tall girl with blonde hair, a tint of red in her hair when the light hit it. Her body slim but not thin. From the side, her nose was a little large. Full-face, when she turned and looked down the bar at him, her face was long and narrow, with a kind of sadness built into it.

The change put away, she placed the empty change bag next to the register. She ducked under the bar and stood there, hesitating, and Kane found himself talking to her in his mind. *Down here. One drink.*

As if she'd heard him, she walked down the length of the bar and stopped two stools away from him. She eased up onto the stool and waited.

"What'll it be, Karen?"

Karen? The girl who'd been with the brother, Barton, the night George Webb had visited him back in August?

The girl said, "J. and B., rocks."

"Right." The bartender scooped ice into a glass and placed it on the bar in front of her. He brought the bottle and poured about a shot and a half over the ice. "First one tonight?"

"Maybe."

He looked at the drink and for a moment Kane thought he'd pick it up and take it away. Karen got there first. She cupped a hand around the glass and slid it toward her.

The bartender leaned close and dropped his voice. "Don't get me in trouble, Karen."

"Not a chance."

"You be sure." Down the bar one of the other drinkers tapped his empty glass on the bar top. The bartender moved in that direction. When he reached for the bottle to pour a refill, he turned and gave the girl a bleak, assessing look.

The girl gulped at the drink and looked away. Away happened to be in the direction of Kane and their eyes brushed over each other. Kane looked away first, down into his coffee cup. He didn't want to seem too eager. That was the first lesson and the last lesson. It would have to be handled right or not at all.

When he lifted his eyes, she'd emptied the glass and pushed it toward the back of the bar counter. And she was waiting, the twitch of tension in the movement of her hands.

The bartender ignored her as long as he could. Maybe he hoped she'd give up and leave the bar. When that didn't work he came down the bar, shaking his head, and leaned toward her. "No, Karen."

It was a whisper or meant to be but there was a shotgun final-
ity to it.

"One more," the girl said. It wasn't the plea Kane had heard
in so many bars, from the eighty-sixed drunks in this city or that
one. For all the tension in her body, there was a touch of amusement in her voice.

"I can't."

"Why?"

"You know why," the bartender said.

Kane heard the weakening in him. It wasn't a shotgun final-
ity after all, only the bluff imitation of one. Karen must have read
that in him too. She stepped down from the stool and walked the
length of the bar. She ducked through the opening and appeared
on the other side of the bar. She got a glass from the tray below
the bar, added some ice, and poured herself about a double shot
from the bar scotch bottle.

Kane swung his attention toward the bartender. It wasn't
necessary. Shaking his head slowly, the bartender lifted the girl's
first glass and dropped it in the sink. Without looking at him,
the girl returned to the customer side of the bar. Back at the same
stool near Kane, she must have felt the intensity of his stare. Just
before she lifted the glass to her mouth, she swung on the stool
toward him and tipped the glass in a kind of mock salute.

Kane nodded and smiled. "Luck."

"You too."

Beyond her, Kane watched the bartender. He put a hand
below the cash register, out of sight, and held it there for a count
of two or three. After he pulled the hand away, the bartender
moved to the far end of the bar and stood there, his back against
the curve of the counter, staring at the girl.

A trouble buzzer of some kind. That was Kane's guess. So it
was changing, happening, shifting. And he'd have to consider
how to play it. If he played it. And feeling the dull ache in the
back of his neck, he knew he was pressing too hard. He relaxed

and lifted the Bisquit. It wouldn't be any of his business until somebody made it his. That was how he'd treat it.

Right about the buzzer. Within seconds, the door marked OFFICE opened and a man came out. He was short and blocky, almost as wide as the door he came through. Wearing a dark suit, off the rack and baggy, but he'd have looked more at home in trunks, in the ring on Saturday Night Wrestling.

The blocky man put a hand on the bar and looked down the length of it. He lifted an eyebrow toward the bartender who leaned close, almost nose-to-nose. The bartender said something. Maybe twenty words, maybe less. At the end of it, the blocky man nodded and stepped around the end of the bar and headed toward the girl. He was smiling as he came. There wasn't a gram of amusement in that smile.

Kane watched him. Short body and even shorter legs. The arms too long for the body, dangling. Closer, only paces from the girl, Kane saw the scar that sliced through the left eyebrow. "Eddie wants to see you, Miss Karen."

He passed her and stepped in close to the bar. He was behind her now and positioned between her and Kane. If he saw Kane at all, he'd dismissed him as a tourist.

The girl didn't answer. The blocky man touched her shoulder. "He said right away."

"In a minute, Franco." She put the glass to her lips and sucked at the scotch.

"Now," Franco said.

"When I'm ready." She'd lowered the glass but now some impulse made her lift it again. It was an inch or so from her mouth when Franco put out a huge hand and grabbed it by the top. He pulled it toward him. The girl tried to hold on. She couldn't. Franco jerked the glass out of her hand. The ice and the remainder of the scotch looped in a thick stream down the length of the bar. A few drops landed on the front of Kane's shirt.

It wasn't much. Maybe it was enough. It put Kane in the center of it. He said, "Damn it," and pushed back his bar stool. He dug a handkerchief from his hip pocket and blotted the front of his shirt. Franco turned to face him. "Watch it, huh?" Kane said.

"You say something to me, friend?"

"I'm not your friend," Kane said. He unfolded the handkerchief and wiped his face. "How about doing your roughhouse somewhere else?"

"Fuck off, friend," Franco said.

"You're not listening." Kane folded the handkerchief and jammed it in his pocket. "I'm not your friend."

"Fancy yourself, huh?"

Past the man's bulk, Kane could see the bright eyes of the girl. Amusement gone now, concern showing. And from down the bar, the bartender edged toward them to make the fourth corner of the design.

Kane waited until the bartender was a step away. He wanted the right amount of outrage to build up. It had to sound right. "Look, I came in here for dinner and a few drinks," he said to the bartender. "I didn't come here to get scotch poured all over me."

"Drink your drink, buddy," the bartender said.

"I'm not your buddy or his friend," Kane said.

"The next drink's on the house." The bartender looked at Franco and back at him. "Just calm it down, huh?"

"And this roughhouse with the girl. If you're not going to do something about it, I want to talk to the manager."

The smile came then. It was on Franco's face.

"I'm the assistant manager," Franco said. "You can talk to me all you want to."

It was designed to shut him up. It didn't. Kane said, "In that case, I'd better call the police. Maybe the police will have something to say about the way he's roughing up ..."

He knew it was coming. Franco had reached his limit. But he wasn't a professional and there wasn't any way he could hide his slowness or the way he set himself to throw the punch.

Given that time, knowing he was going to have to take it, Kane turned slightly and lowered his head toward the hollow of his shoulder. He took most of the punch on his shoulder and fell away, letting it look like Franco had hit him full in the face. Falling away, he could hear the choked off scream of the girl. The second punch he couldn't fake, not if he wanted it to look right. He heard the shuffle of Franco's feet and the second blow, when it came, had brute strength in it but not much more. The big fist hit Kane about heart high and drove him off balance and down to the floor.

The girl's scream, following him down, wasn't choked off this time.

He took his time in the Men's Room. He spent most of it bent over a basin filled with cold water. Afterwards, he wet his hair and combed it and took five minutes more to dust off his clothing. Twenty minutes had passed before he pushed open the door and walked back to the bar. Franco and the bartender were at his end of the bar waiting for him.

"Thought you fell in," Franco said.

"The tab," Kane said.

"It's taken care of," the bartender said.

Franco slapped an open palm down on the bar. "Run along, tough boy."

"It was two cognacs," Kane said. He dug out a wad of money and waited.

"Two fifty," the bartender said.

Kane dropped a five on the bar. He waited for his change. While the bartender was at the cash register, Franco said, "Don't come back here. I see you here again and it really gets rough."

Kane took his change and turned away.

He gave a dollar to the cloak room girl.

Wasted. All that for nothing. No sign of the girl, Karen, in the bar. Probably back in the office. And now he'd have to find some way to meet her again.

He walked across the parking lot, first under the flare of the club lights and then in the near darkness where he'd parked the Duster. His hand was on the car door when he heard her calling him. "Hey ... hey ... you."

A car door slammed in one of the rows of cars back toward the light. Turning, he watched her run out of the light into the darkness. She was wearing a leather coat and had a scarf tied over her hair. A few feet from him, in the space between the Duster and the battered Mercury, she slowed to a walk. In the bad light he could see that she was breathing hard and the smile was shaky.

"Do you do that often?"

"What?" He waited.

"Get into bar brawls?"

"Was that what that was?"

"No." Her face was serious. "I guess you thought you were helping me."

"For all that was worth," he said.

"How do you feel? I mean, he really hit you pretty hard."

"I feel a little stupid." He turned away and fumbled with the door lock. It clicked. *It was time.* He swung the door open. *Time.* He lurched away from her and staggered toward the front of the Duster. He put a hand out and braced himself against the fender and bent over, retching. Nothing came up. But most people didn't have the stomach to inspect what might be on the ground. *Waiting.* And then he felt her hands on his shoulders.

"You're not all right."

He choked and coughed. He clawed for the balled-up handkerchief and covered his mouth. He could smell the few drops of scotch in it. He straightened up and turned, the handkerchief still pressed to his mouth.

"I'm fine." He pulled away from her hands. "I'll be fine when I get back to my motel." He stepped past her and hesitated, one hand on the open car door and the other on the car roof. He took a deep breath, like it might happen again. And, as he'd planned it in his mind, she moved around the door and close to him. He slid into the seat behind the wheel.

"No, you don't." She pushed at his shoulder. "Move over. I'll drive."

"I'm all right." He protested. He fought it for a time. He didn't want it to seem too easy. But in the end, he allowed himself to be pushed from behind the wheel. She said, "God, you're stubborn." She kicked the engine over and backed out of the parking space.

CHAPTER TEN

"You have anything to drink in there, John?" she asked.

She'd parked the car in the slot directly in front of Unit 10. Now she leaned forward and slapped the wheel with the palm of her hand. It was an impatient gesture. Her raw nerves were showing.

"Cognac," Kane said, "But the last thing I need right now."

"I'm the one needs the drink." she said. "And cognac won't cut it."

"I'll see if they've got anything at the desk." Kane passed the motel key to her and got out. "Go on in."

The same burned-out blonde was in the motel office. Late at night now, the tired sexuality pressing out, filling the overheated room. "Yes, Mr. Cassidy?"

"Is there a package store near here?"

"What do you need?"

"Scotch."

"I can save you the trip." She squatted behind the counter and unlocked a cabinet. He heard the dull rattle of bottles and when she stood up she held a fifth of Walker Red in one hand. "This okay?"

"Don't see why not."

"It's my brand too," she said.

"It tastes like medicine to me." He ignored the offer and got out some bills.

"It's twenty," she said. She picked up the twenty when it dropped on the counter in front of her and held it. A thumbnail scratched a thread line down the center of the bill. "You like our town, Mr. Cassidy?"

"I saw the backside tonight." He shook his head. "I'll try the main street tomorrow."

He nodded his thanks and carried the bottle out onto the windy walkway that ran the length of the motel. There was an ice machine outside the office and he dropped in two quarters and got the bag of cubes from the compartment below. Behind him, as he started for his room, he knew the woman was in the doorway watching him. He could feel the warm air blowing past her and he could smell her perfume.

❧ ❧ ❧

Karen was seated on the bed. Kane broke the seal and placed the bottle on the dresser next to a plastic ice bucket. With his back to her he tore off the bag of ice and poured most of the cubes into the bucket. "I hope this meets with your approval, Karen."

She stiffened. "How do you know my name?"

"The bartender called you that. So did the guy who worked me over."

"I guess that's right." She relaxed once more. "I didn't know you were listening."

"Every bit of it," he said. He got two wrapped tumblers from the bathroom and placed them next to the bottle and the ice bucket. "You want me to fix yours?"

"If you don't mind."

He tore the wrapper from one glass and mixed her one the way she'd been drinking in the bar. A stiff one over ice. He carried it to her and turned away.

"You're not drinking?" she said.

He stopped in the bathroom door and faced her. He made a face, like he was tasting his mouth and not liking what he found. "I thought I'd brush my teeth first."

After he brushed and rinsed with a mouthwash, he returned to the bedroom. She'd finished about half her drink. He got the pint flask from the dresser drawer and poured himself about an inch or so in the second tumbler. He cupped the glass in the palm of his hand and warmed the cognac.

"You a fugitive from A.A. or something, Karen?"

"What's that supposed to mean?"

"The way they acted at the club," he said. "The eighty-six they had on you."

"They're afraid," Karen said.

"Afraid of what?" *The ghost of Barton Riker,* he thought. *That the ghost will be too much for you one night. That even scotch won't keep that ghost in the grave.*

She shook her head, red glints flashing in her hair.

"You can stay the night." He said.

A third of the bottle of scotch gone, heading toward the half-way mark. Shoes off, the slim, fine legs crossed at the ankles, she was seated upright on the bed, her back against the headboard. "Is it that easy?"

"Nothing is that easy."

"But you think I am?"

Kane let the question hang in the air. He poured a thin stream of cognac in his glass. "I thought questions like that went out in the forties and fifties."

"Not for me. It was my convent schooling."

"You were a child then." He sipped at the cognac, feeling the burn to it. He stood up and placed the glass on the dresser. "I'll give you a ride home or call you a cab. it's your choice." He got his coat from the closet. He turned with one arm in the sleeve and found that she was sitting like he'd struck her. Eyes closed, lips trembling.

"You all right, Karen?"

"I don't want to go home."

"Stay then," he said. "Pick your side of the bed. The only way I'll bother you is if I snore."

"Promise?" She opened her eyes. Her shoulders shook slightly, as if from a mild chill.

"My solid gold promise." He dropped the coat over the back of a chair and walked over to the dresser. He found a long-sleeved tie shirt and tore the wrappings away. "This ought to work as a nightgown and there's a spare toothbrush in my shaving kit."

"You always bring an extra along?"

"Not usually." He grinned at her and saw the tension leave her. "Only when the moon is right."

She went into the bathroom to change and he turned down the bed, turned off the overhead light and put the lamp on its lowest setting. She came out of the bathroom. The sleeves on the shirt were too long and she'd rolled them up until they balled around her thin wrists. The shirt tail reached down past her knees.

He passed by her into the bathroom with hardly more than a casual look. It wouldn't do to show her anything that would push her away from him. He wanted her to trust him and if that meant he had to ignore her as a woman, then he'd have to do just that.

After a shower, he dressed in a clean t-shirt and boxer shorts. He came out to find that she'd taken one of the blankets and wrapped herself in it. The other blanket was folded on his pillow.

He sat on the edge of the bed and looked at the lamp. "You sleep with the light on?"

"If you don't mind." She was on her back, staring up at the ceiling, arms outside the blanket pressed the blanket to her, like walls she'd constructed.

"It's all right with me." He shook out the blanket and covered himself. "You always do that ... sleep with the lights on?"

"Lately," Karen said.

"Bad dreams?"

"Nightmares," she said.

"It's all that bad?"

"What?" She'd drawn away from him. He could hear it in her voice.

"Why you're not supposed to drink. What you're not to tell anyone."

"Yes."

He waited. Karen didn't say any more and after five minutes he realized from the evenness of her breathing that she'd dropped off to sleep. Like falling down an elevator shaft. That was what the scotch did and that was why she needed it. To go out of the light into the darkness without dreams.

He waited for a few more seconds and when she didn't move he closed his eyes and fell asleep.

"You're snoring."

Kane could feel her hand on his shoulder. "Huh?"

"You're snoring."

Gray morning showed at the bottom of the window, where one part of the drapes rucked up. It was somewhere between seven thirty and eight: that was his guess. The lamp still burned at its lowest setting and he reached up and switched it off.

"Sorry," he said. "I guess it's wake-up time anyway."

During the night she'd spread the blanket. It was no longer wrapped around her like a cocoon. Perhaps it had been the heat in the room or sometime during the night, when he hadn't moved toward her, she'd relaxed and trusted him.

"You talked in your sleep." Karen moved to an elbow. leaning over him, and he watched the tangle of her mussed hair as it fell toward him.

"Learn anything?" The fear was there, deep in him, but he kept it in check.

"Not a thing. It sounded like a foreign language."

He laughed. "So much for those language courses they make you take in college. You can't remember anything during the exams and you dream in conversational German fifteen or twenty years later."

Eyes regarding him frankly, but with no suspicion. "It didn't sound like German."

"Vietnamese then," Kane said. "I know a few words of that."

"The war?"

He nodded.

"Poor baby." It was mocking but there was a gentleness in it.

"It wasn't that bad."

He could feel her weight shifting toward him and he closed his eyes and waited. First her hand under his blanket, stroking the hard angle of his shoulder. "Poor baby." And then a burst of air as she lifted his blanket and slipped under it and pressed against him. The shirt was open and he could feel the waves of body heat she gave off. And, against his arm, the smoothness of her skin.

"Karen, this doesn't have to happen."

In a brief moment there she'd made up her mind. She'd willed it and when they were naked he could feel the hard trip of her heart and the shivering.

"It's been so long," she whispered.

"We can still stop."

"Don't you dare."

A kind of laughter and a go-to-hell all mixed together. He was gentle, easy with her and, after a time, he could feel her moving with him and when he knew she rocked on the edge he told himself to let it go, to turn it all loose and it fell away. It had been like throwing a bailed-up scarf into the air and when it all fell apart it, was like the scarf weighed a hundred pounds and he couldn't lift it anymore. She reached up and caught him by the shoulders and shuddered.

❧ ❧ ❧

Later. The breathing easy. Side-by-side. Her hands moved over him and she found the slick scar tissue, the old wounds. "What are those?"

"Acne scars," he said.

"No."

"Old war wounds."

"Oh." And her hands touched him with a difference. There was the tenderness and the magic of a healer.

Beyond the window he could see the grayness burn away and they slept again.

❧ ❧ ❧

Kane placed the two plastic cups of coffee on the night table beside the bed. She was still sleeping. Then he emptied the second bag. In this there were two smaller cups, fresh pressed orange juice, and at the bottom foil wrapped egg sandwiches.

He sat on the side of the bed. "Breakfast, Karen."

"Did you say breakfast?" Her eyes were open, bright, no longer tired.

"Juice, coffee and a fried egg sandwich."

"The juice and the coffee sound fine." She doubled the pillow behind her and sat up. She pulled the sheet up to her neck. "And no peeking."

"I don't need to. I have a good memory." Kane opened the juice cups and drank his in a couple of long swallows. He watched as she took the little cat sips that emptied hers. He crushed both cups and dropped them in one of the paper bags. After he handed her a cup of coffee, he unwrapped both egg sandwiches.

"Just the coffee," Karen said.

He shook his head. "The sandwich too. More nutrition than in the Johnny Walker."

"You too?"

"Me too … what?"

"You're like the rest of them," she said.

"You think that?" He waited. Serious, no smile. It was important.

"Yes."

He took a long sip of his coffee. "I hide your glass or water your drinks?"

"No."

"Then don't talk foolishness." He bit into the egg sandwich, chewed slowly and swallowed. "If somebody tries to do something for you, don't be so hardheaded. Let it happen."

"All right, John." Like a meek child she took the sandwich. She ate it, every crumb. After they'd finished the coffee he cleared the bed and the night table while she scooted down and stretched out on the bed. She moved over and patted the space next to her. He kicked off his shoes and swung his legs up onto the bed.

"Better?"

"If it stays down," Karen said. But she was smiling and she put her head in the hollow of his shoulder. They remained that way for a long time until they matched breaths and heartbeats. "John, who are you?"

"A dealer in antiques."

"With a wife and children and a mortgage?"

"No wife and no children," he said. "I had a wife once. You could say I've been between wives for the last five years."

"You're the worst kind," she said. "The ones who've learned to live alone again."

"That something your mother told you?"

"I think I read it in *Dear Abby*."

"You like advice for the lovelorn, Karen?"

"You have some for me?"

"Just this," Kane said. "Don't worry about it. Let it happen."

She waited. "Is that the advice?" She lifted her head from his shoulder and stared at him.

"That's it. All of it."

"I'll think about it." She eased her head back onto his shoulder. "How long will you be in town?"

"How long would you like?"

"That's not the question."

"A week," Kane said. "Maybe two weeks. It depends upon the quality at the auction houses."

"And then ...?"

"Back to Charlotte."

Wistful, the sound of a faraway child in her: "That seems like such a short time."

"You know what my advice to the lovelorn meant?"

"No, not really," she said.

"I meant that you're not to force anything. Let everything happen, let it define itself."

"All right, John."

"You've been asking about me. You get equal time. That ruckus last night, what was it really about?"

"I'm not supposed to drink." A muscle twitched at the corner of her mouth. "Not at all. I've been warned."

"Why?"

"They're afraid of me. Afraid of something I might know." It began as a ripple low in her back and grew until it was a shivering desperation. "I can't talk about it. Not even to you. Especially not to you. If they thought you knew ..." The plea choked her voice, asking him not to push, not to try to force it out of her.

"Forget I asked." Keeping it level. It would come. In a day or two, she'd open it up for him, when she thought she knew him. "The club, except for what happened to me there last night, seemed like a nice enough place."

"It's no better or worse than any other club on the Backbone," she said.

"Backbone?"

"It's what they call it. Those streets off the Main Street."

"The tough who worked me over ...?"

"Franco."

"He owns part of the Club?"

"Him? He hasn't got the head for it. The owner's Eddie Vincent. At least he's got the controlling points in it."

"But he's not the real owner?"

"He's as real as anybody else. His name's on the liquor license."

At one thirty Kane drove her from the motel to the parking lot at the Nineties Club. In the daylight, with the shadows, it didn't seem as sinister. A beer truck was parked at the main entrance and two blacks were unloading cases of Bud. Off to one side a heavy, shambling man was running a vacuum sweeper over the empty parts of the parking lot. From a distance, he lifted one hand from the handle of the sweeper and smiled and waved at Karen.

Karen waved back. Dropping the hand, she leaned back into Kane's car.

"Tonight?" Kane asked. "Maybe a late dinner."

"At ten," she said. "I'll come by your place."

She closed the passenger door and stepped up on the curb. The sky behind her was as dull and gray as a lead slug.

CHAPTER ELEVEN

Kane spent the afternoon in the Main Street auction shops. His business card got him past the locked doors and into the display rooms where the managers and their assistants unpacked the boxes and barrels that held that evening's offerings. After an introduction and a few words of small talk, he was given the run of the auction houses. There he passed an afternoon of slow time, a notebook in his hands, wandering through a vast array of silver, pewter and old glassware.

Because he was not sure he was being watched, it was probably a waste of time. But cover was important and it needed to be reinforced. Especially this cover he'd taken on. It was flimsy. Now and then during the afternoon, faced with a shape in glass or a design in silver, he regretted he hadn't allowed himself the proper time to research his cover. That was haste and the danger that haste brought with it.

At one shop, while he stared down at a single silver candlestick, the owner bustled around him. "I see you've got a good eye for it," the owner finally said.

Kane didn't answer.

"I think it's a Goodnow and Jenks," the owner said. "Of course, it's not authenticated."

Kane took his time. He gave the candlestick a final look before he said, "Perhaps," with just the right amount of disdain.

They were waiting for him when he parked the Duster in the parking slot in front of his motel room. He'd seen the black and white police cruiser with *Ansonville Police Department* on the doors as soon as he turned off the street. It was down five or six slots from his own.

As he left the Duster, and walked toward the door to the motel, he heard the opening and the slamming of the cruiser doors. They converged on him while he fumbled for the motel key.

The young cop in uniform stopped about ten feet away from him, hand on his gun butt. The older cop was in plain clothes. He wore a gray pin stripe that was too expensive and too well tailored for the usual police pay. Coat open, he stopped an arm's reach away from Kane.

"You John Cassidy?"

Kane turned slowly. "Yes."

"I'm Harris," the older cop said. He did a flash of a badge and an I.D.

"What's it about?"

"You beat up any girls lately?"

"Lately?" Kane stared at him.

"You know Karen Fisk?"

"I know her." Kane felt his stomach give a little flip before he controlled it. "I met her last night."

"Must not have liked her," Harris said. "You beat her pretty bad this afternoon."

"She say I did it?"

"No."

Kane unlocked the door and pushed it open. "Mind if we go inside?" Harris didn't object so Kane went in. The maid had made her rounds since Kane had been out. The bed was made and the trash basket empty. He took the top from the plastic ice bucket. A few small chips of ice floated on the stale water. The part bottle of scotch and the glass flask of cognac were arranged next to the bucket and two wrapped tumblers were nearby instead of in the bathroom.

Let them wait. He tore the wrapper from one of the glasses and poured a splash of cognac in it. "What time did this beating take place?"

"An hour ago." Harris pushed back his cuff and looked at his watch. "That would put it at five o'clock, give or take a couple of minutes."

"Where?"

"You seem to be asking all the questions." Harris shrugged. "Her apartment outside of town. Out near the lake."

Kane took part of the drink and rolled it around in his mouth. Back to the door, the young uniformed cop stared at him. Kane put the glass on the dresser top and said, "Got to reach in my pocket for some business cards."

Harris said, "Go ahead."

Kane brought out the thin stack of business cards he'd picked up at the auction houses. There were five cards and he spread them on the dresser and sipped at the rest of the cognac while he reconstructed the afternoon in his mind. In the end, he picked up two of the cards and carried them over to Harris. The first was a card for the Brahaney Gallery. He handed it to Harris and said, "I was there from around four thirty until a bit after five." He gave Harris a few seconds and then he passed him the card for the Stellman Salon. "Right after that, must have been from five ten or so, I was in the Stellman until about ten minutes ago."

Harris held a card in each hand. "Odd thing about this," he said. "Those auction shops don't open until around eight in the evening."

"I'm in the business." Kane peeled off his topcoat and his suit jacket and dropped them on the bed. "I had a private look at the stock." He nodded at the cards. "You know those two?"

"I know them," Harris said.

"Use my phone. And if you don't mind, while you're doing that, I'm going to take a shower."

"Go ahead."

When Kane came out of the bathroom ten minutes later, the young cop was still braced against the doorway. Harris was seated on the edge of the bed. He had the other glass in his hand, chips of ice and a good shot of scotch in it. "It checks out. The time's right and both of them remember you."

"Thought they would." Kane had dressed, except for his shoes and socks, in the bathroom. Now he sat down in the chair and put on a clean pair of socks. "You have any special reason to come looking for me?"

"The bartender at the Nineties said you made trouble there last night. He said you made a play for the girl."

"That's his version of it." Kane dropped his shoes in front of him and pushed his feet in. "How's the girl?"

"Banged up pretty good," Harris said. He tipped back his glass and poured down the last of his drink. "The funny thing is that they didn't mark up her face."

Kane stood. "Sounds like somebody wanted her to stay pretty."

Harris pushed up from the bed. He carried the empty glass to the dresser and banged it on the top. "You in antiques." It wasn't a question. "You don't read right, mister. You've got a wrong smell to you."

"I've been around some." Kane picked up his jacket and put it on. "I was in a war or two. Smelled some smoke."

"It's not that," Harris said.

"I don't know what else it could be." Kane picked up his top-coat and waited. "You got any more questions for me?"

"Not right now. You in a hurry to get somewhere?"

"The hospital," Kane said.

Harris nodded. He walked over to stand beside the young cop. "This is a bad town to mix around in if you don't belong."

"That's one bit of advice I don't need. All I did was try to keep the girl from being roughed up. It wasn't any of my business and I got the crap beat out of me."

"You're not the first one," Harris said. "Franco's trouble."

"Well," Kane said, "he didn't get a cherry."

The young cop laughed. He was too young to have heard it in one of the wars. Harris just nodded and they went out and pulled the door closed behind them.

"Miss Fisk." The nurse stood to the right of the hospital bed and leaned over Karen. "Miss Fisk, your brother's here to see you."

Kane took his hand from the foot rail of the bed and moved over to stand on the left. The cop, Harris, had been right. Whoever had worked on her had kept his fists low. There weren't any marks on her face. Even so, her face looked drawn and older. Lines seemed cut into her face, pain lines, and there were dark shadows around her eyes.

Karen's eyelids fluttered. Kane nodded across the bed at the nurse and she left, rubber heels squeaking on the tile floor.

"Looks like you had an accident," Kane said.

"It wasn't... any accident." Her breath was short, like she might have broken or bruised ribs.

"You see who did it?" He put out his hand and touched her face. "Nod if it's easier."

She nodded yes.

"Know them?"

She nodded yes.

"One man?"

Again a nod.

"Franco?"

She shook her head.

"You know him?"

A nod yes.

"Tell me his name."

She shook her head, harder this time, and the breath hissed through her lips. The movement had started the pain running again.

"Give me his name, Karen."

"Not ... supposed ... to talk ... to you."

"He tell you that?"

A nod yes.

"What's his name?"

"Park Simpson ... but ..."

"Where can I find him?" Kane asked.

"You're ... not in ... his league," she said.

Kane stared down at her and shook his head.

"I don't know ... where ... he lives."

"He hang around the Nineties Club?"

"No."

"Where?"

"Bucket ... of Blood."

"That's a club?"

She nodded.

"What does Simpson look like?"

"Tall ... thin ... dark long hair ... big hands ... one wall-eye ... the left one."

He swung around and eased the weight of one hip onto the bed. When the bed shifted, she gasped and he stood up again quickly. "I'm sorry." He brushed his hand over her face. "Why'd they do this to you?"

"Saw me ... with you ... I guess."

"Who saw us?"

"It must have been ... Dummy."

"Who?"

"The swamper ... at the Nineties ... saw us ... when you ... dropped me ... this afternoon."

He remembered. The shambling man with the vacant face. "Where does he live?"

"He doesn't ... know any ... better. The mind of a child ... don't hurt him."

"All right."

"Promise?"

"My best, pure gold promise." he said.

A smile touched her mouth. "For what that's worth."

"I tried to talk you out of it," he said.

"Not ... very hard."

"Rest now." He grinned at her. "Tonight doesn't count as a date. You owe me a rain check."

"John ... don't ... that Simpson is ..."

"Who? Me? I'm not the type."

Careful not to put any weight on the bed, he leaned over her and kissed her. Her lips trembled under his and he could, in his mind, taste blood. The salt of it.

CHAPTER TWELVE

It was seven thirty or so when he left the hospital. Half an hour before the auction houses opened. At a small diner, a short distance away from the hospital, he ate a small rare strip steak and a salad.

It was a few minutes after eight when he drove through Main Street. The auction houses were open and he drove in a kind of aimless circle through the town, an uneven box step until he found an open pawn shop. That noted, he circled the block and parked on Main Street.

He entered the auction house closest to the pawn shop and worked his way into the mass and sea of people. He drifted about the large room for fifteen minutes. He didn't bid and he spent most of his time watching the front door. None of the people who entered the auction house after him seemed to be anyone but the usual tourists. When the bidding on a silver tea set reached its peak, Kane ducked out the back door and down a long dark alley.

He waited in the dark shadow, out of the light, but no one followed him. He waited five minutes and then he followed the narrow alley until it sliced, at a right angle, into the street where he'd noticed the pawn shop a few minutes before.

When Kane came out of the pawn shop five minutes later, the pocket on the right side of his topcoat sagged with weight. In that pocket, his hand fitted over it, was a shot-loaded blackjack with a braided leather cover.

After a brisk walk back up the alley, and a few minutes of mingling in the auction house, Kane pushed his way back out to Main Street and got into his car. He sat in the Duster for five more minutes and watched the auction house front. No one came out. He kicked the engine over and pulled out into the traffic.

❧ ❧ ❧

Bull Racklin stood at parade rest with his back to the closed door. He'd read the message when it came in a few minutes earlier and now he watched Dundee read it for the second time before he dropped it on the center of his desk and slapped a palm down on it.

BLUE MOLE CONFIRMS KANE OUT OF TOWN. POSSIBLE NEW HARDFIST.

And below that, written in the slashing broad script of a fountain pen, a note had been added.

J. CARTER CONFIRMS BY PHONE 2142 HOURS. KANE IN ANSONVILLE, GA. COVER NAME JOHN CASSIDY.

Dundee, thin and pigeon-chested, a man in his mid-forties, lifted his hand from the message form and tapped it with a single finger. Behind steel-rimmed glasses, his eyes looked red and tired.

"Has Whistler seen this?"

"I thought you knew," Bull said.

"Knew what?"

Bull checked his watch. "Whistler left for Paris less than an hour ago."

"Pryor?"

"Sleeping." A thin smile touched Bull's mouth. "He has a wake-up call for 0600."

"That leaves Burden."

"The choir boy?" There was a naked dislike in Bull's tone. "He's at Valley Farm for the week. Some kind of retraining Whistler put on for him. Something about the screwed-up way he walks."

Dundee laughed. Bull waited a polite beat and joined in.

Bull said, when the harsh laughter died out, "It looks like you're keeping the store."

"Interesting."

Bull nodded.

"And this message is also."

"I thought it might be." Bull let his breath out in a thin whistle. "Otherwise I might have made a copy for Pryor."

"No copy for Pryor?"

Bull met his eyes and shook his head slowly. "In fact, that is the only copy. And there is the chance that one might be filed by mistake in some inactive folder or other. You'd be surprised how messy the housekeeping around here is."

"I bet I would," Dundee removed his glasses and rubbed a slim, soft hand across his eyes. "I have a feeling, Bull, that you've been reading my mail."

"Not exactly," Bull said, "but close to it."

"Kane," Dundee said.

"Kane."

The silence set hard, cured like concrete, before Dundee said, "I guess it must get dull, the kind of work you're doing now."

"Dull as cabbage soup," Bull said.

"I was considering a courier job for you."

"That would be a holiday."

"The word around the Shop, about the time I got here, is that you and Kane had your differences."

"He's the reason I'm not in the field right now."

"Pulled you, huh?"

"Not exactly," Bull said. "He punked up to Whistler and blew in his ear. Said I was too old for the work."

"And you're not?"

"Not by half," Bull said.

Dundee nodded. "I think Jacksonville is the closest airfield."

"A commercial flight?"

A bare shake of Dundee's head. "I think I can lay on a military training flight for you."

"Tonight?"

"Within two hours," Dundee said.

Dundee lifted the message and tore it into a hundred little pieces. He scooped up the bits and pieces and dropped them in a metal ashtray. Just before he touched a lighted match to the fragments, he said, "That probably saved the taxpayer a dollar."

The Bucket of Blood looked like Watts modern. There wasn't a window out front and a thin coat of white stucco covered the cinderblock construction. The double doors, a glaring white, carried most of the decoration: a huge comic book glob of bright red blood. It spread across both doors and the bucket, with the same bright red flowing over the sides, was suspended over the door.

Kane left the shot-loaded blackjack under the seat of the Duster and entered. He found elbow room at the bar and ordered cognac. It was brought to him in a thick shot glass with an ice water chaser.

It was a mixed-motif bar, a long wide room with a low ceiling. Kane decided that two or three people had done the interior designed without consulting each other about the final effect they wanted. On one hand there was the nautical: ship fittings and portholes. Beyond the portholes there was nothing but a badly painted image of the sea with frothy whitecaps. Along with that, but not quite meshing, there was the pirate trappings, the tissue paper costumes hanging on the walls, the displays of wooden swords and plastic flintlock pistols.

He watched the subtle flow of movement about the bar. The hookers moved from table-to-table and along the bar, signaled Kane thought by a nod from this bartender or that one, and he heard the price quoted once.

"It's five-oh," the blonde in the tight knit dress said to the man next to Kane. The man nodded and tossed back his drink and left with the blonde and then there was more room at the bar and Kane took the man's stool and made himself comfortable. The fishing was good and he had to shake his head at a couple of girls who drifted by with the question on their faces.

Mainly he watched for the right man. The man who matched the description Karen had given him of Park Simpson. Thin, tall, long black hair, big hands and a walleyed left eye.

By the time he'd finished his first drink and pushed the shot glass toward the bartender for another drink, he'd decided that Park Simpson wasn't in the club. And impatience pushed at him until he noticed the second flow in the room. Straight in front of him, at the back of the club, there was a plain door. At first he thought it might be a rear entrance. He discarded that after a slow walk-by on the way to the men's room. Up closer, what had seemed to him to be some kind of lettering plaque, turned out to be a glass peephole at eye level.

When he returned from the restroom, he waited until the bartender he'd been dealing with backed toward him. He was a young man with a turkey neck and thyroid eyes. Kane touched him on the elbow and when he turned and looked down at Kane's glass, he said, "Action back there?"

The bartender lifted his eyes and looked Kane over. "It's a private club."

"With action?"

The bartender nodded. He hadn't quite finished his estimate of Kane.

"I'd like to join," Kane said.

"Live here in town?"

"Charlotte. I'm here on business and vacation. About fifty-fifty each way."

"Dues'll cost you ten."

Kane brought out his roll. He shielded it from the rest of the bar but let the bartender have his look while he located a ten and dropped it on the bar counter. The bartender left the ten on the bar and walked away. He returned a few moments later with a cigar box. He opened the box and took out a small dime store ledger and a wire ring of metal disks. He unclipped the ring and took off the top disk. Crudely stamped on the center was a number. 803. The bartender wrote down the number from the disk and looked over at Kane. "Driver's license?"

Kane opened his breast wallet and unfolded the card section. It featured the credit cards. He found the bogus North Carolina license and tapped it with his finger. The bartender leaned over and read the name and wrote it next to the number. Closing the ledger, he dropped the ten into the box and slid the metal disk toward Kane. "That's your membership card."

"What's the name of the club?"

"The Hook and Ladder." The bartender closed the cigar box and moved away.

Kane finished his drink and left a couple of singles under his shot glass.

The disk got him past the door. Eyes beyond the peephole stared at him until he held up the disk. Then he heard locks scrape and he was in a dim hallway. A young man wearing a shoulder rig with the butt of a short barrel Smith & Wesson. looked him over and pointed him down the hall. Kane nodded at him and moved toward the closed door at the end of the short hall. It was a low hubbub he heard at first and when he opened the door it hit him with its full force. The chant of the housemen, the bone-scraping laughter of women and the lower rumble of the men playing.

Smoke hung over the room like a cloud and there was the strong scent of some kind of air freshener being pumped into the room through the ventilation system.

To his left, there were four blackjack tables in a row, the housemen with their backs to the wall. In the center, with some open space around it, was the roulette table. And along the right wall two crap tables. At the right front wall, near the crap tables was a service bar without stools. Straight ahead, past the roulette table, there was a high chair with a houseman seated in it.

Kane drifted to the service bar. He didn't see cognac, so he settled for a bourbon and rocks. Then he walked toward the crap tables. Standing on the fringes, watching the play, he got his first good look at the houseman on the high chair. A man in a blue blazer and gray slacks. Hair long and dark. Seemed thin and tall but Kane couldn't be sure with the man seated. And then the man turned and looked in Kane's direction. And Kane saw the walleye, the left one. His eyes met Kane's and held them, some kind of sharp awareness on his face. Just a new player, Kane told himself, one the house hadn't seen before. As casually as he could Kane lowered his eyes and watched the shooter.

The shooter was on a streak. Kane watched him make his point, an eight, and the houseman raked the table. Kane peeled out his first bet, a twenty, and dropped it on the Horn Bet. It was a foolish bet, one with the odds heavily against him. The shooter threw a natural seven and the houseman raked Kane's twenty away. Before the next roll he leaned in and dropped another twenty on a hard way bet, on double fives. The shooter's luck left him and he rolled a twelve. Once again, Kane watched a twenty raked away.

He risked a look at Simpson. Simpson had turned in his chair and was staring at the action at the blackjack tables. Foolish betting had convinced Simpson that Kane was just another sucker who didn't understand craps or the odds.

Kane left the crap tables and played roulette until he lost a hundred or so. He left the gaming room then and walked back out to the Bucket of Blood bar. The same bartender who'd enrolled him in the club poured a cognac for him and said, "Tell them where you won it."

Kane grinned and said, "Won what?"

Before he left the bar, saying he had to cash a few traveler's checks, he found out that the Hook and Ladder kept the gambling tables open until 3 A.M.

CHAPTER THIRTEEN

Bull Racklin wore his traveling clothes. He'd changed to a dark wool suit, a dark blue shirt and a silver-gray tie. His shoes were black chukka boots, taken the day he bought them to a shoe shop where he'd had the leather soles and heels replaced with rubber. Placed just inside the door to Dundee's office was a small cloth-covered suitcase. In it he'd packed two changes of underwear, spare socks, three shirts and his shaving kit.

Now he stood looking down into the attaché case on the front edge of the desk. There was a length of steel chain attached to it and a lock-cuff. It was open and empty.

Dundee opened the clasp on a brown envelope and shook out three enlarged photos. "You know Kane but you haven't seen him in a few years. These were taken about a month ago. You can assume there might be minor alterations, hair color and the like."

Bull studied the photos and dropped them back on the desk. "I won't need these. I'll know him."

"If you're sure," Dundee said.

"I'm sure."

"Your weapon's a .357 ... right?"

Bull nodded.

Dundee reached into a desk drawer on his right and brought out a cloth wrapped object. He placed it on the desk and unwrapped it, careful that he didn't touch any part of it. It was a blue Dan Wesson .357 with a four-inch barrel. "This one was taken off a shipment two weeks ago. As far as we know it, hasn't been reported missing yet. It's been test-fired, cleaned and reloaded."

"Spares?"

One more reach into the same drawer. Dundee tossed a small cloth sack, like a tobacco bag, on the desk next to the Wesson. It gave off a dull clink when it landed. "Hot loads. Twelve enough?"

"More than enough." Bull rewrapped the Wesson and placed it in the attaché case. He dropped the bag of spares in next to it. "Is that all?"

"Expense money." Dundee drew an envelope from his inside breast pocket and tore the end from it. He held it across the desk toward Bull, who shook out a sheaf of used tens and twenties.

"Five hundred," Dundee said, "and no accounting if there's any left over."

"There won't be," Bull said. "I'm on vacation."

"Another five when the job's done."

"That's fair," Bull said. "I'd do it for nothing."

Bull counted out a hundred and put it in his pocket. The rest he returned to the envelope and dropped it in the attaché case. He closed the case and snapped the locks. He placed the case upright and put the cuff-lock on his left wrist and snapped it closed. "Keys?"

Dundee passed him a key ring on which there were two keys. "From Jacksonville, take the bus up to Ansonville. It'll be a dull ride but it won't leave a rental car around and the questions a loose end like that brings up."

"If something goes wrong," Bull said.

Dundee nodded.

"You sound like you have doubts," Bull said.

"Don't under estimate him," Dundee said. "He's on a job and he's wary."

"Of a tourist like me?"

Dundee smiled. He looked over his shoulder at the wall clock. The time was one ten A.M. "The copter's on the pad."

❧ ❧ ❧

At three A.M., the last three customers wobbled their way out the front door of the Bucket of Blood. The door slammed shut behind them and the floodlights that lit the club front and spilled out into the parking lot went out. After those three cars drove away, there were three cars still parked in front of the double white doors with the comic-book stain on it.

Across the street, the nose of his Duster pointed south down the one-way street, Kane waited. It was cold, and from time-to-time he'd stretch the muscles of his back, trying to get some heat generated under his topcoat. And his feet shifted and danced on the floorboards.

At three twenty, Park Simpson backed out of the Bucket of Blood and pulled the door closed behind him. He shook the door a couple of times to be sure the lock held and then he turned and walked to a blue Electra. Kane recognized the long, thin shadow of him and had that sense confirmed when Simpson opened the door to the Electra and the light hit him for a second or two before he stepped inside and pulled the door closed.

The Electra came out of the lot exit about fifty feet in front of where Kane waited. He didn't even have to duck the headlights. He let the Electra have another fifty yards before he kicked the engine over and pulled into the center lane. The road behind him was empty and he waited another count of ten before he cut on his headlights.

It was a slow, leisurely drive down the center of the Backbone. Simpson didn't seem to be in any special hurry. Kane drifted along about a block behind him. In ten minutes, the town proper was past and they were in the skin layer of apartment houses. Then those were behind also and they drove through a wooded area, tall pines bordering them on both sides of the road. No house, no other structure showing. Kane was about to brace himself for some all-night drive that might take him south to Florida, when he saw that Simpson had pumped the brakes, the lights flashing back at him, and he knew he'd drifted back too far. He lost the Electra. The first time by he missed the cut-off and he had to turn on the side of the road and come back slowly. He found it a few minutes later: a narrow ribbon cut into a thick stand of pines, a road about wide enough for one car. Kane swung into the road and took it slowly. It was a good thing he did. The woods back there had been logged in the last year or so. The heavy trucks had rutted and torn up the dirt road.

About a quarter of a mile in, the road widened. Another quarter of a mile and he found he was approaching some kind of compound. The road was like the handle to a lady's fan and the compound was the fan. To his left, as he moved into the fan, he saw a long low cinderblock building. It was rough, unfinished, with no facing of any kind covering the blocks. The matching and balancing windows were shuttered, with only a weak spill of light.

Kane circled the parking lot until he found the blue Electra. There was an empty space to the left of it and Kane parked there. He turned and put an arm over the back of the seat and watched the front door of the building. It didn't take him long to figure out that Simpson had led him to a backwoods, low-rent and low-overhead whorehouse. Within minutes, he'd heard two customers pass, discussing the girls. And not much later, still watching the door, he saw another man leave while a girl in a thin orange robe stood in the open doorway and yelled for him to come back soon.

It was an hour's slow time. Halfway through that hour, Kane slid across the seat and waited near the passenger door, where he would be close to the driver's door of the Electra. The blackjack rested on his thigh.

Park Simpson came out alone. In the light of the open door, before someone slammed it shut behind him, Kane saw him lift a hand and rub it across his eyes. A headache or he'd had a few shots inside and he was dizzy. But the hand dropped away and he walked slowly toward the Electra. His head still shaking while he sucked in deep breaths. His hand fumbled for the keys.

Kane bent over and gripped the door handle in his left hand. His right hand found the grip of the blackjack. He leaned his right shoulder against the door, his strength and power held in check by the door, his feet pressing hard against the floorboards.

Simpson reached the Electra and bent over to insert the key. His back was to the side of the Duster. While he was in that position, Kane flipped the door handle and swung the door against Simpson with all his strength. The Duster door hit Simpson in the rump and slammed him against the side of the Electra. He was stunned and pinned there. Kane stepped out and jerked the door away from Simpson.

Simpson stumbled back, turning, dazed but bringing his hands up when Kane reached in and swung the blackjack against the side of his head. Kane stepped back as Simpson fell, unconscious.

Kane looked over his shoulder at the building. Nothing moved there.

Kane stood over Simpson.

Twenty minutes had passed and they were in another part of the woods. After he'd loaded Simpson in the back of the Duster and tied his hands behind him with his own necktie, he'd followed the narrow, rutted road back to the main highway. He'd turned right there and gone about another two miles before he found a dirt road that sliced off to the left. It didn't seem to go anywhere. It deadened a bit more than a hundred yards off the highway. It was, Kane guessed, some kind of a lover's lane for high school kids in the spring and summer.

Simpson was still out when Kane parked. He grabbed him under the arms and pulled him out of the car. He dragged him away from the Duster, until he was in a narrow clearing. When Simpson began to stir, Kane took a handkerchief from Simpson's hip pocket. He unfolded it and made a triangle. He tied it over Simpson's eyes, so that it was like a child's bandit mask that had slipped too high.

Simpson kicked out and his shoulders knotted with strain as he pulled against the tie that held his hands. Kane leaned forward and placed a foot in the space between Simpson's shoulder blades. He put his weight on the foot until he felt Simpson give up his struggle. He swung the blackjack and tapped Simpson on the point of his shoulder. His voice was low, almost a whisper. "Tell me about it, Park."

"About what?"

"The job on the girl."

"I don't know anything about any girl."

Kane swung the blackjack, this time harder, and when the blow landed on the same point of his shoulder, Simpson sucked in his breath.

"Tell me about it, Park."

"Who are you? You know you could be crossing the wrong…"

Thud of the blackjack. Simpson choked off a scream. "One more time," Kane said, "and the shoulder's bone meal."

"It was a job. Nothing else."

"Who paid the tab?"

"Eddie Jocks."

"Who's he?"

Simpson didn't answer right away. Kane said, "Don't drag your feet on me."

"His real name's Eddie Vincent. At the Nineties Club."

"The owner?"

"Got some points in it," Simpson said.

"Eddie set this up or Franco?"

"Eddie."

"Why?"

"I don't ask a why," Simpson said.

"What's the going rate on a job like that?"

"Fifty for a friend."

Enough for a visit to a backwoods cathouse. "You should have got more," Kane said. "It'll cost you more than that to leave town."

"I'm not leaving town." Simpson bunched his shoulders and pulled against the tie that bound his hands. "Anyway, who the hell are you?"

"The one you've got to worry about," Kane said. "I see you in town again and I'll kill you. You've got my word on that."

"Fuck your word," Simpson said.

Kane looped the blackjack far back and broke Simpson's left shoulder with one hard slap.

Park Simpson's scream rattled round in his head as Kane drove back to town. In his motel room, ready for bed, it took two stiff shots of cognac to blot it out. To make it into a whimper.

One less hard ass in town. That meant a job opening. Job opportunity the brutal way. Park Simpson would leave town, but before he did, he'd pass the word back to Eddie Vincent and Franco. They'd have to know who swung the blackjack. Couldn't risk not knowing. In time, all the arrows would point to Kane.

It was that simple. Like putting an ad in the paper.

New man in town wants work.

CHAPTER FOURTEEN

It was three thirty A.M. when the Sabreline, Admiral Bender's personal plane, landed at the Jacksonville Naval Air Station. A sleepy white hat met the plane at the edge of the taxi strip in a follow-me Jeep and led it to the V.I.P. apron in front of the Operations Tower. As soon as the engine whine died out, another white hat chocked the plane.

Bull stepped down to the apron and looked around. He didn't wait to thank the pilots. He spotted the government car parked in the driveway with the engine running and a white hat, in dress uniform, standing at a slack attention next to the passenger door. When Bull was three paces away, the white hat swung the door open. He reached for Bull's bag but Bull ignored him. He placed it on the floorboards and ducked into the car.

The smell of a sweet pipe tobacco swirled out at him. In the light before the enlisted man closed the door behind him, Bull got his look at the man seated next to him. He'd seen the man around the Shop for a month or two before he'd been assigned and shipped out. Bull didn't remember his name and it didn't matter. What he saw was a pudgy man who needed a shave, who'd been pulled out of his bed with only an hour of warning.

"Something up?" the pudgy man asked.

Bull placed the attaché case on his knees. "What's your name?"

"Foster."

"What kind of fucking question is that, Foster?"

Foster sucked in his breath like he'd been hit. "Where do you want to go?"

"Downtown to the bus station."

Foster leaned forward and repeated that to the enlisted man. Bull looked out at the base as the car moved through the almost empty streets. He had nothing to say to Foster. At the main gate, Foster's card got them through without any delay. That much was handled well.

On the highway heading into Jacksonville, Bull turned and placed his body between the driver and the attaché case. He unlocked the case and placed the contents on the seat beside him. After he closed the attaché case, he opened the small suitcase and stuffed the .357, the money and the bag of hot loads in with his clothing. He closed that case. Then, using the cuff-lock key, he detached the attaché case from his left wrist. He turned and dropped it in Foster's lap. "That's yours."

The car eased to a stop across the street from the bus station. Foster said, "Anything else I can do for you?"

"Stay available." Hand on the door, Bull turned and looked at him. "That means twenty-four hours-a-day until you hear otherwise."

"How long?"

"As long as you have to."

At seven ten, a Trailways bus left the station. The destination was Atlanta and points north, but it would stop in Ansonville for ten minutes at nine-oh-four.

Bull slept the whole way, his head back, the small suitcase on the floor behind his legs.

The girl had pulled away from him during the night. She'd drawn herself up into a ball, her head low, and she presented him only the two half-moons of her ass. The skin texture like curdled milk.

Franco considered that but the phone was ringing and it had been ringing for a long time. The dial on the clock beside the bed gave the time as five minutes after six. Still ringing. Franco got up and walked barefooted from the small bedroom and into the kitchen-living room. The trailer, even anchored on blocks, shook under his weight. He reached the phone, picked it up and said, "Hold it a minute." He went back to the stove and lit the flame under the water kettle. He gave the kettle a shake to make sure there was enough water in it and lumbered back over to grab the phone again.

"Yeah?"

"You don't know me." There was a hint of a lisp, a kind of feminine breath to the voice.

"If I don't know you, what the fuck are you waking me up for?"

"A man was just brought into the hospital, he said it would be worth a ten to you if I called you."

"Tell me about it."

"I'm an orderly here at the hospital. An old farmer just brought a man in. He's got a busted up shoulder. He said his name is Park and that you'd want to talk to him."

"He say how he got a busted shoulder?"

"No."

"What's your name?" Franco found the pad and pencil and poised over the pad. "What's your name?"

"Johnny Carpenter."

"I'll leave the ten at the desk for you."

"Which desk?"

The water stirred in the kettle. "How many are there?"

"Leave it at the desk downstairs by the main entrance. All right?"

"Okay."

Franco placed the receiver back on the hook and cut the flame under the kettle. He made himself a weak cup of instant and spooned in a couple of ounces of sugar. He carried the cup back to the bedroom. When he cut on the overhead light, the girl jerked upright and sat blinking at him.

The rest of her wasn't much better, Franco thought. Hair carrot-red, though her pubic hair was pale straw-yellow. Mascara looking like dirt smudges under her eyes. The body looking abused, either by her or by the men she sold it to. Nipples spreading and like nothing as much as leather buttons. Sagging breasts, no will to hold them up anymore.

"I got to go to town, Allie," Franco said. "You'd better get dressed unless you want to stay here until I get back."

They dressed at opposite ends of the small bedroom. Once, Franco felt a stir but he talked himself out of it. It was odd but the more clothes she put on the better she looked. Now the breasts looked high and hard and the ass, with the panty girdle on, seemed flat and solid.

Dressed, with his topcoat over his arm, Franco finished off the cup of coffee. She moved close to him and rubbed against him. "Honey, you didn't pay me yet."

Franco pushed past her and carried the cup into the kitchen. She followed him and watched while he rinsed the cup and placed it in the sink.

"Honey, I said that you didn't ..."

Franco got out his wallet. He fumbled through a sheaf of bills and selected a twenty. He passed it to her. She looked at the bill with an open mouth. Her mouth moved a few times without anything coming out. When she did get the words out there was a whine to them.

"But we said forty ..."

"For you?" Franco looked through the clothes and saw the body and she knew what he saw.

"But, honey, a deal is a deal and ..."

Franco held up his huge right hand, the fingers extended. Then he drew the fingers into a fist. "Four of these will add up to forty."

"All right." She unsnapped her purse and dropped the twenty in and closed it. "But just because you're a nice guy, Franco."

"And the Pope has a pussy," Franco said.

The other beds, except for the far one nearest the window, were empty. Franco had gone over to look at the man in that bed. The man was a black, the smell of booze on him, and the hairy tracks of stitches down the right side of his face extended down to his breast bone. A cutting at Tintop Bottoms, Franco figured. And he stood over the man until he was sure he was out. Either the drink had done it or they'd given him some kind of sedation. Then Franco went over to talk to Park.

"You didn't see him?"

Sweat ran down Park Simpson's face. It ran down the natural channels formed by the lines in his cheeks. And the walleye seemed to be watching the door that led out to the hallway. He'd been given something for the pain but it didn't seem to be strong enough. Later, the doctors in the emergency room had said, there'd be an operation to try to repair the shoulder. But, the doctor had told him, I hope you weren't a left-hand pitcher before this happened to you.

"He didn't want me to," Simpson said.

"But he mentioned the job you did on the girl?"

"He mentioned your name too."

Franco lit a cigarette and drew the smoke in deep. Simpson stared at the cigarette and Franco leaned over and placed it in his mouth. It was a gesture out of some old World War II movie, but making it, Franco felt a lot closer to Simpson. In a lot of ways they were alike, men who lived on their hardness and their ability to hurt without being hurt. And now and then, no matter how well you planned it out, there were mistakes.

"In what way?"

"Asked if you set up the beating."

"And you said ...?"

"That Eddie Jocks did it."

Franco reached over and took the cigarette from Simpson's lips. An ash fell on the sheet. "Eddie won't like that. A loose mouth bothers him."

"It wasn't Eddie he was whapping on the shoulder with about a pound of shot."

"Still ..." Franco looked at the wet tip of the cigarette and ground it out on the floor and kicked it under the bed.

"Look," Simpson said, "the guy whoever he is, he'd have killed me if I hadn't told him what he wanted to know."

"So you told him and he didn't kill you."

Simpson grimaced and a fresh oil sweat ran down his face. "The way this feels right now, I'd be better off if he had killed me."

"And there's always Eddie Jocks."

"Look. All right, so I might have put Eddie on the hot stove. You know what else? This stud told me to leave town. He'd kill me if he saw me again. With that over me, I've got to worry about Eddie Jocks?"

"You leaving?"

"Does a bear shit in the woods or a Greyhound bus station pay toilet?" Park Simpson's laugh had the burn of fever in it.

⚜   ⚜   ⚜

Bull Racklin left his suitcase in a pay locker in the bus station and walked the two blocks over to Main Street. He looked in the doorways of three cafes before he settled upon one on the ground-floor level of the Town Square Hotel. It was expensive as breakfasts went in town and mostly only the tourists who stayed in the hotel ate there.

Bull ordered bacon and eggs and coffee. When his order came, he asked for a saucer and when it was brought to him, he had the waitress wait while he scooped the steaming grits from his plate and onto the saucer. Then he handed the saucer to the stunned waitress and bent his head over the plate. He finished within five minutes and shook his head at the offer of a second cup of coffee.

He made a call from a pay phone in the lobby of the Town Square Hotel. He used a credit card number. When the operator asked his name he said, "Burt Archer," and waited until the switchboard girl came on and said, "Federal Board," and he asked for extension Four.

"I'm here," he said when Dundee answered.

"Good flight?"

"All right." He turned and looked across the lobby. "You hear any more?"

"Blue Mole's been busy. He traced him to Hartsfield. But he didn't take a plane. Left his car and rented one. A blue Duster. Wait a minute." There was a rattle of papers and Dundee gave him the tag numbers. Bull had him repeat them while he wrote them down in the back of a checkbook.

"Anything else?" Bull closed the checkbook and slipped it in the breast pocket.

"Nothing. I'd rather not contact Carter right now. He might get a smell about it."

"It's not necessary anyway," Bull said. "It's a two-day job."

Bull left the hotel and walked back to the bus station. He retrieved his suitcase and waited at the cab stand until a cab pulled in. He told the driver to take him to the nearest car rental lot.

By eleven, he'd rented a Fury in the name of Burt Archer and checked into a motel. It was a Days Inn and he asked for and got the commercial rate.

CHAPTER FIFTEEN

In the night, Kane dreamed.

Someone he couldn't see threw a bucket of something on him. And he thought, *oh, that's just red paint and it will wash off.* And then he touched it and it wasn't paint. It was blood and he could taste it and smell the salt of it. He used his hands to try to wipe the blood away but there was some kind of texture to the blood, not like a liquid, and he could feel this as shreds of something. Skin and tissue and he thought, *it is my skin and my tissue,* but it wasn't. He thought, *who would throw blood and skin and tissue on me?* As soon as he'd asked, he got his answer. It was a dark-haired, slim and childlike girl. *Vietnamese,* he said, but the features softened and shaped by other blood. French, perhaps.

He asked, *why?*

And the girl said, "I had no choice."

He said, *I don't believe that.*

And she said, "I wouldn't do it if I didn't have to."

He said, *why?*

And she said, "There is no answer to why. It is a Western question."

And Kane awoke, sweating in the warm room. And it was two hours and some drinks later before he could sleep again.

"John, what did you do last night?"

Karen looked rested and most of the pain was gone. Beyond her, on the night table on the other side of the hospital bed, the yellow roses that he'd brought her that afternoon warmed the room. The nurse had furnished a vase and she'd arranged them before she left them alone.

"Me?" He gave her a gentle, loose smile. "I had a few drinks and lost a few dollars in one of the private clubs."

"Franco was here early this morning."

"Did he bring you roses?"

"He said somebody worked Park Simpson over last night and left him in the woods. He wanted to know if I had any protectors here in town."

"And you said...?"

"That I didn't."

"That sounds like the truth to me." He edged a chair close to the bed with the toe of his shoe and sat down. "You think I look like I could handle somebody like Simpson?"

She shook her head. "But you remind me of somebody."

"Anybody I ought to know?"

"No."

"You mean Barton Riker?"

"I knew it." The voice a kind of hurt sigh now.

"Knew what?"

"That you were a cop."

"That's not a good guess. No, not a cop. Something else."

"What else is there?"

Kane said, "A friend of the family."

"A friend of his brother?" She asked. Kane nodded. "What does the brother look like?" Kane described him, briefly and to the point. "Then you're both crazy. There's nothing you can do here."

"I can find out what happened to Barton. I can do that much."

"If I told someone else about what you just told me, it could get you killed."

"Perhaps."

"No perhaps," she said. "Perhaps is not a word they know."

"All I need is a few words from you."

"I can't say those words."

"You will. Maybe not now. But you will." Kane got his top-coat from the back of the other chair and put it on. "When will you be leaving the hospital?"

"Tomorrow morning."

"I'll come back in the morning and drive you home."

"No, John."

"Tomorrow morning," he said.

He leaned over the bed to kiss her. At the last moment, she turned her head away and took the kiss on the cheek.

At the desk he got directions to the cashier's office. It was downstairs near the main entrance. A fleshy young girl left her typewriter and met him at the counter.

"My sister's a patient here. Karen Fisk. I'd like to take care of her bill."

The girl returned a few moments later with a folder. She skimmed down the folder and looked at Kane. "It's already been settled by her employer, a Mr. Franco Terck."

"That's through tomorrow ... when she checks out?"

"Tomorrow?" The girl gave him a puzzled look. "Just a min-ute." She left him and made a call. Her back was to him and he couldn't hear the telephone conversation. When she returned she said, "I checked with Dr. Mattson. I guess you got it mixed up. She'll be leaving this evening after the late rounds."

"I guess I did." He grinned at her and shook his head. "What time are late rounds?"

"Around eight," she said.

At the hospital entrance he stood a long time. Torn between leaving and going back up to Karen's room. In the end, he decided against returning to her floor. She'd lied to him for some reason and there might be better ways to find out the why of it. *Why?*

And he remembered the nightmare. It took him the walk across the parking lot to shake it out of his head.

As Kane drove past the parking lot, stopping just long enough to pay the fee, two other cars in the lot kicked over their engines and backed out.

In the black Fairlane, squat, powerful Franco sat in the front passenger seat. Next to him a lean young man drove. The young man had the five o'clock shadow that looked like ingrained coal dust.

In the other car, the rented Fury, Bull Racklin read the Fairlane for what it was. He smiled to himself. It was a rough game and Kane had bought more company than he could probably handle. And because Bull did nothing without being sure what the risk was, he let the Fury stall. He let the Fairlane fall in behind Kane and then remained far behind.

After a couple of blocks, Bull knew where Kane was going and he dropped back even farther. It would not do for the people in the Fairlane to spot him.

Kane was returning to his motel. And Bull knew where that was because he'd spent almost two hours finding the right one. He'd known Kane's patterns so he'd passed up the hotel. The motels would give Kane the kind of freedom he needed for the job. The coming and going at all hours without being seen. So Bull had split the town into four parts and he'd checked the motels. A slow drive past each one, sometimes going through the parking lot. And then, at twelve thirty, he'd found the blue Duster in the lot of the Restaway Motel. He'd driven past it slowly while he checked the tag numbers against the ones he'd scribbled in the back of his checkbook.

And he'd been waiting across the street five minutes later when Kane came out of his room and drove downtown for a hurried breakfast. From that time on, either Kane or the Duster would be in Bull's vision. Until the job was done.

Kane spotted the Fairlane tailing him within a block of leaving the hospital. He slowed and watched the Fairlane ease down to keep the distance constant. The urge was in him to play games with them, to lead them down the back streets and side alleys. It was a strong impulse. Instead he drove toward his motel. Two blocks from the motel, he caught a yellow traffic light and passed through. The Fairlane caught the red and had to wait.

Kane was seated in a chair facing the door when the knock sounded at his motel room five minutes later. The Woodsman Sport was on his knee angled toward the door, waist high. The traffic light had given him that edge, time to unscrew the back from the television set and take the Sport out.

"It's unlocked," he said.

Franco entered alone and closed the door behind him with the kick of his heel. He looked at the Sport and kept his hands spread wide. "I knew there was something that didn't read right about you, soldier."

"This?" Kane nodded down at the Sport. "This is for plinking."

"And the sap you used on Park?"

"You must be thinking about somebody else." Kane tapped the Sport against his knee. Behind Franco, to his left, there was the other chair, now placed against the wall. Kane nodded at the chair. "Hands on your knees where I can see them."

"I'm not carrying," Franco said. "I don't use iron."

"Hands on your knees anyway," Kane said. "Just humor me."

Franco sat. He tried to make it slow and gracefully but there wasn't that much grace in him. "I thought we ought to talk."

"Talk," Kane said.

"You're no cop."

"It wasn't one of my ambitions. All the time I was a kid, I wanted to be a fireman."

"The job on Park, that wasn't cop work."

"I don't know anybody named Park."

"The thing with Park, was that because of the girl? Or just your way of telling us something about you?"

"You've got a slow mind," Kane said. "You sound queer for some guy named Park."

"The way I see it," Franco said, "you want some of the action."

Kane kept his eyes level. "Action?"

"Come on." Franco sounded impatient. "I know one of the hard ones when I see him."

"That right?" Kane grinned at him.

"You might have fooled me the other night. Not anymore."

"The sucker punch? That was the initiation fee."

Franco's right hand balled and tapped against his thigh. "I can still take you, soldier."

"With a hole in your kneecap?"

"Straight up," Franco said. "Fists."

"You come on your own or did Jocks send you?"

"I knew it. That was what Park said…"

"Before he left town?"

"Not yet. Soon as they fix his shoulder." Franco shook his head slowly, as if he couldn't believe it. "Park is a hard ass, but you scared it out of him."

"Jocks send you?"

Franco nodded. "He wants to see you."

"Now?"

"Now," Franco said. "Two hours ago."

❧ ❧ ❧

The redwood plaque on the front edge of the desk had EDWARD S. VINCENT on it in raised brass lettering. The desk was about as big as a regulation pool table, but the man who sat behind it made it seem like a child's school desk.

"Tell me about yourself," Eddie Vincent said.

The office was in the back of the Nineties Club. At the closed door, before Franco had knocked, he'd held out his hand and Kane had placed the Woodsman Sport in it. "Be sure to leave a few of your prints on it," Kane had said. And he'd watched Franco flinch.

"Not much to tell," Kane said to Eddie Vincent.

The man behind the desk looked like a sausage casing that had been overstuffed, almost to bursting. But it wasn't solid weight. It was kind of liquid, flowing fat. His face, as he looked up at Kane who was still standing, was flushed and sweating.

"Where'd you come from?"

"North."

"Who'd you work with up there?"

"I work alone," Kane said.

"Name me who you know up there."

"Nobody."

"Maybe that's why nobody seems to know you."

"That could be," Kane said.

"A record?"

Kane shook his head.

"No time?"

The door opened behind Kane and Franco came in. After he closed the door, he leaned back against it. Kane looked over his shoulder at Franco and then back at Eddie Vincent.

"I said, ever do any time?"

"I was careful," Kane said.

"Maybe you have a careful specialty," Vincent said.

Behind Kane, Franco said, "Yeah, like conning old ladies."

Kane watched Vincent's face. There was no break in it, only a downward curl at the left side of his mouth. "About specialties. For five hundred, I'll off Franco here and put the bones where they'll never be found."

Franco said, "That's not funny."

"It wasn't supposed to be," Kane said.

Vincent looked past Kane. "Shut up, Franco."

Franco grunted and closed his mouth.

"Your interest in Karen, what's that?"

"The interest any man has in a woman. Short-term favors."

"Nothing else?"

"You mean middle-class shit like love?"

Vincent shook his head. "You do much talking to her?"

"No more than I need to."

"The thing with Park Simpson..." Eddie Vincent began.

"I protect even short-term things that belong to me."

"How'd you tag Simpson for it?"

"Looked around," Kane said.

"You good at that?"

"When I want to be."

"You talk a good one," Vincent said. "You want to tell me what you're doing in town?"

"Not especially."

"Tell him anyway," Franco said.

"Not because you're pressing me. It's this way. I heard there were pickings here in town."

"You heard wrong," Vincent said.

"During my time in town, I've seen a few."

"They're not open to freelancing," Vincent said.

"Who says?"

"I do. We do."

"I've seen you and your pet ape here. So far I'm not convinced."

"Take my word for it."

Kane shook his head. "No chance. There's pickings on the street and you think I'm going to starve?"

"You won't be asked to. Not if you fit in."

"One thing," Kane said. "I don't do the time as a stock boy. All that working my way up, that's a waste of my time. If I work, it's where the good money is."

"Are there many more like you at home?" Eddie Vincent nodded past Kane at Franco. "You know where to reach him?"

"I know," Franco said.

Then to Kane: "You sit tight. A day or two and we ought to know whether we have a place for you."

"All right."

"And maybe you ought to stay away from the girl for the time being."

Kane said, "No way."

"If you work for me ..."

"When I work for you, I might consider taking orders."

Vincent didn't push it.

✥ ✥ ✥

Bull Racklin stood next to the rented Fury and watched Kane come out of the Nineties Club. He'd parked the Fury in a spot between the club door and the blue Duster that Kane drove. Now, when Kane was almost past the tail of the Fury, Bull stepped out and held up an unlighted cigarette.

"Sure." Kane dug into his topcoat pocket and brought out a pack of matches. "Keep them."

"Thanks."

Eyes still on Kane's face. No sign of recognition.

He watched Kane walk to the Duster. Not now. Not in the daylight. At night when he could walk right up to him on a dark street or outside his motel room. Just another stranger, another tourist. It was, he knew, going to be one of the easy ones.

CHAPTER SIXTEEN

Eight thirty, a dark and cold night, with the wind whipping around in the street facing the hospital. Kane watched the main entrance from across the street. A fire-truck red 1974 Ford pickup was parked in the loading and unloading zone. After a few minutes, a young man came out of the hospital, following a stiff and upright Karen. He carried her overnight case and he rushed past her to hold open the door of the truck for her. She got in the pickup, her movements slow and almost those of an old woman. That was the pain from the beating.

The young man placed the overnight case at her feet and closed the door. Moments later he drove the wide loop out of the hospital grounds and headed north.

It was a slow drive. The man in the pickup didn't seem in much of a hurry. Kane drifted and dipped through the traffic behind him. The traffic thinned some outside the city limits. An old Mercury convertible wedged itself between the pickup and Kane's Duster. That was as Kane wanted it.

Tall pines bordered both sides of the road. Up in the distance, now and then there was a wink of light, a house set far back off the highway, and then Kane could smell the lake. Lake Tarver, he'd heard it called, and the smell made him suspect that the lake was still polluted, though not to the degree it had been twenty years ago when Hardy Winston returned from the Korean War and had his dream for the town.

The highway ended abruptly and there was a fork where two roads cut away. The Mercury convertible took the left part of the fork and ahead Kane could see the lights of the pickup. It had taken the right fork, a hard-packed clay road that ran along the edge of the lake. Kane slowed and took the right fork also.

The lake spread off to his right, dark and oily, with the stumps of cypresses breaking the smoothness. The road followed the curve of the lake for another mile until, from his careful distance, Kane saw the driver of the pickup pump his brakes. The pickup turned left into a notch in the pines. By the time Kane reached the turnoff, the pickup had parked and cut its lights. It was in front of a lighted house. The house was a split-level that perched on the side of a rocky slope.

Kane continued on. He found a break in the timber about a quarter of a mile away and parked the Duster and walked back up the road.

The mail box next to the road was the simple black tin one, the kind that dotted most rural roads. The name on the side in white letters about an inch high. HARDY WINSTON. Kane read it without having to use a light. Nodding to himself, puzzled, Kane walked up the gravel road, passed the pickup, and stopped to stare up at the house. Only one room was lighted on the top level, that one on the front left corner. The whole ground floor was lit, some light leaking from beyond drawn drapes.

After his long look, Kane climbed the low flight of stairs to the narrow porch. On each side of the porch, framing the doorway, there were huge stone urns with some kind of waxy plant in each. Kane reached into his pocket and brought the Sport out. He bent over the stone urn on his right and placed the Sport, butt down and the barrel clear, in a depression at the back. Straightening up, he found the door bell and gave it one long push.

"You want something?" The man who opened the door was the one who'd driven Karen from the hospital. A hard young man in jeans and a faded denim jacket. Flint dark eyes and a drooping lower lip.

Kane said, "Karen's expecting me."

"I don't know any Karen."

"That's funny," Kane said. "You drove her here from the hospital."

"Mister ..." The quick anger was there and Kane braced himself. "Mister, you've come to the wrong place."

From a distance, from the room beyond, Kane heard the bull voice of another man. A strong voice with the twang of the South in it. "What is it, Art?"

Art turned his head, looking back into the room. "Some crazy guy who says that ..."

Kane rammed a shoulder against the door. Art was off balance. He lost his grip on the door as it struck his shoulder and threw him back into the room. He shouted something that broke apart in the noise of his fall. Kane stepped through the doorway and slammed the door closed behind him. He was in a kind of hallway. In front of him, a set of carpeted steps led down into a deep, sunken living room. Art was on one knee at the bottom of the steps. While he gathered himself for a lunge at Kane, Kane took the time to look across the living room. A large man in his late forties had just pushed himself up and out of an overstuffed chair. Short bristle-cut gray hair, thick shoulders, a round face going to age and fat, but with a kind of angry strength in it. Kane saw this and he saw the big hands closing into fists.

It was all the time he had. Art was on his feet and coming up the steps. He reached the last step and took a swing at Kane, who slipped the punch and kicked Art in the right knee. It was the leg holding all of Art's weight and when it buckled under him he tumbled down the steps. Art landed on his back. Even on the carpeted floor the impact stunned him.

Kane looked down at him and then across the living room at the other man. "We can do this another half-hour and it still won't get us anywhere."

"I don't know you," the heavy man said.

"You're Hardy Winston?"

The heavy man nodded.

"Karen knows me."

Art rolled over and got on all fours. He scooted around until he faced Kane. Tears of anger and frustration streaked his face. Hardy Winston stared down at him. "You all right, Art?"

"Yeah."

"Get Karen."

Art used the steps to pull himself up. Standing, he favored the right leg. "You could have crippled me."

"That's right," Kane said.

Art limped off to Kane's left. There was a wide staircase there constructed from thick, heavy beams that looked like railroad ties. As soon as Art started up the stairs, Kane stepped down into the living room. It was a wide, large room. To the right, opposite the staircase, there was a raised dining room and a door beyond that which probably led to a kitchen.

The sofa against the wall was dark red leather. Low slung chairs on each side matched it. The coffee table in front of the sofa was made of the same heavy beam wood that had been used in the staircase. And, at the far end of this table, stood the old overstuffed chair. It seemed a holdover from some other home, some other room.

All in all, it was a man's room. There wasn't a hint of a woman's touch anywhere. Gun racks and cabinets covered the wall that faced the sofa.

"You hunt?" Winston asked.

The question moved Kane's eyes from the gun racks and back to Hardy Winston. "Some."

"You want a drink?"

"Cognac if you've got it," Kane said.

Winston brought a decanter and two glasses from a dark wood cabinet near the dining room. The glasses were shaped somewhat like a shot glass though they were larger and the mouth was a bit wider.

"My design," Winston said as he placed both glasses on the coffee table and poured double shots in each. "I hate those puny things you're supposed to drink brandy out of."

Kane picked up one of the glasses. "Thanks."

Winston looked at Kane over the thick rim of the glass. "That kicking ... that how you do all your fighting?"

"One of the ways," Kane said. "I didn't feel like jamming a knuckle on his head."

"You got me interested." Winston sipped from his glass and his eyes drew down to narrow slits. "I used to like a brawl myself now and then. You think you could take me?"

Kane had the glass almost at his lips and he had to lower it so that he could laugh. The warmed aroma of the cognac told him it was a good aged one and he didn't want to risk spilling any of it. When the laugh came it was free and easy, without a trace of contempt in it.

"You laughing at me?"

"Just at the idea," Kane said. "I have a feeling it would be a long, hard way to spend an afternoon."

"More like it," Winston said. He waved a hand at the leather sofa. "I'd like to think you'd earn your breakfast and dinner doing it."

Kane didn't answer. He held the cognac, warming it, and after a few seconds he took his first sip. He rolled it on his tongue, feeling the soft burn of it, and then he swallowed. "Hard to be sure," he said to Winston, "but this is thirty years in the barrel if it's a day."

"About that. And it's still in the barrel until I draw off a bottle now and again."

Kane heard footsteps on the staircase. He stood up when he saw Karen coming down, still shaky and pale, one hand sliding down the bannister. Behind her, taking one step at a time, Art limped his way down toward the living room.

There wasn't any surprise on Karen's face. Whatever Art had said to her upstairs had removed that. When she moved closer,

Kane could see anger and impatience in the set of her mouth. "You couldn't leave it alone, could you, John?"

"You broke a date with me," Kane said.

"A date?" Art had reached the bottom of the stairs. "You do all this just because you got stood up?"

Winston said, "Shut up, Art. One day you're going to grow up and find out that words don't mean the same things to different people."

"Aw, Hardy…"

"Go put some ice on that knee before it swells and busts your britches."

After Art closed the kitchen door behind him, Karen walked around Kane and stood next to Winston. "This is the one I told you about. The one who broke Park Simpson's shoulder."

"You do that?" Winston asked. Kane sipped his cognac and didn't answer. "The word is that Simpson was a tough one."

"The lady has me mixed up with somebody else. Some other knight in rusty armor."

Karen insisted. "I'm sure of it, Hardy."

"Don't know why a man would be ashamed to admit a thing like that," Winston said.

Kane smiled. "Me either. This is a girl worth fighting a dragon over now and then."

Winston matched his grin. "When I was a boy my favorite was the Lone Ranger and he never stopped to be thanked either."

"A foolish man," Kane said.

"There's a connection I didn't tell you about," Karen said. "He claims he's a friend of the family. Of Barton's family."

"That so?" Winston lifted the decanter and brought it over and tipped cognac into Kane's glass. "Doing what?"

"Asking questions. Looking around."

"A cop? A private investigator?"

Kane shook his head. "Nothing like that."

Karen said, "I can call George Webb in Atlanta."

"He'll say he doesn't know me," Kane said. "That's part of the deal."

Hardy Winston shook his head slowly. "I don't know if we can take you for what you say you are."

"It's the only way."

Winston put a hand on Karen's shoulder. "I've got a feeling you trust him."

A hesitation, a flicker, before Karen said, "Some."

"A bushel or a peck?"

"More like a bushel," she said.

Winston put his head back and poured the cognac down in a steady stream. When he moved the glass away from his mouth he said, "Then I guess we ought to let him see what he came to see."

The words didn't come out but Kane watched her face. Her mouth shaped the "no, no, no."

❧   ❧   ❧

It was a smell like a hospital. The scent blew down the hallway on the warm air of the heating system. A male nurse, a slim dark man who looked Cuban, heard them in the hall and came out and stood beside the door. The door was open and Kane could see, in the gloom of the half-light, the regulation hospital bed.

Karen entered first. Kane followed and Winston came in last and closed the door behind them.

There was a man in the bed. Kane knew that by the shape of the body. It had been a large and powerful body once. Now it was wasting down to the bone.

Kane stopped at the foot of the bed and looked down at the shrouded and bandaged head. "Who is it?"

Karen stood to his left. He saw her face then, tight and drawn and even paler than it had been in the living room.

Behind them, Winston opened the door. "Carlo."

The male nurse entered. "Yes, sir."

"Have you changed the bandage already?"

"Yes, sir."

"Do it again."

It took a few minutes. Kane remained at the foot of the bed. The male nurse leaned over the bed, his slim body blocking Kane as he removed the bandages. The only sound was Karen's strained breathing and the snip of the scissors. When it was done, Hardy Winston said. "Step away for a minute, Carlo."

Carlo stepped away from the bed and stood with his back to the wall.

Behind them, Winston turned on the overhead light.

The man in the bed had only about half of a face. The skull, shaved now, was intact, but the left side of the face, from the ear to the nose, was gone. It was one red crusted scar.

Kane knew then. He didn't need to hear what Hardy Winston said.

"That's Barton Riker," he said. "Also known as Barton Webb."

CHAPTER SEVENTEEN

"It's my town," Hardy Winston said. "I made it with my own hands and then they took it away from me."

They'd left the hospital room upstairs and walked slowly back down to the sunken living room. Karen had needed Kane's arm to get her down the stairs and now she sat next to him on the leather sofa. Winston's hand shook when he'd topped off the brandy glasses.

"Who?" Kane asked.

"They call themselves the Inner Circle."

"A fancy name."

"Three men." Winston ticked them off on his fingers as he named them. "Eddie Vincent."

Kane nodded. "I've met him. Today." He saw the raised eyebrow. "I'm beginning to bother him. I think he wants to recruit me."

Winston pinched the second finger, frozen there. "And ... ?"

"I let him talk."

"Red Stamper," Winston said.

Karen said, "He's the lawyer. He has an office but as far as we can tell he doesn't have any clients."

"Three. That's Benjamin Turner. He's the money man. Real estate in Atlanta for years before he moved down here. Sells some land around here."

"Let me see if I have it," Kane said. "Eddie Vincent ..."

"The rackets," Winston said. "Gambling and the girls."

"Red Stamper ..."

"Enforcement. Protects his own and punishes his own."

"Benjamin Turner…"

"The money man," Winston said. "The way we put it together, Vincent and Stamper came in about the same time. They saw what they could do here. But they needed big money to get it underway. They settled on Benjamin Turner. They laid it out for him. This is the pie and this is the way we can cut it up. And he bought it. But so far we think Turner's stayed away from the hard decisions. They're made by Vincent and Stamper."

"He might be the weak link," Karen said. "He's ruthless in money matters, but he's never had to be ruthless with human life."

"The Inner Circle." Kane let it hang in the stillness of the room. He stood up and waved an arm toward the flight of stairs that led up to the hallway where the hospital bed was. "Tell me about that."

Late in the evening, Bull Racklin checked out of the Days Inn and drove down the Backbone until he reached the Restaway Motel. The thin washed-out blonde woman registered him and reached for the door key to Unit # 1.

Bull stopped her. "I'm superstitious."

"What?"

"I worry about numbers," Bull said.

"Really?"

"What other rooms are available?"

"Eight and twelve," she said.

"If it's all right with you," Bull said, "I'll take eight. It's one of my good numbers."

Her hand moved down the key box until it touched the plastic tag on the key to Unit #8. "Why is it a good number?"

"I was born on the eighth," Bull said.

Bull unpacked his bag and placed it in the back of the closet. He'd dropped the Dan Wesson and the sack of hot loads on the bed. He was reaching for the Dan Wesson when the knock came at the door. He scooped up the .357 and the sack of shells and dropped them in a bureau drawer with his socks and underwear. One hand spread the underwear over the Wesson while the other closed the drawer.

The blonde was in the doorway. "This isn't part of the management plan to make guests feel welcome," she said, "but I have a couple of miniatures of good bourbon and I know how you traveling men need a drink after a long drive."

She held four miniatures of I. W. Harper stacked in one hand

"You've got a good heart," Bull said. He waved her into the room with a gesture that was almost a bow. "I don't think I know your name."

"It's Carol."

"That's a name with five letters," Bull said. "Five is also one of my good numbers." Up close, he could see the blue and tired veins behind the transparent skin of her face.

"I didn't bring any ice."

"In this kind of weather?" Bull laughed on the way to the bathroom to get the glasses. He emptied two of the miniatures into each of the glasses while she sat on the edge of the bed and watched. That done, he carried her drink to her and stood looking at her breasts and thighs.

"I guess you must think this is awfully forward of me," Carol said.

"You know how I feel about numbers?"

"Yes."

"I believe in fate too," Bull said.

He held her eyes and then with the gesture he'd seen a man make in a German bar once, a man he would kill less than an hour later, he touched his glass to hers and they drank.

❧ ❧ ❧

"It was two years ago," Winston said. "I got fed up. I saw they'd taken my town away from me and I made up my mind to take it back."

"How?" Kane asked.

"Any way I could. Any way I had to."

Karen came from the kitchen with a cup of coffee. She sat on the sofa again, this time between Kane and Hardy Winston.

"One way was through the law. But I couldn't go to the state Attorney General until I could prove what was happening here. That's where Barton came in."

Hardy Winston had known old Judge Martin Webb for years. So, on a trip to Atlanta, he'd visited the Webb home. After dinner, in the Judge's study, he'd explained his problem. It was much later, when the Judge had listened him out, that Barton Webb came in from a night on the town. A handsome man, a strong man, a charming and witty man. Winston hadn't seen Barton in a number of years and now he got the impression of a man whose only weakness was a kind of misdirection.

After Barton left for bed, the Judge explained his options. The Judge needed to know exactly what was going on, step by step documentation. With that in his hands, he could go straight to the Attorney General and, if necessary, the Attorney General would send the National Guard and the Highway Patrol in to clean the town up.

The Judge was dead within a week. A heart attack.

Winston had driven back to Atlanta for the funeral and afterwards he'd had another talk with Barton Webb. The impression he had of Barton was so strong that he made his offer: $100,000.00 in cash if Barton took the job. To be paid ahead of time in cash. The money was an important factor, he was certain of that. Barton knew how bad the Judge's investments had been.

Barton Webb, now Barton Riker, arrived in Ansonville a week later. He drove a white Caddy and his clothes were expensive and flashy and there was about him the hard edge of a man who took what he wanted from the world. He wasn't in any hurry. He took his time finding his spot. It took him six months to get close to the first of the Inner Circle, Eddie Vincent. It was another two or three months, using all his wit and charm and his hardness, before Eddie Vincent offered him the job as manager of the Nineties Club.

That first year, while Barton worked his way toward the center, the agreement was that there'd be no meetings between Winston and Barton. In the second year, now with access to ledgers and other kinds of documents, Barton had to risk it. There were meetings from time-to-time in another city. And never in the same city twice. At the meetings, Barton would turn over documents and ledgers he'd photographed and he would talk by the hour into a tape recorder about what he knew about the Inner Circle's operations in town, what he'd experienced and what he'd heard. Over that second year the proof began to add up. What had seemed impossible for two years now seemed possible."

Kane said, "What went wrong?"

"We don't know." Winston looked at Karen. "We've tried to look back at it. Some small mistake. Maybe somebody saw us in Macon or Savannah or New Orleans. Someone who knew us when we didn't know them. Or Barton got careless. One of those. Anyway, they set up the kill. They didn't need a lot of proof to do that. All they needed was just a bit of doubt."

"How did it happen?"

Winston nodded at Karen.

"I guess you've been wondering how I got involved in this," she said. "I didn't know Barton until he took over as manager of the club. But I did some of the bookkeeping and it wasn't long before I had a suspicion about him. That he wasn't what he said he was. But by then I cared for him and I wouldn't have hurt him for anything. And, because I cared for him, I wanted what he wanted. Call that love if you want to."

Winston leaned forward, out of his overstuffed chair, and covered her hands with one of his. "That's enough, Karen. Just tell him about that night. The rest of it isn't any of his business."

"It seemed ordinary enough at the time," Karen said. "A small time player at one of the clubs came to Barton. He said he'd got in trouble and he was leaving town. He needed moving money. The little he told Barton about the trouble he was in made Barton think it might be worth checking into. The small timer wouldn't meet Barton at the club or any of the usual places. They settled upon a street that's usually deserted late at night. H Street."

Winston said, "That section of the street's mostly garages and auto parts shops."

"I knew about the meeting. I knew the when and the where. Around closing time, right after Barton left, I passed through the club about the time the last call was being given. I saw the small timer over at a booth with Franco. He must have waited outside until Barton drove off and then came in."

"She called me then," Winston said. "Art and I got there a few minutes after it happened. We loaded Barton into my car and drove him here. I bought myself a doctor for life. And since then, I've bought a few more. Specialists. And they're able to do nothing."

"Hopeless?" Kane said.

"He's a vegetable and a miracle at the same time."

"You could help us," Hardy Winston said.

"How?" Kane stood on the raised hallway near the front door, putting on his topcoat.

Winston placed one foot on the bottom step and stared up at Kane. "Let them recruit you."

RALPH DENNIS

Past Winston, Kane could see Karen's eyes. He couldn't read on her face what she wanted him to do. Not that it would have mattered. What they wanted was another spy in the organization to replace Barton Riker. There was danger in that. And their objectives weren't the same.

"I work my own way," Kane said.

"Which way is that?"

Kane shook his head and backed out of the door.

After Kane closed the door behind him, he reached into the stone urn and lifted out the Sport. He stuffed it into his waistband. On the way down the driveway he turned once and looked at the lighted window at the left front corner of the top floor.

Sometimes living could be worse than death.

CHAPTER EIGHTEEN

The call awoke Jackson Carter. He sounded angry until he recognized Kane's voice.

The smell of old grease and coffee swirled around Kane. On the outskirts of town he'd pulled into an all-night truck stop. He'd parked next to a semi. At the counter he ordered and got a mug of coffee. He carried it into the phone booth at the back of the cafe. Sipping at it, he spoke the kind of roundabout code that told Carter why the call was necessary.

At the end, Carter said, "That does change it."

"But you have to play this carefully," Kane said. "If you have to go back to the client you have to cover up some of the facts. You let him know where his brother is and you could blow up this town and me with it. I don't want the client down here poking around."

"Understood," Carter said. "Call me at noon tomorrow and I'll know how much this changes it."

Kane replaced the receiver and carried the coffee mug back to the counter. He sat between two sleepy truck drivers and listened to them talk about faraway places. Places he'd probably been some time or other but had forgotten.

They came at Kane from two directions. One from the left of the door as he swung it open and walked into the motel room. The other from the front, from the direction of the bed. The one who'd been flattened against the wall to the left of the door hit him with a right that scraped the doorframe before it landed on the left side of Kane's head. The force of it threw him back against the open door. The second man reached him then and caught him by the lapels of his topcoat. He swung Kane around and threw him into the center of the room. That was so they could close the door.

Kane hit the bed, stunned, deaf in his left ear. But he still had his reflexes and when his back hit the bed he swung his legs back high, over him, and tumbled across the bed and onto the rug on the other side. The first man, the one who'd thrown the punch, lunged across the room after him and ran into the bed. The second man closed the door and locked it before he also moved toward the center of the room.

Head still ringing. The whole left side of his face numb. Kane pulled at the Woodsman Sport. It caught in the lining of the pocket but he drew it free and flipped the safety off. His right hand shook so he lifted his left hand and wrapped his fingers around his right wrist. Both hands were shaking but they were steady enough.

The first man was a thin shape. He'd bounced away from the bed. Now circling the foot of it. The second man was a thicker shape. He moved straight for the side of the bed.

"Right there," Kane said. "One more move and somebody is dead." He heard his voice as a thin, reedy sound, like a voice on a phone.

Both men stopped. Kane dropped his left hand from his right wrist and used his left hand to push himself up. Neither of the two men moved but their harsh breathing filled the room.

Kane edged to his left. His knees brushed the side of the bed. His left hand found the night table. He fumbled around until he found the base of the lamp and slipped his fingers upward until he found the switch. He pressed it and the room lighted up.

The man who faced him across the bed was the one who'd thrown the punch. He was thick-necked, a fat face with puffy lids over cold, gray eyes. The other man, the one near the foot of the bed, Kane had seen him before. He was the driver who'd been with Franco earlier in the day, the man with the five o'clock shadow grained into his face. Both men stared at the Sport in Kane's hand.

"What's the message?" Kane said.

The thick-necked one looked at Franco's driver.

"I assume there's some message." Neither spoke. Kane moved to his right, backing away slightly.

"The beating was the message," Franco's driver said.

Kane smiled. He felt like the left side of his face hadn't moved. "I guess there's no opening at the store. Is that it?"

Franco's driver nodded. A single jerk of his head.

"Too bad about that," Kane said. "Just when I was beginning to like everybody who worked over there."

"It's a job," Franco's driver said. Behind the five o'clock shadow his skin was pale as fresh milk.

"You," Kane said to the thick-necked man. "Cross your legs and sit back on them."

The thick-necked man looked at Franco's driver. "Do it, Ned," the driver said.

Kane watched while Ned crossed his legs and sat back on them. "Hands locked behind your head."

Ned locked his fingers together and clasped them behind his neck. Kane looked at Franco's driver. "What's your name?"

"They call me Julie."

"This way, Julie."

Julie took one step toward Kane and stopped. Then another step.

"One more," Kane said.

Julie sucked in his breath and took the step. He was close enough. Kane swung back his left and hit Julie in the nose. The bones crushed under his fist. Julie fell back on his rump and sat there. He rubbed at his nose. After a few seconds, a thick smear of blood covered his upper lip and ran down into his mouth.

Kane looked at Ned.

Ned sat still, not moving.

Kane said, "Come here, Julie."

Julie shook his head. Strings of mucous and blood sprayed down the front of his coat.

"One more time, Julie. You're not hurt enough to leave the game yet."

Julie put his hands on the rug and pushed himself up to his feet. He swayed and clawed at the dresser top. He moved toward Kane.

"You're dead," Julie said. "You know you're dead."

"Not yet," Kane said. He looked down at the Woodsman Sport. When Julie's eyes widened and dropped to the pistol, Kane swung his left again. Julie's upper front teeth gave under the fist. Kane felt the cutting edge of them before they gave. Then Julie was on his back. He choked and spat out broken teeth.

"You," Kane said to Ned, "take him back to Franco."

Ned helped Julie to his feet and the two men staggered out.

Kane locked the door after them and propped the chair against the doorknob. He carried the Sport into the bathroom and kept it near while he soaked his left hand in cold water. He washed the cuts where Julie's teeth had dug in. He studied the left side of his face in the mirror. The ear was red and swollen. His jawline was puffy.

Later, ready for bed and barefoot, he stepped on something near the dresser that hurt the sole of his foot. He found two broken teeth in the rug. The teeth were clean on the front side but stained on the back. He wrapped them in tissue and dropped them in the trash basket in the bathroom.

Bull slept light. He awoke when he heard the thump a few doors off to the right of his room. He didn't know what the thump meant but he moved to the window on the chance that the noise might be connected with Kane. He stood for a time at the window and stared out into the lighted parking lot. Behind him, in the bed, Carol blubbered and snored.

He saw the two men come out of the motel room a few minutes later. From the direction of Unit # 10. A broad-shouldered man supported a slim, thin one. The man being supported could hardly move his legs and he was shaking his head from side to side.

Thicker and thicker, the soup was boiling.

Bull watched the heavier man dump the hurt one in the passenger seat.

Too thick. He'd have to wait his time. He'd have to be sure he didn't walk into the middle of something when he did the hit. And, he decided, there was always the chance that he wouldn't have to do it at all. Flies were around the soup. Some might fall in but some others might make a meal.

It was that simple. That easy.

The connection was in-town clear. Kane could hear the frost in Jackson Carter's voice. "The client wants the contract finalized."

"How?"

Kane had passed up the outdoor pay phones on the road from the motel. He didn't like being so exposed. He'd driven to the Town Square Hotel and had coffee and toast in the coffee shop. At twelve noon, exactly he'd made the call to Atlanta from one of the lobby phones.

"He wants the ones responsible. All three, if necessary."

"That's a big order."

"It's his money," Carter said. "And he's agreed to an increase in the fee. He understands that there is a greater risk now."

"All three?"

"But not if only one of them was responsible. I was firm on that point."

"It's heating up here." He put up one hand and cupped the bruised left ear. It felt hot under his palm.

"Can you find which one was responsible?"

"Maybe."

"You want to turn the contract back?"

"Not yet," Kane said. "I'll see what I can do."

"The client has mixed feelings about what I told him concerning his brother."

"You told him what?"

"The brother's true condition. And that the brother is in a private hospital in Florida, the location kept secret to protect him."

The operator cut in. "It will be two dollars for three more minutes."

Kane said, "We've finished," and hung up.

He turned toward the lobby and found Franco standing twenty feet away from him. A brown tweed coat was over one arm, but both hands showed. They were empty and he'd pulled his dark blazer open so that Kane could see the waistband of his pants. Nothing there either.

"Just talk," Franco said.

"You follow me? I didn't see you."

"Someone," Franco said. "Not me."

Kane let his eyes drift over the lobby. It was empty. There was a sofa and a low brass coffee table next to the escalator that ran down to the lounges and shops below. Kane turned in that direction. Franco matched him step for step. When they reached the sofa, Franco said. "There's no reason to sit down unless you're tired."

"What does that mean?"

"They're waiting to talk to you," Franco said.

"They?"

"The people who own this town."

"Talk about what?"

"It might be a job offer," Franco said.

"Why today and not yesterday?"

"Things change. We got your message. Julie isn't talking much right now. Ned, the big one, looks dumb but he isn't. He told it the way he saw it. I guess you could say he was impressed."

"No games," Kane said. "I've had games up to my teeth."

Franco shook his head. "It's for real."

CHAPTER NINETEEN

hrough the open doorway, past Franco, Kane could see the three of them over lunch. It was in the private dining room in the rear of Pucci's, an Italian restaurant on the outskirts northwest of town. Franco had parked in the back lot and they'd entered through the steamy kitchen. At the private dining room doorway, Franco had knocked and waited until he heard the "Come" from inside.

The dining room was olive green and trimmed in gold. Off to one side, still covered by white linen, was the long banquet table that could seat thirty or so people. It had been pushed there to make room for the smaller round table where the three man sat. Behind them, near the gold drapes, a hard young man with a cowlick and a shock of dark hair leaned against the wall, his hands in his topcoat pockets.

Kane knew Eddie Vincent. He overflowed the chair he sat in, and even as he looked toward the doorway, he stuffed veal marsala into his mouth, whole piece by whole piece.

To his Vincent's left there was a tall, thin-chested man with gray-peppered red hair. Probably Red Stamper, the lawyer of the combine. He had freckles, too, though at his age they might have been liver spots.

The man to the right of Vincent, that end of the semicircle, Kane figured had to be Benjamin Turner. He looked of a small town businessman. The one who had the Ford or Chevrolet dealership. The man who'd been the Junior Chamber of Commerce Young Man of the Year when he was twenty-five. Now, in his forties, the comfortable weight was settling on him. Milky blue eyes found Kane, read him, and slid away.

Vincent straightened up and wiped his mouth with a napkin. When he lowered the napkin his mouth was still wet. "Come on in, Cassidy."

Next to him Red Stamper twisted around in his chair and said, "Bill, you and Franco wait outside."

Kane cleared the doorway. The bodyguard passed him, brushing him with a shoulder. Behind Kane, the door closed.

"Over here," Stamper said.

Kane moved over toward them until he was a couple of feet from the table. The three men stared at him from the semicircle. Benjamin Turner lifted the two carafes of wine, one red and one white, and placed them on the edge of the table near Kane. "Have a glass of wine."

Kane turned a spare wine glass and poured himself a glass of the white. His hand was steady and he realized that the three men were watching his hands. "Thanks."

"John ... that's right, isn't it?"

Kane nodded. He looked over the rim of the glass at Red Stamper while he drank.

"You're making some problems for us."

"I hadn't intended to," Kane said.

"Nevertheless, you have," Stamper said.

"I got you to notice me," Kane said. He drank the rest of the wine in one gulp and placed the empty glass on the front edge of the table.

"All that ... just to get noticed?" Turner stopped with a thick wedge of steak inches away from his mouth.

"I had my look at the pickings here. All I want is some of the table scraps. That's not much to ask for."

Eddie Vincent crossed his knife and fork in the center of his empty plate. He took a long gulp of wine. When he lowered the glass Kane could see the curved grease mark on the lip of the glass.

"All this small talk aside," Vincent said, "I've got my feeling about you, I think you've made your dead bones."

Benjamin Turner whipped his head in the direction of Vincent. "We don't need to talk like that."

Red Stamper said, "Shut up, Ben."

Kane shrugged, "I was in one of the less popular wars. Men die in those. They walk right in front of a bullet without seeing it."

"Not that," Vincent said. "I mean in the streets. In the alleys."

"It's important for you to know?" Kane said.

Vincent nodded.

Kane said, "I've scraped a bone or two."

"Many times?"

"Some."

"On contract?" Vincent said.

"When the money was right."

Turner's fork clattered on his plate. He'd been trying to put it down quietly but it'd dropped from his fingers. "I don't want to listen to this. If I'd known..."

Stamper's eyes didn't move from his appraisal of Kane. "Ben, go sell a duplex or something."

Turner pushed back his chair. "I don't know anything about this."

"If you're so goddam innocent, how the hell do you know what we're talking about?"

Turner dug into the topcoats stacked across the seat of a spare chair. He came up with brown herringbone and, struggling to get his suitcoat sleeves into the arms, he flapped his way toward the door. Like a fat, awkward bird.

Kane watched Stamper and Vincent. He read the contempt on their faces.

Stamper said, "Glad you enjoyed your lunch, Ben." The door opened and slammed. Stamper turned to Kane. "We need something done."

"Done right. No loose ends and no arrows pointing back here." Eddie Vincent lifted the napkin from beside his plate and wiped the grease mark from his glass. He filled the glass from the carafe of white. "You might be the man for it."

"No local talent?" Kane said.

"You wouldn't believe how punk the local talent is," Stamper said. "You met Park Simpson, I think, and there's Franco and that dumb kid, Julie. That's about the lot."

"You left out Ned." Kane said.

"That one. He can't even find his way across town on a bus."

"Let me see if I understand you. You want somebody killed."

"That's it," Stamper said.

"Exactly." Eddie Vincent nodded.

"Big fish? Little fish?"

"Medium," Stamper said.

"Medium to medium-big," Eddie Vincent added. "You interested?"

"If the money's right," Kane said. "That's what it turns on."

"It has to be done in the right way. Can't be done here in town. Maybe in Atlanta where it can look like a mugging that went rank."

Kane nodded. "Better that way."

As if on cue, Red Stamper and Eddie Vincent turned and faced each other. Neither nodded but the agreement was there.

"It's a man named Hardy Winston," Eddie Vincent said.

It started right after Kane left the private dining room at Pucci's. Franco spent a minute or two in the dining room while Kane found his way to the Naples Lounge out front and had a cognac. Franco eased his weight onto the bar stool on Kane's right a few minutes later. Franco's whole attitude had changed. All the hostility had washed away and he acted like he and Kane were the best of new friends.

From Pucci's, they moved on to Ryan's, a tavern designed like an English pub. Around six, they left Ryan's and drove on to the Nineties Club. All that time Franco was buying. He kept saying, "Not a chance, old buddy."

Not long after they arrived at the Nineties, Kane looked toward the bar and saw Julie sitting there. There was a mass of white tape over his nose and he kept his mouth closed over broken teeth.

"Your boy over there," Kane said.

"Dumb shit," Franco said. "Ought to know he couldn't handle you like some fat drunk." The admiration showed now. "The way Ned told it, he thinks you move like a cat and you see in the dark."

"Ned was the one I should have hurt." He reached up and touched his swollen left ear. "But I thought he might be pick-up help. I thought Julie might carry the message better."

Franco touched the side of his head with his finger. "Always thinking, that's you."

At eight, Kane had a small steak and a salad. The drinking went on. At nine, Franco left the booth and remained on the phone for a few minutes. When he returned to the booth, he said, "Got a couple of girls coming over to my place. You up for a party?"

"Any choice?" Kane said.

"Just between the girls," Franco said. "You can pick the one you want. It don't matter to me."

Kane sat on the sofa in the living room-kitchen section of Franco's trailer. The sliding door that led to the bedroom had closed behind Franco and the red-haired girl he called Allie.

Next to him, the girl who'd been furnished for him, a small-boned and delicate brunette named Charlotte, took a long, deep breath. Through the drinking part of the party, all the talk that led up to the grand exit Franco made with his hand on Allie's rear end, she'd been prim and proper. Now, with the door closed behind Franco, she placed a hand lightly on Kane's crotch.

"Everything all right, honey?"

Kane got out his cash roll and peeled off a couple of twenties. "My head's not on it tonight. Some other girl's walking around heavy in there." He held out the two twenties. "If it's all right with you, let's don't and say that we did."

"You sure, honey?" Her hand moved from his crotch and closed over the bills. She had them folded and tucked away in her purse before he could blink twice.

"Dumb thing," Kane said, "but it's kinda like love."

"I think that's sweet," Charlotte said.

"But since Franco's putting on the party, I wouldn't want him to think I was backing away from the dessert."

"That's sweet, too," She leaned across him and kissed him. He got the strawberry taste of her lip gloss. "Wish I met more nice men like you." The thin, phony sadness made Kane want to laugh.

When Franco came out of the bedroom half an hour later, he'd dressed in a t-shirt and trousers. His feet were bare. Kane's tie was off, a couple of buttons open on his shirt and he'd kicked off his shoes.

"Good?" Franco asked from behind the low refrigerator where he was filling a glass with ice.

"None better," Kane said.

Next to him, Charlotte smiled. "Your friend here, Franco, is a mean horse."

"Why the fuck not?" Franco said. "Ain't he hard ass of the year?"

❧ ❧ ❧

The last bottle. Halfway gone. It was near midnight. Charlotte had taken Kane's money and the cash that Franco had paid her and left. The other girl, Allie, was stored away in the bedroom. Watching Franco, the glazed stare and the lumbering way he moved, Kane decided that it was time to pick some at Franco's head and see how much he knew.

"You know what those guys want of me?"

Franco nodded and said. "And it's about time too."

"Got to think on that," Kane said. "Got to think about it tomorrow. After I get over tonight. If I get over tonight."

"Shit, friend, tonight is worth the headache." Franco lifted his scotch and almost missed his mouth. A dribble ran down his chin and darkened the neck of his t-shirt. "Nothing else, you and me, we got over raising our backs at each other."

"And raised them at the broads instead."

"You bet." Franco nodded toward the back of the trailer. "You want some of Allie, you go help yourself."

"Not tonight. Got the edge taken off by Charlotte." Kane got a cigarette from a crumpled pack and watched Franco's hand wag and waver as he tried to touch a match to the tip of it. "This offing people, that's the extreme way to deal with troubles."

"Got to do it sometimes. Hell, you know that better than I do."

"Not me," Kane said. "You got me mixed up with some other dude who makes that kind of living."

"Sure." Franco grinned. "Anything you say, friend."

"That thing today at Pucci's. Hard to figure."

"How?"

"The three of them sitting there. Two of them for it. Right down the line, all the way to the boneyard. The other one backing off, chicken guts showing."

"That's the democratic way."

"Bothers me," Kane said. He lifted his arms and stretched. "Lord, that girl almost broke my lower back. Guess I'm not in training like you are."

"Why'd it bother you?"

"You do this kind of work and you got to believe that you got good backing. That nobody'll blow whistles around town and put your ass in a crack."

"Nothing to worry about," Franco said. "You take the last one…"

"Huh?"

"Forget it."

Kane stood up and looked down at him. "No, man, I got to know everything. Anything that might tell me about the deal here. Shit, you're talking about us getting our backs down. You got to show me you're talking straight to me."

"The last one. Won't talk names. No percentage in that. Let's just say the guy had big eyes and a mouth that might have been moving when it wasn't supposed to be."

"And the three of them backed it?"

"Didn't have time for that," Franco said.

"Two then?"

"One," Franco said.

"Stamper or Vincent?" Kane said. "I can't see Turner writing an X on anybody."

A hesitation. A flicker, then Franco said: "Vincent."

In the dream, the childlike Vietnamese girl said. "Western thought is so odd."

In the darkness, Kane could not even see her face.

"Why?"

"In your society you think of death as some kind of harsh intruder. Some stranger who comes without being invited. In the East death always sits on the lip of the rice bowl."

Kane said, *"Go away, leave me alone."*

He heard a knocking, a tapping, and he thought that it was the sound of her high heels as she moved away from him. The knocking went on and on and it didn't have the pace of someone's walk. He awoke and realized that the knocking was at his motel door.

His watch on the night table placed the time at 3:10.

CHAPTER TWENTY

The package arrived from Jacksonville on the eight ten P.M. bus. The package was ten inches long, about six inches wide and about seven inches high. Printed on the outside of the carton was SUPREMACYAM-FM CLOCK RADIO.

On the way back to the Restaway Motel, Bull stopped under a street lamp on a deserted street and opened the carton. The large item in the package was the receiver. He lifted that out and placed it on the seat next to his leg. He had to dig around in the packing material until he found the bug. It was taped to one side, in a box about the size of a small matchbox. He opened the container and found the bug nestled in a wad of surgical cotton. He closed the box and placed the bug in his jacket pocket. He returned the receiver to the carton and drove on to the motel.

The parking slot in front of Kane's room was still empty. Bull parked in his space and walked down to the office. Carol closed a ledger she was working with and hurried to the counter.

"I was wondering where you were." She said.

"A late call on a client," Bull said. "Had to get that business finished before nine o'clock." He grinned at her. Letting it show. "Hey, you know what? I left my key in my room. I'm locked out. How about letting me have the master key for a few seconds?"

"For you, anything." She lifted the master from the hook on the side of the key rack and brought it to the counter. The look she gave him was a parody of all the seductive looks she'd seen in hundreds of movies during the fifties and sixties. "You said something about nine o'clock?"

He looked up at the clock. It was twenty to nine.

"You bet your ass I did."

When he went into Kane's dark room, he took no time at all to attach the bug. Even before he'd called the Agency contact in Jacksonville, he'd paced out his own room and located the best spot for the bug. He went straight for the lamp on Kane's night table. He tilted it to one side. When the bug touched the flat metal screw at the base, he could feel the magnet hold.

Total time in the room was only a minute. As it turned out, he had all the time in the world. There was time for Carol when she got relieved at nine.

Carol dressed and left his room at eleven. As soon as she was out the door, Bull got the receiver from the dresser and placed it on the night table beside his bed. He flipped the ON switch and stretched out on the bed.

Bull awoke from a light sleep at a few minutes after one. Kane had entered the motel room. He seemed to have trouble moving around, like he'd had too much to drink. Bull listened to the fumbling as he undressed, water running in the basin and the toilet flushing. And, not much later, he heard Kane settle into the bed and the light, breathy snore when Kane was sleeping. Bull went back to sleep.

Bull awoke quickly. What had awakened him was a loud groan. The time on the clock was 3:09. After the groan, he heard Kane ask, "Why?"

There were a few seconds of silence and then Kane said, "Go away, leave me alone."

Dreaming. That was what Bull decided it was. And he'd stretched out once more and fitted his head into the pillow when he heard the knocking at Kane's door.

Something after all.

Bull kicked his legs over the side of the bed and leaned close to the receiver. He shook a cigarette from the pack on the table and lit it and waited.

The girl said, "You don't look in very good shape, John."

"I'm not. I feel like I tried to drink a whole river of booze. But I had to if I wanted to get close to Franco."

Dull footsteps. The girl said, "Where're you going?"

"To run some cold water over my face. Or, if I'm lucky, to drown myself in the basin." The bathroom door closed behind him.

Sound of a zipper, cloth rustling and the muted tap of her shoes hitting the carpet. When the bathroom door opened, there was a gurgle of the toilet for a few seconds and then Kane said, "The bruises haven't gone away yet."

"I think they'll be with me for a long time."

Footsteps and the sound of the bed giving under Kane's weight. "You come here for any special reason, Karen?"

"I thought you'd know … when you saw me like this."

"I am not a thing," Kane said.

"What?"

"I'm not a dildo for lonely ladies."

"You saw him," the girl said. "The way Barton is now."

"Go love him," Kane said.

"I did, until somebody blew away half of his face."

"Love him or stop loving him," Kane said.

"That's easy for you to say. You didn't know Barton Riker the way I did. Before it happened he was as much a man as you are. All the things a man ought to be."

In his motel room, Bull wrote *Barton Riker* on a pad next to the receiver. He didn't need to add a question mark.

"Go tell that to his ghost," Kane said.

"I do. I love him. I still love him. But I'm a woman just like any woman and I need...I need. Before you there wasn't anybody. Before you..." Her voice was husky, pleading.

Kane said, "Oh, God."

The bed squeaked under his shifting weight. The girl was crying.

Kissing and the crying stopped. A gasp from the girl and the bed began to stir under their movement. The girl was saying, over and over, "Love me, love me, love me. ..."

Bull went into the bathroom. Urinating, he listened to their strong bed movement. He heard it while he stood and looked at his face in the bathroom mirror. The cold flint eyes stared back at him.

What is the Chinese philosopher's question? Am I a man dreaming that I am a butterfly or a butterfly dreaming that I am a man dreaming that I am a butterfly?

The two water tumblers were on the cover of the toilet. Hers showed the mark of her lipstick. Bull pushed that one away, rinsed his and carried it into the bedroom. He got the pint of I. W. Harper from the dresser and poured himself a shot. His ear near the receiver while he drank, he heard a shift in the motion and thought, in the short rows, there was something like the cry of a bird and Kane said, "Oh, God damn," and the movement stopped.

In the silence, waiting to see if there would be pillow talk, Bull said to himself, "I am not a God damn butterfly. What kind of fucking nonsense is that?"

"I've pretended to take a contract," Kane said.

The voices were low now, the intensity gone. Bull leaned forward and turned up the volume.

"The contract is on Hardy Winston," Kane added.

"But you're not...?"

"Of course not," Kane said. "It's a matter of acting like I'm looking for the right time and place. That will buy us some time."

A pause, a scratch and the flare of a match. "As long as they think I'm going to make the hit, they won't bring in anybody from outside to try it."

"If they try it, they'll find Barton," the girl said.

"I doubt it. They want the job done away from town. Somewhere else. So it'll look like a mugging that went bad. The last thing they want is for it to happen at Winston's house."

Bull wrote down *Hardy Winston*. Then he wrote below that *Barton Riker there?*

The girl said, yawning, "I feel so much better. I almost feel human again."

Kane said, "Anytime, lady."

"And I do thank you, John, for understanding."

"Don't thank me," Kane said. "Leave the money on the table on your way out and please be generous."

The girl left about daylight. Long before that, Bull turned the volume down and slept. It was a restless sleep. He could hear their breathing, the snoring, and the tossing and turning. At times, like a nightmare, it seemed to him that all three of them slept together in the same huge, restless bed.

⚜ ⚜ ⚜

At the *Ansonville Telegram-Star,* Bull hunched over the counter in the Want Ads section, writing on the pad that the gray-haired lady had furnished him.

Newcomer to city interested in good business proposition. Have medium amount of capital available for investment.

There was space left at the bottom of the form for the newspaper to assign it a box number. At the top of the form, Bull wrote: *Orin B. Travis, Days Inn Motel.*

"So you thinking of going into business here, Mr. Travis?" The tip of her pencil tapped each word, counting, and he watched while she figured what he owed on the basis of a week of daily runs.

"I'm not sure," he said. "It depends upon the kind of response I get."

"Oh, you'll get a lot of good offers," she said. "Money's tight right now."

Bull placed a twenty on the counter. She gave him his change and a receipt for the payment.

"That could be," Bull said. "Still, there's a question or two. Things that bother me about this town."

"Is that so?"

"Now, mind you, I don't say they're true. And I've only been in town a day or two."

"What kind of things?"

"Well … stories about organized crime. How it's got a good hold here. And about the violence."

The mouth prim. "I can't imagine what you've heard."

Bull got out a cigarette and lit it and waited. The pump was in, and it was primed.

"Of course," she said, "you always hear those stories about any town."

"It was something about a shooting here in town a while back. I'm not sure I heard the name right. It was Richter or Riker or …"

The pursed mouth relaxed. "Yes, that happened. But as my Frank says, it's all right if it's just criminals killing each other."

"Killing? I thought it was just a shooting. I didn't hear anything …"

"They never found the body if that's what you mean. Frank said there was enough blood and bone and all that in the car when they found it … well, enough so you could be sure that the Riker man couldn't have lived after that. And Frank says they always take the body off somewhere and bury it. And lots of times they pour quick lime over it."

"They do that?"

"That's what Frank says."

"But they never found the body?"

"From what I heard, they didn't even look very hard. They knew he was dead. Frank says you wouldn't believe the way these criminals just disappear. One day they're here and overnight they're gone. And everybody says that they left for New York or Chicago but they all know better."

"This Riker fellow, he was in with the mobs?"

Within another eight or ten minutes, carefully directing her back to the information he wanted each time she strayed, Bull stored away almost all he wanted to know about Barton Riker.

CHAPTER TWENTY ONE

Kane entered the Nineties Club a few minutes after two in the afternoon. The bartender, the one who'd been on duty the night Kane and Franco had their run-in, gave him a good buddy wave from behind the bar. So the word was out. He was in and that meant he had the run of the place. Kane nodded at the bartender and headed for the dining room. A sullen waiter met him at the doorway and said that the dining room had closed at two. Kane swung back to the bar.

"A beer," he said.

"Any special kind?" The bartender used a damp rag to wipe the already clean surface of the bar where Kane sat.

"It all tastes like piss to me," Kane said.

"Try this one then," the bartender said. He placed a bottle of Beck's in front of Kane. He stood and waited until Kane had his first sip. He took Kane's bland nod as a compliment.

"The kitchen closed?"

Kane said that it was.

"You want something?"

"Prime rib and a salad."

"How you want it?" the bartender asked.

"The ribs bleeding and the salad with oil and vinegar."

Rounding the bar and heading for the kitchen, the bartender winked at Kane.

One of the bus boys brought his lunch to him at the bar fifteen minutes later. Kane finished the prime rib under the eyes of the bartender and he was on a second Beck's when Franco rushed in the front door. He found Kane at the bar and a relaxed smile replaced the tense, worried expression on his face.

"I've been looking all over for you," Franco said. "Something just went down and …"

Kane whirled his stool around and put his back to the bar. He shook his head at Franco, silencing him. He caught Franco by the topcoat sleeve and pulled him toward a corner table some distance from the bar.

"Don't talk my business in front of people," he said.

"Him?" Franco looked at the bartender. "He's all right."

"Nobody is all right," Kane said. "Now tell me about it and keep your voice down."

Franco leaned close to him. "Word we have is that Hardy Winston is flying to Atlanta later this afternoon."

"How do you know?"

"I put some cash on the mech who services his plane. He called an hour or so ago, said Winston wanted the plane ready about four." He looked at his watch. "In about an hour or less."

"Then it's on?"

"It's on."

"How do I get there?"

"Charter," Franco said. "It's waiting now. A Beechcraft. You leave right now and you can be waiting for him when he touches down."

"His flight plan filed?"

"Not yet, but the mech says he'll be landing at the DeKalb airport."

Kane left him and went to the bar. He got his topcoat from the stool next to the one where he'd been sitting. He put it on and got out his cash roll. He took out a ten. The bartender moved down and looked at the ten on the bar and shook his head. "I'm told it's on the house for you, anything you want."

Kane pushed the ten toward him. "Then Lord knows who this belongs to." He heard the bartender's thank you as he followed Franco out to the parking lot.

He stopped at the motel on the way to the Ansonville airport. Franco parked next to him and waited while he went inside. He got the Sport from inside the television set. He left the Duster parked at the motel and Franco drove him out to the airport.

Twilight in Atlanta. The flight took a bit more than an hour. Kane was met out front by a faceless hood, as Franco said he would, who gave him the keys to a black Impala. Then he'd gotten into a white Continental with another hood and they'd driven away without looking back.

Kane waited an hour in the Impala before Hardy Winston walked out next to a still limping Art and waved at a waiting cab. After the driver packed a couple of suitcases away in the trunk, the cab headed for Atlanta.

Sometime later Kane saw the cab pull into the oval driveway in front of the Regency Hyatt House. From the street, Kane saw the suitcases unloaded before the car behind him started honking at him, forcing him to drive on.

At 590 West, the club high above Stouffers on West Peachtree, Kane sat at a small table overlooking West Peachtree Street. The lights of northeast Atlanta spread out below him. Off in the distance, near Peachtree and 14th, he could see the lights of the Colony Square development and the new Fairmont Hotel.

Jackson Carter arrived while he was still on his first drink. At first, Jackson seemed to be drifting, searching for a table, but his eyes caught Kane's and Kane nodded. Carter sat down.

The waitress who'd followed Carter over to the table took his order for a vodka martini with a lemon twist. When she moved away, Carter watched the movement of her rump with a keen, hot interest.

"What do you need?"

"Human blood. A quart or so of it. With tissue in it. In Winston's blood type, if you can find out what it is."

"Ought to be a way," Carter said.

"And a place for Winston to hide out for a week or so, until the job is done."

"The house on Tenth. It's empty." Carter brought out a key ring and worked a key off. He slid it across the table toward Kane.

"How soon can you have the blood for me?"

"An hour or an hour and a half. I know this friendly undertaker." He looked around when the waitress placed the drink in front of him. "The problem is finding out the right blood type." He took a quick sip of the martini. "Back in a couple of minutes."

He was gone for ten minutes. He nodded before he sat down. "Got it from his service record. Pays to know a few people here and there." He sipped the warm martini. "Pick it up in an hour at the corner of Tenth and Peachtree. You know the Chinese place, Eng's? In the parking lot behind that."

"Payment?" Kane asked.

"Give him fifty."

"He trustworthy?"

"I own his ass," Carter said. "I tell him when to breathe." He fished the lemon peel from the martini with one finger and chewed it slowly and swallowed it.

The quart of blood and tissue was in a brown bag on the floorboards of the back seat. Kane drove out Peachtree until he found an open service station just past Pershing Point. He told the attendant to fill the tank and check the oil. A quick look at the phone book and he dialed the Regency Hyatt number and asked for Hardy Winston's room.

Winston answered.

"No names," Kane said. "I'm your visitor from the other night."

"Karen's new friend?"

"That's the one. You talk to her today?"

"She told me some wild assed story."

"It's not that wild. I've got to see you and set it up." Kane felt the hesitation. "Either you believe me or you don't. It's that simple."

He heard the nasal breathing and then a kind of grunt of decision. "I guess I have to."

"You got a car?"

"Art rented one."

"Make and color?"

"Brown Mustang. Art's taste runs to cars that girls will like."

"You know that string of clubs down from the Hyatt? The Nitery and the Copy Cat, those places?"

"Yeah."

"Have a few drinks at each. Be seen. And park the Mustang in the motel parking lot across from the Copy Cat."

"I come alone?"

"Bring your flunky with you if it makes you feel better. But get noticed. Do some big tips. Pinch a butt or two."

"That ought to be easy," Winston said. "How long do I do this?"

"Put in an hour or so. Half of it at the Nitery and half at the Copy Cat." Kane looked at his watch. "It's ten now. Give yourself a bit of an edge. Leave the Copy Cat and head for the Mustang at about eleven twenty-five."

"What happens then?"

"We do a charade."

❧   ❧   ❧

At eleven twenty-five, Kane pulled the Impala into the narrow lot next to the motel. He turned it around and pointed it back toward the street. He left the engine running. At eleven thirty he heard footsteps coming across the street and into the lot. He recognized the thick shape of Hardy Winston. Next to him, limping, the smaller shape of Art.

Kane got out of the Impala. The Sport was in his coat pocket and the brown bag with the quart of blood and tissue in it in his left hand.

Hardy Winston looked at him and said, "What's this about a charade?"

"Just that," Kane said. "I'm going to make some people think I killed you." He touched Winston's heavy tweed jacket. "I hope you're not in love with this. I'm going to ruin it."

Winston shucked off the jacket. He reached for the thin wallet in the breast pocket. Kane stopped him. "I'll need that, too. Much cash in it?"

"Four or five hundred."

"That stays too." Kane waved a hand toward the Mustang. "Start it up."

He turned to Art. "You get behind the wheel of the Impala."

As soon as Art was in the Impala's driver's seat, Kane walked over to the Mustang and waited until Winston had the engine going.

He motioned Hardy to the Impala. He placed the tweed jacket on the seat of the Mustang and poured about half of the dark liquid on the coat. The rest of the contents of the bottle he poured on the dashboard, from the center of it toward the passenger side. He replaced the bottle in the bag and placed it at his feet. He lifted the tweed coat and held it at a height that he estimated it would be if Hardy were seated behind the wheel. He took out the Sport, held it about a foot from the back of the coat, and fired two rounds into it, about heart high.

He lifted the bag with the bottle in it and still holding the coat he made his run for the Impala. He got in the back seat and said, "Take a left." He looked back and saw the Mustang's door open, the lights, and the dark splashes.

While they headed out Peachtree, he stuffed the coat into a plastic bag he'd placed there for that purpose.

At Ponce de Leon, he had Art take a left and after a block, another left that had them heading up West Peachtree, back toward the Regency Hyatt House.

"Your story," Kane said to Art, "is that you got tired of drinking and decided to go back to the hotel. Hardy wanted to try a few more bars. You walked back to the Hyatt and went to bed. The police ought to be in touch with you in a half-hour or so. Maybe an hour. That is, if anybody heard the shots. Maybe not. All you do is play dumb. If they haven't contacted you by morning, call the police. Say you're worried that Hardy might have got in some trouble."

"The cops who know me will believe that."

"Tell them you think Hardy had a few hundred on him and that he was flashing it around in the bars."

"Where'll you be?" Art asked Winston.

"Hidden away for a week or so," Kane said.

They stopped for a red light at the corner of Baker and Peachtree. Kane got out of the back seat. He opened the door on the driver's side and motioned Art out. Art rounded the Impala and stood on the curb. Kane said, "As soon as the police are through with you, head back to Ansonville."

Art stood on the curb and watched Kane drive away.

CHAPTER
TWENTY TWO

Franco pushed the trailer door open and stood there blinking down at Kane. He wore only a pair of white boxer shorts. The upper part of his body, covered with black wire-hair, seemed constructed out of sheets and chunks and scraps of steel.

"Got something for you," Kane said. He held out the plastic bag with Hardy Winston's tweed jacket in it. "Found it at a Goodwill shop in Atlanta and thought you might like it. The guy who'd owned it probably decided he didn't like the fit anymore."

Franco took the bag and hefted it. "You bastard. Already?"

The blood hadn't dried yet. It was still tacky to the fingers. Franco spread the jacket over the back of a chair and touched the two small holes in the back that the Sport had made. He found the weight in the breast pocket and reached around and slipped out the wallet. He looked through the credit cards and the sheaf of bills. "Winston's all right. He dead?"

"If he's not," Kane said after a sip of Franco's instant coffee, "that old dude is trying to dig himself out from under about five feet of rocks and dirt."

The afternoon before, Bull had followed Kane and Franco when they'd driven away from the motel. He'd watched helplessly while Kane got into the Beechcraft, its props already turning, and the plane taxied down the strip to the runway.

It took Bull a few minutes of asking around to find out that the Beechcraft was booked for a one-way flight to Atlanta. Angry with himself, the burn like acid in his stomach, he found a pay phone and put in a call to Dundee at the Agency.

"He's gone up to Atlanta. I don't think it's worth a trip up there. His things and the rented car are still at the motel. I'll have to sit on the egg and wait."

"What going on down there?"

Bull read the irritation in Dundee's voice. "I wish I knew. One thing I do know. I think he's got himself caught in the middle. He's getting in tight with the mob. At the same time, he might be playing against them."

Dundee said, "Now you've got me curious. You sure you're not making all this up to lengthen your vacation?"

"Not much," Bull said. "This place is a shithole. One thing you can help me with. I'd like to know why he came to Ansonville. Must have been some kind of job. Who took it out? Who's he after?"

Silence on the other end of the line for a few seconds. Bull heard the flick of a lighter and the thin hiss as Dundee exhaled the smoke. "That could be hard. Approaching Carter, that could alert them and put the risk on your side."

"Blue Mole's a good man. He's got more hustles than a five dollar whore. He can find out without Carter getting his nose in the right part of the wind."

Dundee said, "I'll get it out to him now. Call me back at ten in the morning. I'm still running the store."

Carol came by that night a few minutes after nine. Bull toyed with her for a couple of hours, pushing her more and more toward the grotesque forms of lovemaking. It was, he knew, his way of fighting against the boredom that she'd planted in him.

When she left him, she walked like a broken, damaged person who'd found out that there were more openings and orifices than she'd known existed before and more ways of violating them than she'd ever dreamed of even in her hot, blue movie fantasies.

At seven the next morning, he was in the bathroom shaving when he heard the car pull up in front and the car doors slam. The lather still on his face, he hurried to the window. Kane was there and the big man, Franco. Kane opened the motel door and Franco followed him and stood in the doorway. Bull flipped on the receiver and turned up the gain.

Kane was saying "... time for the eagle to scream, like we used to say in the service."

"When we're sure," Franco said.

"Listen to the radio," Kane said. "Read the Atlanta papers. It'll be there by now."

"When we're sure, it'll be right there on the barrelhead. Where'll you be?"

"Here," Kane said. "Sleeping."

"I'll be in touch," Franco said.

Slam of the door. Bull returned to the bathroom and finished his shave while he listened to Kane undressing and stretching cut on the bed. After he wiped the excess lather away, Bull got back into bed. He heard the rolling, the turning, the restlessness until Kane slept. Bull turned off the receiver and dozed until nine.

At ten, Bull bought an *Atlanta Constitution* from a rack in the lobby of the Town Square Hotel. He ran his eyes down the front page while he waited for his call to go through. *Nothing.* But he knew that this was the early edition of the morning paper, the one that was printed for home delivery and for shipment out of town. Dundee came on and talked while Bull ran his fingers down the inside pages. By the time the operator cut in at the three minute mark, Bull knew enough to put the pieces together. Bull saw the overall shape of it and he realized how vulnerable Kane was. He'd made a mistake that he couldn't take back. He'd shined a light on himself.

There were a lot of ways you could get dead doing that. Even a beginner knew that. On a job you were a shadow man. You couldn't even breathe in the light. Only in the darkness, in the shadow world. Kane in the light, that brought up some interesting possibilities. He'd have to look at them from all sides, the way a person walked around a piece of sculpture.

Dundee said, "Soon?"

"Today," Bull said.

On the way back to the motel, he stopped at a discount store and bought a cheap transistor radio and a few spare batteries. Within the hour, he heard the same news item three times on the local station.

In Atlanta police are trying to piece together the puzzling slaying of Ansonville businessman, Hardy Winston, whose blood-stained rental car was discovered by police in a nightclub area of downtown Atlanta last night…

Kane awoke at three P.M. with the faint elusive memory of a dream he'd had. It was too weak, too dim for him to remember. The feeling of the dream remained with him while he showered and shaved. *Something. Something.* There wasn't a handle and he couldn't hold it. It kept slipping away.

He was dressed and taking down his topcoat when the knock came at the door. It was the thin, faded blonde woman from the motel office. "There's a call for you at the desk."

"Don't say anything," Carter said on the phone. "Just listen. The man we'd salted away on Tenth street got restless. He checked out. I'm looking for him at this end. My feeling is he's headed in your direction."

"When?"

"This morning. I got to worrying about him and sent over some booze around noon. He was gone."

Kane looked at the blonde woman. She had her head down, thumbing through registration cards.

"Interesting," he said.

"I thought you'd think so. My feeling is that you ought to pack this one in. The hardfist has gone sour."

"Not if I can reach him first. I'll offer him a better deal."

"If you can't," Carter said, "dig a hole."

Kane broke the connection.

Across the room, the blonde woman lifted her head and smiled at him as he walked out.

Franco's Fairlane was in the space on the other side of Kane's Duster. When he saw Kane returning from the motel office, he gave the horn a short tap.

Kane opened the passenger door and leaned in. "Yeah?"

"Get enough sleep?"

Kane nodded.

"They want to see you."

"Who?"

"Vincent and Stamper."

"Now?"

"Now," Franco said.

Kane got in and leaned his head back. Dark clouds covered the sky as far as he could see. They looked like snow clouds and might have been in some other part of the country. Here, this far south, it was unlikely.

"The radio's having a field day," Red Stamper said.

It was the same private dining room at Pucci's. A huge platter of fettucine made of spinach noodles and covered with a creamy cheese and butter sauce was in front of Eddie Vincent. Stamper was eating shells with a thick meat sauce. Both men were eating raw mushroom salads.

"It was supposed to look like a mugging," Eddie Vincent said.

"Bitch, bitch," Kane said. "It was the only good angle I had at him all night. But it was tight. I didn't have time to beat his brains in. I did the hit the only way I could."

"Why plant the body?" Stamper looked past Kane at Franco. "You did say he planted it, didn't you?"

Franco said, "Yes."

"That's the way I work," Kane said. "It gives the cops one more thing to worry about. They're not even sure a hit's been made. Got to split their attention. Have to look for the body, got to be sure there is a body. How can you look for a killer when you're not even sure there's a killing?"

Stamper dropped his fork on his plate. "All that logical horse-shit aside, you didn't follow instructions. You could have waited another day. You could have waited until you got the right chance."

"It's easy to say that from all the way back here. The problem is that he wasn't alone. There was this other dude with him most of the time. Some guy who was limping. He'd been with him all day. It just happened he got tired and decided to go back to the hotel. Winston was alone...hell, maybe for the only time that whole trip to Atlanta." Kane turned over a spare glass and poured himself about half a glass of the red from a carafe. Before drinking it, he said, "Either of you ever try to mug two guys at once?"

Franco moved up a step or two. "Anyway you look at it, he did the fucking job."

Kane turned his head and winked at Franco over the rim of the wine glass, then looked back at Stamper. "The job nobody else in this town could be trusted to do at all."

Stamper took a sheaf of bills out of his inside coat pocket and tossed it, shovel fashion, toward Kane. Kane flipped through it. About three thousand in hundreds.

"Stay around," Eddie Vincent said. "There might be more work for you."

"Same kind of work?" Kane said.

Vincent chewed a mouthful of the fettucine and wiped his mouth with the back of his hand. "Right down your line. But it won't be right away. It might be a month. Maybe a bit more. If your cash gives out, we'll put an advance on you."

Kane looked at Stamper, who said, "One of our partners has just about run out of guts. He's getting nervous. He's about to get religion, join the church and ask if he can sing tenor in the choir."

"But nothing about this outside this room," Vincent said.

"About what?" Kane gave them a lazy grin and followed Franco out.

❧ ❧ ❧

He had two drinks with Franco. He paid for them with one of the hundreds. Franco tapped the change on the table. "Running close, huh?"

"Now I can afford my motel room," Kane said.

"You ought to look around for a place," Franco said. "Maybe get a trailer and move out next to me..."

"I'll think on it," Kane said.

"You do it. We could be good neighbors." Franco leaned forward and dropped his voice. "The price was right?"

"This time. Next time I set it firm before the job." Kane winked. "This was the cut-rate one, the one to show I could do what I said."

By the time, he'd finished his second drink he'd yawned a few times for Franco's benefit. When Franco suggested another drink, he shook his head. He said he needed sleep. Maybe later, if Franco was around, they could run a couple of girls to ground. And this time it was Kane's party.

"I'm up for it," Franco said.

After saying he'd call the Nineties around ten or so, Kane went out and flagged down a cab that dropped him off at the motel. Within minutes, he'd picked up the Sport and was driving toward the lake. If Hardy Winston was back in town, he'd be at his place. He was that easy to figure.

The voice wasn't that of anybody Franco knew. It had a twang to it, a touch of somewhere like Boston. The clock over the bar showed the time as five thirty-five.

"You don't know me," the man said.

Oh, shit, this is my week. Franco said, "All right then, I don't know you."

After Kane left Pucci's he'd driven over to the Nineties. It was getting dark already. There were a few freelance hookers in the club early and Franco had said a few words to one pair of them. He'd told them to do short times only, that there might be a party later in the evening.

"I know a few things you ought to know."

"Tell me about them," Franco said.

"The first thing. Barton Riker is not dead."

"The shit you say." Franco lowered his drink and some of it sloshed over the side. "Who is this?" He pressed the receiver hard against his ear, closing off the sound of the juke box.

"The second thing. The killing in Atlanta last night was a fake. A con job somebody did on you."

"Look, buddy, I don't know what the hell you're talking about. Why don't you come over here to the club and…?"

"Riker's out at Winston's place. You know where that is?"

Franco felt the chill. It was a chill like the first time they'd put the arm on him. He'd been eighteen and he'd been screwing around with the cash from the numbers collection. Joey Black sent two of his best to talk to him. In the end they hadn't said much. He'd taken his lumps.

"Why're you telling me this? What's in it for you?"

"Just say I'm a friend."

The line went dead.

Franco remained at the phone, letting the receiver dig into his ear, hurting him. When he moved away, he could feel hard blood pumping in him. His right hand, when he held it out and sighted down it, had a slight but hardly noticeable tremor to it.

The burn was on. The mad was there. It was under control.

God help anybody who craps on me. On the way out of the club he stopped beside one of the hookers. He told her the party was off for the night. Might as well keep it friendly for another time.

CHAPTER
TWENTY THREE

"Come to kill me again?" Hardy Winston came to the door with one of his oversized shot glasses in his hand. He grinned and waved Kane inside and slammed the door behind him.

Kane faced him. "You're messing it up. I need a few days. The word gets out you're alive and I'm walking the high wire."

"I couldn't help it," Winston said. "I knew Art wouldn't be here until the police finish with him. I wasn't sure Karen could be here all the time. And somebody ought to be with Barton."

"How'd you get here?"

"Took a cab. Told him to drive me here."

"You didn't have any money," Kane said.

"Not on me. He didn't know that."

"Nobody saw you?"

"I'm not dumb," Winston said. "I had the cab bypass the town and come in on the Old Lake Road."

"That's a blessing." Kane said. "You been listening to your obituaries?"

"They're not half bad," Winston said.

Kane got a glass from the cabinet and poured himself a long shot of cognac. "Maybe, just maybe, it's not ruined yet. Things are falling apart out there. Vincent and Stamper are getting edgy about Turner. They think he'll get dangerous to them. I'm to make that hit, too, when they've made up their minds."

"Turner could be the wedge that breaks it open."

"If he's shaky," Kane said. He looked around. "Karen here yet?"

"Should be soon," Winston said. He picked up a red hunting jacket from the back of a chair. He put it on. "I thought I'd walk down to the lake while we wait for her."

Kane nodded. After they refilled their glasses, Winston led him up through the dining room, through the kitchen, and out the back. There was a flight of heavy oak steps leading down to a meadow. The meadow sloped down to the lake, stopping only feet away from the sandy band where the lake met the shore.

A granite bench perched on the lip of the meadow. Kane sat down beside Winston and turned up his topcoat collar. The wind off the lake was chill, but it was a fresh, head-clearing wind and they were silent there for a time.

"That job back in Atlanta," Winston said, "you seemed to know what you were doing."

"Just being creative," Kane said.

Off to the right, where the lake curved away behind a cluster of dark pines, an owl hooted. Once, then again.

"That's the death sound," Winston said.

"Only if you hear it when you're by yourself," Kane said. He turned and saw that the huge man was shivering, his eyes closed tight against the darkness.

The first two blasts were from a shotgun. Kane knew the sound. It could have been both barrels, fired separately, or a pump-action shotgun. What followed seemed a flat series of echoes. Small arms, handguns, he thought, as he counted the five flat cracks.

Kane ran for the house. The Sport out and ready, though he knew that it was the wrong weapon to stack against a shotgun. Behind him, just past his right shoulder he could hear the forced, harsh breathing of the huge man. Kane reached the steps. "You're not carrying anything?"

"All in the gun cabinets," Winston said.

At the top of the flight of stairs, Kane waited with his hand on the knob. He took the short, doggy breaths that would still and steady him. When he was sure he was ready, he opened the door and stepped sideways through the doorway and into the kitchen.

The kitchen was empty. Near the center table, Kane paused long enough to unbuckle his shoes and step out of them. He handed them to Winston and walked, now light-footed, to the door that led to the raised dining room. One more pause while he tried to remember if there'd been any squeak to the door when they'd gone through only minutes before. He couldn't. It hadn't seemed important. So he'd have to gut it up this time.

He pressed his left hand flat against the door and swung it outward. He stepped through at the ready. Eyes straight ahead, he saw the man at the bottom of the stairs. His back was to Kane, a sawed-off shotgun under his right arm, pointed downward. There was something vaguely familiar about the man's back. Maybe it was some shift in the airflow. The man felt the difference and turned, swinging up the shotgun.

It was Julie, the man whose nose and teeth Kane had broken. Kane saw the band of dirty tape across Julie's nose and then he fired. The tape exploded into blood. The other two rounds Kane fired, whether they hit him or not, that didn't matter. The one that struck his nose tore the back of his head away. He fell back against the steps.

Winston dropped Kane's shoes at his feet and ran toward the gun cabinets. Kane didn't wait to watch him. He sprinted for the stairs. He grabbed up the sawed-off shotgun and, placing the Sport on the floor beside his knee, he broke it and checked the shells. Loaded, neither chamber fired.

He stood. He shoved the Sport into his waistband. He was backing away from the stairs when he heard the thunder of footsteps approaching the landing high above him. He lifted the shotgun and braced himself.

Ned, the big thick-necked one who'd been with Julie that night in the motel room, reached the landing and looked down at Kane. There was a .45 automatic in his hand. Kane swung the shotgun toward him, a kind of fast tracking but before he'd lined up on him, he heard two blasts behind him. Both hit Ned high in the chest. The rounds tore the breath and the life out of him.

Winston stood beside the gun cabinet with a Winchester .30-.30 at his shoulder.

Kane said, "Watch the stairs."

He ran for the dining room. He found his shoes and slipped them on and buckled them. When he stood up he asked, "Any other way down from up there?"

Winston stared at him like he didn't understand the question. Stunned, Kane thought, by the killing he'd just done.

"Any other way down?"

The question got through to him this time. "Stairs that lead to a back porch."

"You hold this end." Kane passed him and ran for the front door.

Outside, going down the stairs, he could see the Fairlane parked in the driveway, out near the road.

Franco's Fairlane, he thought, and he ducked low as he rounded the front corner of the house. He could see the dark shape of the porch. It extended beyond the frame of the house. Dark there. No lights from the rooms. The moon was there, beyond the porch, but dark clouds masked it. No help there. Kane stopped and waited. After a minute or so he could see the lines of the railing that ran around the porch. Another minute passed and he could see the narrow flight of steps that had seemed a part of the beams that supported the porch. The steps began right in front of him, twenty or thirty feet from him, and ran up to the front corner of the porch.

As soon as he shows, as soon as he breaks the line of the porch railing. That would be the time. Waiting. A muscle jumped in his shoulder.

He heard it then. A sob. Crying. A woman's crying. A hissed warning, "Shut up."

Karen. It had to be Karen. That changed it. It was a different war. He shook himself out of his frozen stance and backed away. He reached the corner of the house. He swung himself around the corner, hidden by it. One look toward the road and he saw the Fairlane. It would have to be there. Franco would have to get there one way or another. He'd need the car to get him back to town.

Kane bent almost double and ran for the Fairlane. He reached it and sprinted beyond, turning to crouch behind the trunk, his hand on the rear bumper.

Five minutes.

The whimpering first, the low choking sobs. Kane saw the shape of the corner of the house change, as if a growth had settled upon it. The growth pulled away. It was a large shadow that pressed a thin shape to it. It limped and plodded in a straight line toward the Fairlane.

Kane put the shotgun on the ground. Not much chance he could use that. Not with Karen there. It would be the Sport. Still, to be sure, he closed his eyes and felt for the shotgun. He would have to know where it was if he needed it.

Twenty feet from the car. He could see where the huge shape of Franco ended and the smaller shape of Karen began. He could see that the limping movement he'd noticed was the result of the slackness of Karen, that Franco was all but carrying her.

The front door opened and Hardy Winston stood there, the Winchester at his hip, back-lighted, the ribbon of light cutting down the driveway toward the Fairlane.

Franco whirled into the light and fired twice. The .38 in his big hand seemed like a child's toy. Both shots missed Winston.

Wood splintered from the doorway beside him and Winston fell away.

Franco said. "We get to the car, I'll open the door. Stay in front of me until I tell you to move. When I tell you, slide past the wheel but you keep your head up. And don't touch the other door. That makes me dead. Before that happens you're dead too. You hear me?"

Karen didn't answer.

They reached the side of the car. Franco shifted the arm that supported her. Now the arm that held the gun was around her neck. He turned and grabbed the car door and swung it open. The light flared out at them. Franco pushed her forward until she was behind the door but still between him and the lighted doorway.

"Now," Franco said. He gave Karen a shove.

Kane straightened up. Before Franco could turn and follow Karen, Kane shot him in the back three times. The force of the slugs threw him against the car door.

Inside the car, Karen screamed until she ran out of breath.

Hardy Winston brought out a powerful flashlight and, leaning against the Fairlane, he held the light on Franco. Kane turned him and picked up the .38 from the driveway where he'd kicked it a minute ago, right after he shot Franco.

In the light, Kane could see the pink blood bubbles on Franco's lips. One of the slugs had torn a lung. It made him think of the bullfight he'd seen in Mexico. A year or so before when he'd been there on a contract. Those same blood bubbles after the sword hit the bull's lungs.

Kane said, "Up at the house?"

"Barton's dead. So's Carlo, the male nurse."

Franco moved his head. "Glad," he said. "Should have been ... the last time."

"Vincent ordered that one?" Kane said.

"Him?" Franco coughed, choking on blood. "Not him. Me. I ordered ... it. Wasn't time ...."

"You were in the club that night," Kane said. "Who was the trigger?"

"Julie. Ned drove."

"It's done then," Kane said. "Give it up, Franco. It's not worth fighting for."

"You," Franco said. He coughed and sprayed blood down the front of his coat. "I liked you. I thought ...."

"You don't have good taste in friends," Kane said.

Franco closed his mouth in a tight line and drowned in his own blood. He didn't say another word.

It took longer than Kane thought it would.

CHAPTER
TWENTY FOUR

By nine that night, Bull was sure it was over. The call to Franco had thrown Kane to the pack and they'd rip and tear him until it was done. Just a matter now of waiting for confirmation. It was that easy if you knew your way around the game.

Carol dropped by with a pint of I. W. Harper and he could see by the expectant way she looked at him that she wanted him to teach her the other debased ways of satisfaction. She wanted him to push her deeper into the pit, where you went blindfolded, where you waited to see what happened next, where it happened. The interest wasn't in him and he said he thought he might be coming down with a virus.

"Tomorrow morning," he said, "you can drop by and see if I'm alive or dead." When he said *alive* and *dead,* he patted his crotch.

After she left, he packed his bag. He left out his shaving gear and the drip-dry shirt and the pair of shorts that were still damp. They'd be dry by the time he left. Or he'd wear them damp until his body dried them. In the field, it was that way sometimes.

By ten, he'd cracked the cap on the new bottle Carol had left with him. A couple of drinks in him and he'd mentally outlined the verbal report he'd make to Dundee. It was the kind of operation Dundee would appreciate. Minimum risk and maximum results.

And maybe, just maybe, if Dundee liked the way it had gone, he could use the influence he had to ...

He heard a car pull into a parking space down the way. He reached the window in time to see Kane step out of the Duster.

Over. The way Karen had looked at him after Franco died. Horror on her face. Like she'd seen inside him and what she'd seen was a mass of crawling, wriggling things. Slugs and maggots and worms. *Done.*

Kane stood in the center of the motel room and looked around him. Like all the rooms where he spent days and hours and minutes, this one didn't show any mark that was a part of him. The impersonality of the room still without the slightest print of his personality.

He undressed and stood under the shower for a long time. He washed the dry salt sweat away. He told himself that more than the perspiration washed down the length of him, down the drain. All the deceit, the sham, the bad faith and the killings. All down the drain. Even as he told himself this, he knew that he didn't believe it.

Over. Done. If only she'd been twenty minutes later arriving at Hardy Winston's house. Hadn't arrived there just seconds before Franco and the other two. Hadn't been in the room with Barton Riker when Franco killed him. All those if's. *Done.*

At ten thirty, dressed and with his bags packed, Kane walked down to the motel office. He paid his bill in cash and took the receipt without looking at it and crushed it into a ball in his pocket.

Going back down the breezeway, he saw a man putting a small traveling bag in the trunk of a Fury. That was in front of room #8. The man didn't lift his face or seem to notice Kane. Just as Kane entered his room, he heard the trunk slam with a flattened out report like that of a shot fired at a distance.

❖   ❖   ❖

He would write the bug off. It would be neater to retrieve it, that was true. The risk, Bull decided, was acceptable. It might be years before the bug was found, if at all. Then, if found, it would not be connected with what would happen in the next few minutes: The death of some unknown man. No, a whole new kind of story would be created around the bug. A man and a woman had stayed in that room and, without knowing it, they had manufactured the evidence for a divorce. Nameless people.

The Dan Wesson .357 was on his thigh. The window down on the driver's side. No safety on the Wesson to worry about. Right hand closed over the butt, finger on the trigger guard. When Kane came out, he'd lift the Wesson, place it on the window frame, put his finger on the trigger, and tracking Kane, he'd get off three or four rounds before Kane knew what had happened to him. If there was time, he'd leave the car, run to Kane and fire another time or two into his head. The to-be-sure shots. If there was time.

Waiting. Breath even. Hand steady. That was how it was done. That was what it was all about.

He lifted his hand from the butt of the Wesson and turned the ignition key. The engine kicked over and held. There was a flutter and a plume of exhaust swirling behind him in the cold night air.

Kane heard the car engine roar to life outside. He noticed that and placed it somewhere back in his catlike awareness. He sat on the edge of the bed and cleaned the Sport. His bags were stacked beside the door, ready to be placed in the Duster for the long night drive back to Atlanta. He reloaded the Sport when he finished cleaning it and went into the bathroom and washed the oil from his hands. He stood in the bathroom doorway, drying his hands, and he felt the vibration of the engine hard against his body. *Nothing.* It is cold and the man, whoever he is, is warming up the engine.

Five minutes more and the car still hadn't moved. Kane went to the window and through a space at the side, where the drapes had rucked away from the window casement, he saw the flicker of a cigarette. A man sat behind the wheel.

Strange, but it might not be anything after all. Nerves, perhaps. The jumpy edges that hadn't settled in him. The residue of suspicion that touched everything. That made even the commonplace appear to be dangerous.

Still....

He lifted the Sport from the bed and carried it to the door with him. He put a hand on the light switch. Within a split second, after he'd flipped the switch into the OFF position and thrown the room into total darkness, he was at the window. He saw the arc of the cigarette tip as it was tossed through the window. There was a shower of sparks before the wind rolled the cigarette away.

Kane knew then.

He crossed the room and stepped into the bathroom. He closed the door and switched on the light. A low window at the back. There was hardly room for him to step through it. A strain but he made it. He was outside, in a clay expanse of ground. Feeble winter grass tried to cover the clay. A hundred yards away, he could see the dark shape of tall pines.

He knew. It was a certainty now.

Kane walked away from the light that came out of the bathroom window. He moved out into the clay field until he was in the darkness where the light ended abruptly. He squatted here and waited.

⚜ ⚜ ⚜

Bull threw the cigarette away as soon as the light went out in Kane's room. Stupid to be smoking it anyway. It was against all the rules he'd set for himself all those years ago, those years when he'd been in the field. Still, he'd been sure that Kane would be longer, that it would take him more time to ready himself for the drive north.

He placed the Wesson on the window frame, angled toward the motel door. It was the kind of shot he'd made many times before. That time in front of the hotel in Munich. Another time in Chicago. Three or four rounds to down him. The to-be-sure shot in the head. Then, before the crowd gathered, he'd be out of the lot and heading south toward Jacksonville. Back into the nest that the Agency offered him.

Two minutes. Three minutes. Too long since the light had gone out. It had gone sour.

He slid across the seat and ducked his head. He pushed open the door on the passenger side and rolled out. He landed on the asphalt and duckwalked away until he could close the door. Away, away. It had gone sour and he would have to try to salvage it.

He sprinted for the end of the motel where the office was. He rounded the corner and headed for the back of the motel. He reached the corner and stood there, letting his breath even out. The short, dog breaths that they taught you to use at Valley Farm.

Kane waited. His legs ached from the muscle strain. But the hand that held the Sport was steady.

Bull stood at the corner and sighted down the length of the back of the motel. Only one light there. He counted in his mind and thought, yes, that is the bathroom of unit #10. Maybe he is in the shower, maybe he is on the john. That would be the fun. Blow him away while he is on his pot. What a story to tell Dundee.

He walked in that direction. So close to the motel building that his shoulder brushed the concrete blocks. He counted the units as he passed them. Eight, nine ... and stopped.

The light came from unit #10. Right so far. He flattened himself next to the window. He lifted the Wesson. He swung himself around, into the light as he looked into the bathroom. Empty. No one there. There was something else also. He could feel, about chest high, the warm air pouring out of the open window.

Panic ripped at him. His stomach shook. Caught. Foxed. He turned to face the darkness beyond. The pines were there. As he turned, the first shot from the Sport slammed into his kidney. He felt that one. He didn't feel the second one that splattered his right eyeball across his face and exploded into his brain.

Kane stood to the side, out of the light, and looked down at the man. He was slumped back against the concrete block wall below the window. Enough light spilled there for Kane to see him clearly. The ruined face and the blood congealing in the cold wind.

He wasn't, Kane decided, anyone he knew.

Jackson Carter sat in the wreath of light and looked across the desk.

George Webb stood there with a hand clenched on the back of the chair there. Karen Fisk, wearing a simple black wool dress, sat in the chair. Above the black collar of the dress, her skin seemed pale, almost luminous.

"You know, of course," Carter said to Webb, "that this violates our agreement."

"But Karen said ..."

Karen put out a hand and touched Webb's arm. "I want to see him."

"That is not possible," Carter said. "He is out of town."

"Then you can tell me where he is," Karen said.

"I do not know myself," Carter said.

Behind the mirror, in the closet-like room, Kane pushed back his chair and stood up. He drank from the plastic cup, the water tepid, and the whole time he drank he stared at Karen. He placed the cup on the shelf, mashed out the cigarette that burned in the ashtray, and walked out the back door.

Kane closed the door behind him and walked down the flight of steps to the parking lot.

It was cold and windy and the sky was so clear that he could count stars as he drove across town toward his house near Jenner Park.

CHAPTER
TWENTY FIVE

From: Blue Mole (Atlanta)
Subject still inactive. No hardfists in the three months since his previous job in Ansonville. Contact with him leads me to believe that he still has no memory of his true past. That he still accepts the created past of his New Identity File.

Subject spent last weekend with Mary Ann Spencer, stewardess with Eastern Airlines, Not likely that Spencer girl represents any kind of intrusion threat, but check might be called for.

It began with the scam.

It was a middle-sized, impossible to duplicate and dangerous right up to the graveyard gate scam. Harley Wynn, almost as old as God and with some of the fox fur still on him, took three weeks to set it up. Unlike most scam men, he didn't seem to spend much time looking around for the back door. The danger, for some reason, didn't seem to bother him. He walked the wire. He floated on that wire, one foot in the air, that foot dipping down or to the side now and then, and he moved with all the assurance of a man out for a Sunday walk in a town that had banned cars. He was that sure of himself or he just didn't care.

On Tuesday morning, with the hook in gut deep, he played it. Harley's room was on the 5th floor of the Imperial Hotel in Atlanta. He was seated on the edge of the unmade bed, alternately putting on a sock or a shoe and sipping at the plastic cup of coffee one of the Cubans had brought him from the coffee shop downstairs. That same Cuban, James, placed a cheap transistor radio on the night table and flipped it on. The station it was tuned to was WPLO, the country western station. That didn't matter. Not one of the three men in the room listened to it anyway. It was, Harley had decided a couple of days before, the Cuban's way of trying to jam any bugging that might be going on. There'd been a weapons sale bust by the Feds a month before and it had taken Harley a full week to convince the two Cubans that he wasn't an undercover man for the government.

Harley Wynn, pale and thin, wearing tan plastic rimmed glasses, tied both shoe laces and stood up. The suit had been well cut about five or six years before. Now it was a relic of another fashion age. In spite of that, the crease in the trousers was blade edges and the narrow cuff pressed so flat that you had to feel the cloth to realize that it had a cuff.

Harley stopped at the dresser and picked up a silver backed hair brush. He gave his collar length gray hair a sweep or two before he faced the two Cubans.

"The problem is," he said, "that they want to see some earnest money."

Harley looked away while the two Cubans turned and stared at each other. They were an odd, a mixed pair and, in the time Harley had been working the scam, he'd spent a few hours figuring out their relationship. The younger one who called himself Carl had the pock scars across his nose, a butterfly design of them that ran outward into his cheeks. He looked dumb but he wasn't. He carried the scuffed black leather bag with him all the time. Now it was placed exactly between his feet. The other Cuban, James, was older and taller and he looked like the prototype of the revolutionary. The thin bitter face, the dark hard eyes. James used his silence like a cover. It was a way of hiding the fact he wasn't the leader and that his mind was slow.

"You mind if we talk?" James moved over to stand next to Carl's left shoulder.

Harley reached into the closet and got a tie from the rail bar. It was his only new purchase. The ties he'd stored away were thin and narrow. He'd bought a new one at Davison's Department Store the day he arrived in Atlanta.

"Go ahead and talk," Harley said. "I don't understand the language."

Carl, the seated one, shook his head. He pointed at the bathroom. "Privately, if you don't mind."

"Not at all." Harley went into the bathroom and closed the door behind him. He smiled when he heard the volume twisted to full on the radio. While he waited, he tried a couple of knots in the tie and settled for a half-Windsor. He waited three or four minutes more before there was a knock at the door. When he came out, he saw that James had been the one who'd knocked. One more clue. James was the low man.

From his chair beside the bed, Carl said, "How much earnest money?"

"One quarter," Harley said. "Twenty thousand."

"That's a lot of money," James said.

Harley didn't even look at him. The one he had to convince was Carl. "Look, this is as much a surprise to me as it is to you."

"Why?" Carl touched the side of the transistor radio and lowered the volume.

"It's just the way they do business. There was a certain amount of expense getting the merchandise together and transporting it from all over the country."

"It's here already?" James sucked in his breath and moved around Harley to look at Carl.

"That's the kind of people they are. It's business straight down the line. Now, they've taken my word for a part of it, that you seem to be people they can trust, all that, but now they've got to be sure you've got the cash."

"You could not convince them of that?" Carl said.

"How could I?" Harley spread his hands. "You showed me the top of what's in that bag and I could see some hundreds there. But for all I know it's like one of those wedding cakes. One layer of cake and the rest of it is cardboard."

Carl said stood up and placed the scuffed bag on the bed. He unlocked the clasp with a key that was on a long cord around his neck. He opened the bag and dumped the contents on the bed.

Harley edged forward until his knees were against the bed. Bundles of hundreds and fifties. His mind did a fast count. Around eighty bundles, a thousand to the bundle. It was eighty thousand dollars.

Carl watched him from across the bed. "Now you can tell them."

"It's past that now," Harley said. "They've said how they'll deal and they won't back off one step. It won't matter what I tell them."

Carl leaned over the bed and began picking up the bundles. He stacked them carefully in the bag. "Then, I think the deal is off."

"That's sudden," Harley said. "And that could be dangerous to me and to you. Let's look at it like good business. That other party, call them Mafia if you want to, went to a lot of trouble. You wanted automatic weapons and you specified the ones you'd accept. And you wanted ammo to fit those weapons. That's the order. It's given and it's confirmed and for ten percent I'm the middleman. I've had to deal with them and they know me and I'd bet half of what's coming to me that they know both of you too. We won't talk about what that means. It'll just confuse the real issue here."

Harley looked at James and saw a thin film of sweat had broken on his face. He'd convinced one of the men, but the wrong one. He went on: "So it's a business deal and you didn't ask any questions about where the weapons were coming from. Have you read the papers lately? If you had, you'd know about a couple of break-ins at Army storage depots." He saw a flick of Carl's eyes. It had registered. "And there are probably a couple of break-ins the Army doesn't know about yet. So, without making this a scare story, the party of the second part has already gone to a lot of trouble to get that order together. And risk too. The Feds don't like people stealing from them. So there's been risk and time and trouble. All these people want is some proof you've got the money together. Let's say about one-quarter of the money there, that twenty thousand, is expense money. What it cost to get the weapons together and transport them down to Atlanta. All they want to be sure of is that they didn't go to all that trouble for nothing."

Carl closed the top of the bag but didn't lock it. "What is to keep them from taking the twenty thousand and not delivering the weapons to us?"

Harley smiled and shook his head. "The profit. The other sixty thousand. Look at the good side of that. They've got the weapons together and they've brought them here to town. And you're the only buyer they've got. Who else wants enough equipment to start a small war? One of the black movements? Not a chance, I'll tell you. They want donations. They can't put cash on the barrel the way you can."

"It makes sense," the tall one, James, said.

Carl ignored him. "And the weapons? You've seen the weapons?"

"Walked right through them," Harley said. "They look clean. Most of them even look brand new."

"And the ammunition?"

"Boxes and boxes of it," Harley said.

"The proper amounts?"

"I didn't count it. That's for you to do until you're satisfied."

"The twenty thousand …"

Harley said, "What about it?"

"If I make that payment and the order is not satisfactory...?"

"It's like any other business deal. You don't take anything less than what you ordered. You show why it's not what you wanted and you'll get the twenty big ones back."

"And there will be no tricks in this?"

"I'll be there. You've got my word on it. And you've got the word of the lawyer in New Orleans. The one I told you about, the one I talked to and set up the deal."

"I have his name," Carl said. "And he will back us in this?"

"If we're right."

Carl spread the top of the bag and began to count out the bundles. Harley turned away. He got his suit jacket from the closet. He put it on and took his time adjusting the fit. When he turned around he still didn't look at the money.

"When can we see the weapons?"

"Tonight," Harley said.

Carl closed the scuffed bag and locked it. "And you will not be careless with this money?"

"Me? You think I'm crazy?"

"That would be crazy," James said.

The two Cubans moved toward the door to the hallway. Harley waited until they reached the door. He wanted it to sound right. "Look, I know a deal is a deal and I'm not supposed to get my finder's fee until the deal is over, but I wonder if you'd let me have a hundred on account...?"

The tall Cuban laughed. The contempt was there, the bare boned dislike.

In the end, Carl let him have fifty.

Harley waited alone in the hotel room for another hour. When he left, he carried the twenty thousand under his arm in a rolled up brown paper bag.

CHAPTER TWENTY SIX

Kane did his running early in the mornings. He'd be up and out of his house before the leftover chill from the winter had melted away in the sun. That was the best time, the early spring or the early fall.

For the first hour, he jogged in the road that circled the narrow park. As he ran, he watched the lights, one by one, go on in the bedrooms and the kitchens of the homes that bordered Jenner Park. And after a time, he almost believed he could smell the frying eggs, the bacon and sausage and the delicate aroma of melting butter.

One hour and there were cars on the road. He'd walk down the long flight of steps. There would be dew on the grass. He'd cross the narrow footbridge to the low side of the park. Off to one side, there was a level area where the neighborhood children played touch football in the fall and baseball in the spring. It was about a hundred yards long and Kane would run his Windsprints there. Twenty yards as fast as he could go. A pause and a deep breath and another twenty yards. When he reached the ends, the sloping bank or the children's' swings, he'd turn and head in the other direction.

During this hour, the traffic was thick on both sides of the road, above and below him. Harvard Drive had become a shortcut, a way to avoid the rush hour clogs on the way to Colony Square and beyond. At the peak hour, eight-thirty or so, Kane would pass on to a series of slow hundred-yard jogs before he quit for the day.

Kane was in one of his trots when his neighbor Bill Gordon crossed the road and seated himself in the glider near the children's' swings. He carried two large ceramic mugs, one covered with aluminum foil. He placed the covered mug off to one side as Kane slowed to a walk. Kane wiped his face on the sweatshirt sleeve and headed for the glider.

Bill lifted a large ceramic mug from his knee and sipped at the steaming tea. He nodded at a matching mug on the grass at his feet. "It's Irish this morning. I felt kind of rank today."

Kane peeled the foil away and leaned his face over the steam. There was something just a little harsh about the scent of the tea. He took a small sip. "I can't taste the Bushmill's, Bill."

"Irish tea, you fool."

"Thought you might have taken up morning drinking."

"Not this year."

Kane sat on the grass at the side of the glider and drank the tea. The sun warmed him and began today the perspiration on him. The mug seemed bottomless.

Bill said, "You ever hunt big game, John?"

The question took Kane by surprise. He drew a blank. He didn't, for a time, really know. And then, because nothing floated up, he shook his head.

"Ought to," Bill said. "There was one hunt I did in Kenya..."

Kane closed his eyes and listened. Bill Gordon had been most places and done almost everything. While Bill told about bagging a bull elephant part of Kane listened and the other part asked himself a question. *What was big game? Was man defined as big game?*

A *yes* and Kane could have nodded. It was a matter of sour pride. At the same time, each killing brought with it the taste of ashes and a brief, small death in himself. The hardfist job in Ansonville three months ago had been like that. Not so much because of the actual men he'd killed this time, they'd needed killing, but because of the broken woman he'd left in his wake.

Bill talked on. The bull charged from fifty yards.

Kane shivered in the warm sun.

❦   ❦   ❦

Jackson Carter leaned back in his chair and shook his head. He'd been laughing and the laughter ran down until it was like a bubbling, a low rumble.

"I'm surprised at you, Harley."

"At me?" Harley's expression was an innocent as that of a senile old man. "What have I done?"

"How long you been out?"

"Four weeks," Harley said.

"And already in the middle of a hornet's nest?"

"Me?"

"You," Carter said. "Word's out all over town. Somebody pulled a scam and burned both parties. And these are rough parties. Not the kind of boys you play scam games with. Word is they're mad, mad enough to kill." Carter shook his head sadly at the little man. "You should have stuck with the widows and their savings accounts."

"I know my limits," Harley said. "And you might say that I have not lost my charm with the ladies. In fact, I just plucked three of them for a grand total just on the other side of twenty thousand."

"Odd," Carter said. "Twenty thousand is the figure they're throwing around out there on the street."

"Coincidence," Harley said. "If my name is being used in connection with that scam, I may just have to go over and see them and straighten this out. A man's good name is all he has if he doesn't have any money."

"Harley, you talk shit with the best of them." Carter looked at the brown paper bag on the edge of the desk. "You said you wanted to see me about something."

"I bypassed the middleman. Knowing you I thought that would be okay with you. What's old friendship for if it won't round a corner for you now and then?"

"Exactly," Carter said.

"And I've got the contract price if you don't mind that it came from three old ladies who are going to be bitching to the police in a day or two ... when I don't show up with a marriage license."

"I thought the man and the woman had to show up to get the license."

"You can't fault these ladies for not knowing that." Harley gave his impish smile. "All of these ladies have been widows for better than twenty years."

"And even if they knew better?"

"I have an in at the court house. Why, these ladies are so brittle they break bones leaning over to pick up the morning paper out of the driveway. A gentleman would spare them that trouble. Those ladies, right now, are home getting beautiful and saving up their energy for the wedding night."

Carter grinned. "You give them a taste of what it'll be like?"

"A refined gentleman like me?"

Kane stretched and watched the meeting from his room behind the two-way mirror. On the shelf below the mirror, there was the usual ash tray, a plastic glass of water and a note pad.

He was ready to work. The last job three months ago, the harshness of it, was washed away, the blood of that one faded away until it was in black and white, no longer in color.

The spring had arrived. April was only a few days old. He'd been considering a drive into the mountains when the hurry-up call came from Carter. It was walk-in business. Not the kind of trade Carter usually liked. He'd made an exception this time.

He'd known Harley for a number of years, back to New Orleans and beyond.

"He was the king of them all in his day," Carter had said. "He could peel money off people the way boiling water peels a tomato."

A funny little bird of a man, Kane decided. Neat and clean, every hair in place. The prison pallor on him. Not even the time walking in the yards could cover that. It was hard to judge his age. He might be fifty or seventy. A cocky old guy. The lean, honest face, the longish gray hair, probably a month's growth since he got out. The wet, pale blue eyes that begged you to trust him.

⚜ ⚜ ⚜

"How long were you in this time, Harley?"

"Two years." The old man looked around the office, at the bookcases, at the huge abstract behind him, and finally at the cabinet. "It was a bad rap, of course."

"Of course," Carter said.

"That cabinet," Harley said. "I think I see booze in there."

Carter stood up. He walked to the cabinet and got out two shot glasses and placed them on the desk. "Bourbon, if I remember correctly." He carried a decanter back to the desk and sat down. He poured two shots and passed one to Harley. "If the talk is right out on the street, you might end up wishing you were still in."

"Another bad rap." Harley lifted the shot glass. His hand shook but he didn't spill a drop. "Think about all you know about me. Is that my kind of scam?"

Carter watched him sip the bourbon. "Off hand, I'd say it wasn't. Coming here like this, that isn't your kind of thing either."

"You sell a service I need. I'm a buyer of that service unless our past relationship ..."

"Tell me about it, Harley."

"I'm not the injured person. I'm the middleman, taking the contract out for someone else. You know me, I've had my share of bad experiences. I am not the Jesus type. But I've never felt about any of God's creatures the way I feel about this man." He placed the empty shot glass on the front edge of the desk. "I could do this killing myself if I had the time."

"Who?"

"Let me tell you the whole thing."

Carter leaned across the desk and refilled Harley's glass.

"I've got maybe one real friend in the whole world. I met him two years ago at Reidsville Prison. And I'll tell you it scared the hell out of me when I heard what he was in for. I was put in the same cell with him and somebody asked me if I knew what that dude had done. When he told me, I almost pissed in my pants."

"What?"

"The molestation murder of a five-year-old boy."

"I can see why you'd be nervous," Carter said.

"The only thing is, I liked him right away. The guy who'd warned me about him, it turned out, didn't know him at all. The best way to get a laugh going in the slam is to say you'd been bad-rapped. A few days in there and I found out nobody believed Ben Carpenter could have done that. No way, everybody said."

Kane wrote *Ben Carpenter* on the pad in front of him.

Carter lifted his shot glass and sipped at it. His tongue licked at a drop that ran down the side. "He say he was bad-rapped?"

"Not for a whole year," Harley said. "And even then I had to start the conversation. I had to pull it out of him."

"And you believe him?"

"You spend two years with somebody, you get to know when they're telling the truth and what's a lie. He's telling the truth when he says he didn't kill the boy and he doesn't know who did."

"One problem I see here," Carter said. "You've come to the wrong place."

The old man shook his head. "No."

"What you hire here is what we might call it a final solution. It won't get this friend of yours, Carpenter, out of the slammer."

"That's not the problem anymore. You see, he's coming out. It might be two months. It might be six months."

"Parole?"

"No," Harley said. "He's doing four consecutive life sentences. He's on the first one right now."

"You ran past me," Carter said.

"Lung cancer. It's past the point where anything can be done about it. He's over at the Grady prison ward right now. I've tried to see him but I can't get in."

"What does Carpenter want?"

"He wants to know who killed the boy and he wants that man dead, dead, dead." Harley said. "He's a good man but ten years in the slam for something he didn't do, that rots the humanity off the bone." Harley pushed the brown paper bag into the center of the desk. "Twenty big ones in there. You interested?"

Carter's hand touched the bag and moved away. "Ten years? The ground's been rained on a lot since then."

"I didn't say it would be easy."

Carter unrolled the neck of the bag and dumped the money on the desk top. "I can't promise anything, Harley."

"Just your best."

Carter nodded.

"That's good enough for me." Harley stood up and took the shot glass in a cupped hand. He stared down at it a moment before he tossed back the bourbon left in it.

"How will I get in touch with you?" Carter asked.

"You won't," Harley said. "I'm going to be running away and looking over my shoulder for those three pissed off widows. I'll call you."

Kane watched the little man straighten his shoulders and adjust his tie. Carter circled the desk and put an arm around Harley's neck and walked to the door with him.

There goes a dead man, Kane said to himself, and he knows he's dead.

⚜   ⚜   ⚜

Harley caught a bus into town and rode it through the important commercial part of Peachtree Street, past the Regency and Peachtree Center. He got off at the stop close to Houston Street and walked over. It was still bright afternoon and he passed two flophouse hotels, the handwritten cards taped to the windows.

$6 a day.

$25 by the week

Too early, he thought. Carl and James would be checking the hotels. The longer he waited, the better.

Past the flophouse hotels the porno movie houses nudged at him. Why not? It was not a place they'd look for him. He passed up the first theater and entered the second one. He paid his five dollars and fumbled his way down the aisle in the pitch darkness. It was so dark that he found a seat only after one attempt to sit in a startled fat man's lap.

For half an hour, he watched the film with a kind of breathless interest. That is the nasty old man in me, he thought. And then the jumble of organs, the ravaging of each other and the simulated passion tired him and he closed his eyes.

He opened them half an hour later when a man stumbled over his feet. On screen, a blonde girl with a motorcycle tailpipe burn on the inside of her right leg was undressing. When she bared her small, puppy nose breasts, Harley lowered his head once more.

There had been a girl once. Where? The string of towns flashing by, alike, blurring in his mind's eye. One of those tobacco auction towns in North Carolina. The dusty hot summer, the blinding sun all day and the stifling heat at night. The girl had had breasts like that. It was the summer of '40 or '41. He'd been working his version of the pigeon drop scam that time, only once in each town. Using a five carat diamond instead of the "found" envelope with the money in it. He'd made $43,000 or better that summer, plucking a tobacco farmer of his year's profits every three or four days.

That girl, Elvira her name. He'd seen her first in front of the town's only movie theater. He'd followed her inside and sat next to her. He'd offered her his popcorn until she accepted.

Later that night there'd been an open field with the heat of the sun still stored in the earth. The inverted bowl of the stars over them and he'd liked her and she'd liked him. Her body had been warm and cool at the same time and he'd wanted to stay another day, another week, another year. But the auction season was about done for the year and there were other towns and other suckers and he'd told himself they'd be other girls just like Elvira.

When he left her that night he'd said he'd meet her in front of the movie theater the next night but he hadn't. He left town at first light. He moved on to the next town and the next girl and it had been a year or two before he realized there hadn't been another Elvira and that there wouldn't be.

Harley dozed. A fitful dream of that dark field with the baked earth under his knees. The star sputter over them. The cry of night birds in the distance.

A few minutes after seven, Harley left the porno theater. He felt oddly at peace, rested, when he checked into the first hotel he reached on his way back to Peachtree Street.

At four-ten a.m. a patrol car answered a disturbance complaint called in by the night clerk at the Creighton Hotel. In the alley behind the hotel, in an area choked with trash and garbage cans, the two policemen found the broken body of an old man. He was wearing socks and shiny dark trousers. He was bare to the waist. His chest was a sheet of drying blood. Strips of skin had been peeled away. The fingers on both hands had been broken.

The coroner's report, issued a couple of days later, estimated that the man had died of shock and a heart attack.

All the flophouse clerk could tell the police was that the man had registered that afternoon as Harland A. Winters. He'd given an address in Miami.

CHAPTER
TWENTY SEVEN

B en Carpenter opened his eyes when the male nurse swung the door open and waved Jackson Carter in. The room was in half darkness, the only light coming from a slightly open set of blinds off to the right of the bed.

Carter carried a legal pad in one hand, a small tape recorder in the other. He'd had to leave his briefcase with the ward guard at the barred and locked entrance to the floor. Now, his eyes on the man in the bed, he edged a chair close to the bed and placed the portable tape recorder on the night table. He dropped the legal pad into the chair and bent over the recorder until he'd unwound the microphone cable and plugged in the jack. Lifting the legal pad he sat down and looked at the dying prisoner.

Carpenter had been a big man at one time. The frame, the bone structure showed that. He'd been about six-two and he'd probably weighed around two-ten or twenty. Illness had sliced about a hundred pounds of that away. If anything, now he carried about a hundred and twenty pounds wrapped loosely over the bones. He was a year or two over forty. He looked fifty. His hair, in the prison brush cut, was gray and limp, damp and cooling like the fur of a dying animal.

"I don't know you," Carpenter said.

"We have a mutual friend. A man with a lot of scams."

A smile twisted across Carpenter's face. "So he did it?"

Carter nodded. "He's quite a guy."

"All of that and more."

Carter lifted the microphone. "We'd better start off now. I'm not sure how much time we've got. This visit, in case anybody asks, is about a small estate you inherited some time back. I've been handling it for you. At least, that's how I got in here. That and some pull."

"What is it you want?"

Carter placed the microphone a few inches away from Carpenter's lips. "The whole story. Everything you remember." He turned back to the recorder and pressed the RECORD bar.

The voice, in the beginning, was strong, firm. As the tape went on a kind of weary breathing crept in. Kane sat in the client's chair across the desk from Jackson Carter. A shot glass of cognac was on the desk, near Kane's right elbow. Kane hadn't asked for it and he hadn't touched it yet. He stared at the tape recorder on the desk blotter and the slowly spinning reels.

"*... living in an apartment on Saint Charles at the time. It was an old house that had been cut up into eight apartments, what you might call efficiency apartments.*"

Kane lifted his head and looked at Carter. "You have that address?"

Carter nodded and tapped the legal pad with a finger.

"*... working construction ... steel ... with the Dubose Company out on Stewart Avenue. Making a pretty good living but blowing it all on the weekends. You know, on beer, booze and broads.*"

On the tape, Carter said, "Tell me about the boy."

"*He lived two doors down from where I did. He was a good smart kid. Tim Goddard. His mother ... well, she was divorced and wasn't much better than she was supposed to be. I think she worked as a waitress at one of the diners over on Ponce de Leon.*"

Carter asked how well he'd known the boy.

"*Pretty well, I guess. You could say I was a friend of his and not be far from wrong. He had this thing about hard hats, like they were heroes of his. One spring, he started hanging around our porch. We'd be out there drinking some beer and talking. He'd sit very quiet, all eyes and ears and he wouldn't say anything. At first, he was sort of in the way. But after a time, I got to know him and I liked him. You know, in his situation, he needed a friend and that friend needed to be a man who wasn't trying to push him out the house so he could tip his mother over into the nearest bed. By the summer, I'd asked if it was okay with his mother and I took him to a movie now and then or out to Piedmont Park. And sometimes to a Sunday afternoon baseball game.*"

"*His mother didn't mind?*"

"*Not that I could tell. In fact, she seemed to like it. It took the kid off her hands for a few hours. It gave her time for her own... business. That was the hard fact.*"

"*Tell me about the killing.*"

"*It was the first or second Saturday in September. The night before, Friday, I'd gone home from the job and cleaned up. I met some of the guys over at the Driftwood on Piedmont. We got beered up and it must have been midnight before we left there. We rode around for a while and went to bed to sleep it off. The next thing I knew somebody was banging on my door. It was the police. Two of them. They said that Tim's mother, Janice, had been trying to call me. But, like I did when I wanted to sleep it off, I'd taken the phone off the hook. She'd got worried when Tim didn't show up for lunch and she'd come to the apartment house and she'd buzzed me for a time trying to get past the outside door. I hadn't answered the buzzer. If I heard it at all, I'd probably stuffed the pillow over my head and gone back to sleep. So Janice had rung the buzzer of one of the women upstairs and the woman had let her in. She'd knocked at my door and I hadn't answered. She'd tried the apartment next to mine but the lady there had gone grocery shopping. The next one down was empty, the one next to the front door. She tried that door and it was unlocked. She went in and found Tim."*

"Found him how?"

"I didn't see him. I wouldn't even look at the photos they had in court. But from what I heard, he had his t-shirt stuffed in his mouth as a gag and he was all torn up. You know, torn up by the things that were done to him."

"What did the police want with you?"

"It took some time for me to find that out. I'd hardly started talking to the police before Tim's mother made a run at me, scream-ing and clawing at me. By the time the police got her off me, I was so confused and groggy I didn't know what was going on."

"They tell you why they came looking for you?"

"Two reasons, they said. The first was that when Tim left his house around ten that morning he told his mother he was going to see me."

"And the other one?"

"They showed me a cigarette lighter. They asked if it was mine and I had to admit that it was. You see, it was engraved. It was a thing a lot of us had done one time when we were doing some work on Guam. It had the Seabee emblem on one side and my name on the other. It was a silver cover and all you had to do was buy a Zipp and slip the cover on in place of the one that came with it."

"What war was that?"

"The Korean one. Well, I got to asking what my lighter had to do with it and the policemen said they'd found the lighter on the floor next to Tim. All I could remember was that I'd been using the lighter the night before at the Driftwood. But I was groggy and shook up and scared and I guess I didn't make much sense to them. They took me downtown and questioned me for a day or two and the next thing I knew they'd charged me with the murder."

"It doesn't sound like they had much to go on."

"I guess they didn't need much. At the trial a lot was made of the lighter. And there was an outside door, the one that led to the

porch. If they said it once they said it a hundred times. The door was always locked and only a tenant could have let the boy in. There was just no other way he could get in. What really did me in was the mother. She did some shouting and screaming about how Tim didn't lie and how she was sure Tim told the truth when he said he was going to see me. According to her, he'd said I was expecting him."

"That true?"

"No, but he might have said it just to get out of the house."

"And you were convicted?"

"It didn't take the jury long to make up their minds."

"But you didn't get the death sentence?"

"Four consecutive life sentences, that might be worse than death."

There was a time of silence, just the breathing of Ben Carpenter and the thin squeak of the tape head, before Jackson Carter cleared his throat. *"One question I've got to ask you, Ben. Harley Wynn believes in you. I've known Harley for a long time and he's no fool. I don't know you at all. I want to be sure this isn't a wild goose chase. Are you guilty, Ben?"*

Carpenter's voice had grown weaker and weaker. Somehow, from some depth in him, he pulled out the last of the strength. *"No, God damn it, no. I had nothing to do with it."*

⚜ ⚜ ⚜

Carter reached across the desk and punched the STOP bar on the recorder. "The rest of it is just names," he said. "The names of the people he drank with that Friday night and ..."

"That won't do much good," Kane said. He looked down at the shot glass of cognac. He picked it up and wrapped his hand around it, warming it.

"The mother's full name. The names of the people who lived in the apartment building with Carpenter. There were six other tenants. The eighth apartment was empty, unrented."

Carter ripped off the top page of the legal pad. There was an address on Saint Charles at the top of the sheet. Below that there were two lists. One list was headed: *drinking with him that night.* The second list of names had above it: *tenants in the building at the time.* Two of the names on the second list were women. Kane knew he could strike them off. That left four men he'd have to trace if he could.

He sipped the cognac and looked at both lists. The four men on the tenants listing were also on the drinking with him list.

"You believe him?"

Carter's nod came without hesitation. "All you could do was hear him. I saw him. He's one step from the dark edge and he knows it. There's no percentage in lying."

"Ten years." Kane folded the list and looked down at it. "That's a long time to be backtracking on."

"All you need is a good break," Carter said.

"Five or six."

"You'll need credentials of some kind." Carter opened his desk drawer to the left and brought out a thin stack of business cards. It was Carter's standard C.P.A. business card with one addition. At the bottom left of the card *John A. Callan, Associate* was printed.

"It's a bullshit story," Carter said. "Feel free to add to it when you have to. It's a small estate and the will specified that the money wasn't to go to Ben Carpenter unless there was some reasonable doubt about his guilt."

"Nobody will believe that."

"It's just dumb enough to sound like the truth," Carter said. "And it might open some doors."

"And close others." Kane put the business cards in his jacket pocket. "The mother won't want to talk to me at all."

"Use charm," Carter said. "It sounds like she used to like men quite a bit."

"This isn't the usual contract."

Carter's smile was thin. "I thought you'd appreciate the difference after the last one."

Kane pushed his unfinished cognac away and stood up. He reached the door to the outer office before Carter stopped him.

"There's one more thing."

Kane turned. "Yes?"

Carter rounded the desk. He carried a folded newspaper in one hand. "You read the Blue Streak edition of the *Journal* today?"

"No."

Jackson handed him the paper. A headline and a single paragraph had been circled with a felt-tipped pen.

Brutal Slaying at Creighton Hotel

Kane read the single paragraph. The dead man hadn't been identified yet. He passed the paper back to Carter. "Harley Wynn?"

Carter gave a short, final nod. "I did some quiet checking."

"The poor son-of-a-bitch," Kane said.

CHAPTER
TWENTY EIGHT

The ceremony took place during the lunch hour at the Agency. Whistler and Pryor attended. The third director, Dundee, had called in at ten with the excuse of an early spring cold. "The worst kind," he'd said.

About twenty people gathered in the hallway near the guarded main entrance into the building. There, to the left as one entered, was a series of bronze name plaques. Each one gave only a man or woman's name and the year of birth and the year of death. The heading above it was just as simple: ROLL OF HONOR. The first name had been placed there in 1955. There were twenty-three other names added below that one. That was the purpose of the ceremony: the adding of the latest name.

It was a silent tribute. There would be no speeches. Nothing could be said that didn't violate the National Security Act. When he was certain that the full staff was present, Whistler took the name plaque from his pocket and stepped forward.

Matthew R. Racklin 1923–1974

Whistler handed the bronze tag to the building maintenance man and backed away. The maintenance man had already drilled the two holes and driven in the metal sheaths that would accept the bronze screws. Now, as the twenty people watched, he fitted the tag over the holes and took first one screw and then the second one out of his mouth. A few turns with his screwdriver and the name tag was firmly in place.

That done, the people who'd attended the ceremony broke into small groups and drifted away. At the end only the maintenance man and Whistler and Pryor remained.

Whistler waited until the workman packed away his tools, gave them a wave that was almost a salute, and marched out past the guard. Then he stepped forward and leaned over to stare at the new addition to the ROLL OF HONOR. After a few seconds, he straightened up and backed away.

"I don't think it's quite level," he said to Pryor.

Pryor leaned in. "I think you're right. It's high on the right end."

"It might not matter," Whistler said.

"Not in a hundred years," Pryor said.

The two men, almost as if on signal, turned and marched step for step to the elevator. Within seconds the elevator placed them on the top floor of the Agency building. It was the 10th floor. On this level were the executive offices, a steno pool staffed by four women with the highest clearance, a Meeting Room and a private dining room.

Whistler paused with his key in the office door and looked around at Pryor. "I've just made a fresh pot."

Pryor nodded and followed him inside.

Seated, the coffee poured, Whistler tilted his head in the general direction of the main entrance to the building, the foyer where the ceremony had taken place. "I have mixed feelings about that."

"I thought you did." Pryor lifted his cup, blew the steam away and sipped at it. "I've been meaning to ask why."

"Questions," Whistler said. "Questions that I haven't wanted to bring up at the Friday meetings."

"Two of the three who attend those meetings are here now, about to discuss it. I guess I have to assume that it is about Dundee."

"For the sake of the Agency, I don't want this to go out of this room."

"I think I can promise that," Pryor said.

"Let me put it this way. If Bull Racklin had died on the way to work in an automobile accident, I'd have no doubt that his name belongs on that list down there. For fine past service alone."

"The way he died bothers you?"

"Enough so that I did some of my own checking into it." Whistler took a long-stemmed briar pipe from the tray on his desk and packed it with John Cotton's Mixture. The tobacco was as black as twigs. "Blue Mole in Atlanta gave me the first clue. It was in one of his reports on Kane's activities. It was his last hardfist, the one he carried out in the resort town in Georgia. Ansonville, I think it was."

"I remember reading about the town in some other connection," Pryor said.

"That was back in late December," Whistler said. "The Governor and the Attorney General sent in a task force to clean out the criminal elements in the town. It was going toward becoming another ..." Whistler stopped. "What was that city in Alabama?"

"Phenix City."

"Yes, it was becoming another Phenix City."

"I remember," Pryor said.

"An odd thing about that hardfist in Ansonville. From what Blue Mole said, he seems to believe that Kane's involvement in the bloodshed there may have helped to bring in the State. In one evening, Kane was responsible for the death of at least two men, perhaps three." He touched a match to the pipe. The strong acrid tobacco scent filled the room. "What's odd is that Bull Racklin was found dead in an alley in Jacksonville exactly six hours after that bloodbath in Ansonville."

"Close by?"

"No time at all by helicopter," Whistler said. "It might be a couple of hours by car."

"The Jacksonville Police think Bull Racklin died in a mugging that went wrong."

"It was their guess." Whistler took the pipe from his mouth and looked down into the bowl at the white ash. "Did you read the medical report?"

Pryor shook his head. "I don't think it was routed by me."

"That's strange too. I found the medical report and it had been initialed by you and by me."

"I wonder how that happened."

"*Why* might be the better question." Whistler used a finger to tamp the tobacco in his pipe. "And I think I know the answer. Bull was shot twice, once in the side and once in the face. Right in the eye to be exact. Both slugs fragmented to some degree but there was enough there for ballistics to make their estimate that the rounds were .22's."

"Kane."

"It's his weapon," Whistler said. "The Woodsman Sport."

"So what do you think the real story is?"

"I think that Dundee is trying to take our votes away from us. The decision to put Kane on a long rope and let him run was a two-to-one decision. Dundee argued against it and voted against it. He wants Kane dead. I would hate to think that Dundee believes that his is the only vote that counts."

"Of course," Pryor said, "there was some talk of bad blood between Bull and Kane."

"That's true. I was a part of that. On Kane's advice, before Long Rope, I removed Bull from field work. A man like Bull wouldn't accept that kind of demotion with grace."

"It could have been personal then?"

"Perhaps. Bull was supposed to be in Jacksonville on a few days of vacation. But he was met at the Naval Air Station by Foster. Foster was given the impression that Bull was on official business."

"It could have been Bull's bluff."

"And the flight down in the Admiral's plane?"

"That kind of hitch-hiking goes on all the time, " Pryor said. "I'm guilty of it myself now and then."

"One more tricky question," Whistler said. "How can Kane be two places at once? In Ansonville and in Jacksonville?"

"It's what Dundee would say."

"Exactly. I think the key to it might be Foster there in Jacksonville. I think we ought to recall him for a week or so of retraining."

"Without Dundee's knowledge? That seems high-handed."

"It could be an agreement made today. I could always argue that he wasn't available. That spring cold of his, you know."

Pryor stood up. His coffee was only half finished. "You think Bull was in Ansonville to cancel Kane on Dundee's orders. Something went wrong and Kane killed Bull. And then, also on Dundee's orders, Foster went in and cleaned it up and set up the Jacksonville death for Bull."

"That's the way I see it," Whistler said.

Pryor reached the door. He turned with his hand on the knob. "That kind of thinking makes this morning's ceremony even more interesting. That spring cold that kept Dundee away. If Bull was his man, if Bull died trying to do the hardfist for him, the least he could have done was show up for it. That is nothing less than basic loyalty."

Whistler met his eyes. He didn't blink or nod.

After a few seconds, Pryor opened the door. Over his shoulder, as he stepped through the doorway, he said, "Yes, that is something to think about."

The door closed behind him with hardly a sound.

It was a storage warehouse on Stewart Avenue. For about a year a FOR SALE OR LEASE sign had been planted in the dirt border near the building. Now that sign leaned against the wall, showing the dirty and weathered back. A moving van with HARKER MOVES IT ALL painted on the doors was backed into the narrow alleyway that led to the ramp. From the information below that it was clear that the Harker Company was located in Kansas City.

The two Cubans, James and Carl, stood in the refreshment booth of the Gulf station across the street. They were drinking Cokes and eating snack crackers and staring at the warehouse front. The scuffed money bag was on the patio concrete next to Carl's left shoe.

They'd taken a cab to the warehouse and walked across the street to the station. From the clock in the Gulf station they could see that they were five minutes early for the meeting.

"It is the right place?" James asked for the second time.

"The truck makes me think so," Carl said. His real name was Carlo but he'd dropped the "o" the first year in Miami. That was when he'd thought of forgetting his homeland and becoming an American. The bitterness of that first year, his own poverty set against the wealth he saw around him, moved him into the revolution.

"The lawyer ... his name ...?"

"Mr. Ponce," Carl said.

"Do you trust him?"

"It is hard," Carl said, "to make any judgment over a telephone."

"But we have his word?"

Carl smiled. "The word of a man on the telephone? The word of a man we do not know?"

Carl placed the Coke bottle, with still an inch or so of the drink remaining, in the rack. He chewed the last of the snack crackers while he bent over and picked up the bag. He looked at James. "Don't perspire so much. It is either the right day to die or it is the wrong day."

He walked briskly toward the street. James hesitated for a few seconds and had to use his longer strides to catch up before they reached the curb and waited for a break in the traffic.

The albino, Freddie, opened the office door and looked at them. "Yeah?"

"Mr. Ponce sent us," Carl said.

The albino swung the door open. Carl walked right past him. James, with a frightened, pasty look, walked in sideways so that he'd be sure he didn't touch the albino. The albino was death. Hadn't James' grandmother told him that? An albino or the dream of a. white bull that ran down the road or around the house. He looked back and saw the albino go out and pull the door closed behind him.

There were two men behind the desk. One seated at the center, the regular position, and the other off to his left, a bit removed. The one at the center position pushed back the roll-away chair and stood up. He was about six-four, knife edge thin. He wore tan whipcord trousers and a white short sleeved tie shirt, the neck open. His hair was almost blue-black and the hairs on his arms were dark and wire-like. There was a scar on the right nostril, running from the bottom edge to the bridge of his nose.

"First names will do," this man said. "I am Zack."

Carl gave his name and turned to James to give his.

The man, Zack, turned and waved a thin hand at the man still seated to his left. This man looked fat, barrel chested, and his crossed legs showed white cotton socks above cheap low cut black shoes. The man's eyes watched them while he dug at his fingernails with a straightened out paper clip. "This is Gibbs."

Carl nodded at him. The cold eyes watched him, but the head didn't move.

"I talk for us," Zack said. "A two-man conversation is better than a four-man one. Who does the talking for you?"

"I do," Carl said.

"You carry the bag. I thought so." Zack reached behind him and caught the arms of his chair. He pulled it in close and sat down, edging the chair forward until he was against the desk's border. "Does your man know weapons?"

Carl nodded. "He has had the best training."

Zack looked at James and then looked over his left shoulder at Gibbs. "Show him the merchandise. Show him the merchandise for at least ten or fifteen minutes."

Gibbs uncrossed his legs and dropped the paper clip on the floor. Standing he was about five-nine. What had seemed to be fat wasn't when he was upright. The belly seemed sucked in and he moved around the desk with a kind of animal grace.

James followed him out. Zack waited until the albino closed the door before he nodded at the chair across the desk from him. "I understand from a call from New Orleans by way of K.C. that there is some problem with the money."

"The middleman decided that he wanted more than his ten percent."

"But you recovered it?"

Carl shook his head.

"How much is left in the kitty?"

Carl lifted the bag and placed it on the desk. "There is sixty thousand in here."

"Then you are twenty thousand short?"

"Your math is as good as mine," Carl said.

A flicker of irritation passed over Zack's face. It was there and then washed away. "It is not enough. Even with the finder's fee for Harley Wynn, the total to me should be seventy-two thousand. I can't take a dime less than that."

The middleman ..." Carl began.

"You chose him, or rather he chose you. He came from your side of the deal. He is not our responsibility."

"Mr. Ponce knew him and accepted him."

"Ponce is not a big factor in this deal."

Carl reached up slowly and took the bag from the desk. Zack watched him. "Then we have no deal. I will look elsewhere."

"It is not that easy," Zack said. "That is not how we do business." The roll-away chair squeaked on the floor as Zack pushed it back a foot or so. Carl had been watching his eyes, his face, and he didn't see the center desk drawer eased open. Zack reached into the drawer and brought out an army-issue .45 automatic. He placed it on the dusty top of the desk and moved his hand away. "I don't know who you've been doing business with in the past..."

Carl lifted his hands and placed them palm down on the front edge of the desk. "Now I know how you do business."

"Can you come up with another twelve thousand in the next day or two?"

Carl shook his head. "It has taken us three years to collect this sum. Dimes, quarters and sometimes dollars. You do not know the hardship on my people that this eighty thousand has been. If you knew..."

"I don't care if your sisters collected it giving blowjobs to spades," Zack said. "It is twelve thousand short."

Carl's hands jerked away from the desk edge. "In my country one does not talk..."

"Screw it," Zack said. "It is a figure of speech."

It didn't completely satisfy him, but Carl opened his hands and placed them on the desk once more. "There is the twenty thousand that Mr. Wynn took from us."

"From you," Zack corrected him.

"That twenty thousand still exists."

"You think we might make a deal?"

"There is also the matter of eight thousand dollars. What Mr. Wynn was to receive for his part in this."

"Instead of seventy-two thousand you would pay the whole eighty thousand."

"For your help," Carl said.

Zack lifted the .45 from the desk top and placed it in the drawer. He closed the drawer. "I think we might work something out. It shouldn't take but a day or two to find Harley Wynn."

"It is not that simple. We have already found him. He is dead. But he didn't have the money."

"What is this shit anyway?" The hard anger blew across the desk. "What the fuck do you want?"

"I said he did not have the money. Before he died he told us who did have it."

"Give me a name," Zack said.

"Jackson Carter."

"Carter?" Zack put back his head and laughed. When the laugh died down he said, "You know your chance of getting it back from him? The chance of a snowball in hell, that's what."

"He is a powerful man?"

"He's got strings going everywhere," Zack said. "What did Ponce say when you told him this?"

"I didn't," Carl said, "When I talked to him we hadn't found Mr. Wynn yet."

"Jackson Carter, huh?" Zack stood up and reached into his pocket. He brought out a small handful of coins. "I don't have a phone here. I'll have to call from across the street." He dug a finger around in the change. He looked at Carl. "You got any quarters?"

Carl had three. He passed them to Zack. "Then we will work on this together?"

"I'll see what Ponce says." He stopped at the door. He swung it open and the albino looked in. "Freddie, take him back in the warehouse. I'll be across the street."

Carl watched him head for the Gulf station. The albino nodded toward the door in the center of the unloading ramp. Carl followed him. The bag felt like it weighed about fifty pounds.

"It is a tricky question," Charlie Ponce said.

Zack turned and watched two girls in shorts get out of a VW and head for the refreshment patio. One girl's shorts were so high and tight he could see the hard cheeks of her ass.

"The ties he had with old Carlo, do they still have any clout?"

"I'll have to ask around."

"I have to know this afternoon," Zack said.

"That is quick."

"Time is money like they say in the Chamber of Commerce." The girl with the high, tight shorts leaned over to take an orange drink from the mouth of the drink machine. Zack watched the ass and felt a strong stirring. "I don't think my principal back in K.C. gives a shit for Jackson Carter. I am just touching the bases by asking you. I can always make a call to K.C."

"Where can I reach you?"

"I don't have a phone. I'll call back by six. In two hours."

Ponce said, "I might not have it by then."

"In that case, I'll call K.C."

"You're pushing hard," Ponce said.

"You cleared Harley Wynn with us," Zack said. "Think about that." He hung up the phone and backed out of the booth. As he passed the refreshment patio, he had his close look at the girls. The one who'd stirred him some had a face like a mule.

CHAPTER
TWENTY NINE

Kane sat in the glider in Jenner Park, across the street from his house. The park was about half a block wide and about two blocks long. A thin trashy stream ran through the center of it. The glider, as he swung slowly back and forth, faced the low brick house. The grass below the porch, sloping down toward the walk and the dogwood trees, was blue-green and needed cutting. It was a single-floored cottage and from the outside it looked smaller than it really was. It extended deep into the lot. There were two bedrooms, one of which he'd converted into a library-study. There was a large living room. This was divided from the dining room by a two-faced fireplace, one fireplace facing into the living room and the other the dining room. Kane never used the dining room. There was a large kitchen. He lived at that table in the center of it.

The basement door was always locked. He'd spent some time right after buying the house putting in extra insulation and sound proofing down there. He'd put in a firing range and every day, or at least six days a week, he fired fifty rounds. Though he had his choice of weapons he preferred the Woodsman Sport. It said something about his sense of the killing range that the targets, side and front views, were only twenty-five yards from the rail.

Today he had not fired his fifty rounds. It was Wednesday and, as he did on those days, he'd awakened to the sound of Reba's light step in the other parts of the house.

It is almost four in the afternoon now. The hunt was on. There were things to do but he waited. At four, Reba came out the front door and closed it carefully behind her. Kane stilled the glider and stepped out of it. He walked toward the driveway, where she waited for him. The blue, two-year-old Duster was there. He'd have preferred a better car, but the Duster fit his cover as John Callan, a heavy equipment salesman.

Kane opened the door on the passenger side for Reba. "Thank you, Mr. Callan," she said just before he closed the door.

He got behind the wheel. "One day, Reba, you're going to call me John."

"Just before my funeral," she said.

"That'll be too long."

"I could, I suppose, call you Mr. John."

He laughed as he backed the Duster out of the driveway.

After he dropped Reba at her home, Kane drove back to Ponce de Leon and started working his way from cafe-to-cafe. He was looking for the dead boy's mother, Janice Goddard. It took him an hour and a half to find her. The name wasn't the same. She'd remarried.

⚜   ⚜   ⚜

At five, Zack sent the albino, Freddie, down the road to the pizza house to pick up some sandwiches and beer. He gave him a twenty and said that he wanted about three or four dollars in change. Freddie was back in half an hour. There were enough sandwiches and beer for twice the number of people in the warehouse office.

Zack nodded at the cardboard box that was on the desk. He said to Carl and James, "Be our guests."

At five of six, after eating a meatball sandwich and a pepper and steak one, Zack finished off his beer and stood up. He scooped the change Freddie had brought back to him from the desk. "I have to make another call to New Orleans," he said.

James, who'd approached his first sandwich like he thought it might be poisoned, had his eye on the two remaining sandwiches. He wanted a second one but pride was holding him back.

Zack said, "The weapons, the count and the ammo, they are all as you contracted for? It might be important to know for this call."

"The condition and the count are fine," Carl said. "It is now a matter of the money."

Zack smiled and went out to the phone booth at the Gulf station to call Ponce.

Charlie Ponce said, "Jackson Carter still has some ties here. Some of them are strong."

"Does that mean …?"

"Let me finish," Ponce said. "Some people here in the Gambino group would take it hard if Carter got hurt. On the other hand, after I explained the matter of the money, they believe that you have a right to it. If Carter were still a part of the organization, it would be a simple matter of telling him to turn the money over to you."

"And it's not that simple anymore?"

"Carter's father was a man who built up a collection of I.O.U.'s that he never called in. And the son, before he moved away, did some service for the organization."

"All that fancy sounding crap aside," Zack said.

"It is this: the money is yours. You can use whatever means it takes to recover it. That is, up to the point where any serious harm is done to Jackson Carter."

"That makes it easy," Zack said. "That is a piece of cake the way you've got it laid out."

"That's the way it is."

"Thanks for nothing, Ponce." Zack hung up and fished out a dime. He made a collect call to the Harker Transportation Company in Kansas City. In a roundabout way, using the business words that covered his real meaning in case there was a tap on the line, he explained the situation to the man.

At the end, after a few questions, also around about, that clarified a point or two, the man said, "Give it no more than a week. Think of it as a vacation. The sixty, if we settled for it, would still give us a healthy profit, but I don't want to do cut-rate business."

Zack said he understood.

Back at the warehouse office, Zack opened a can of beer, now warm, and nodded at Carl. "It seems that we are in business together."

James took that moment to pick up one of the last sandwiches. It was veal and pepper.

The supper rush was over at the Windom Steak House on Ponce de Leon. The short order man at the grill was cooking some sirloin tips in a liberal sprinkle of oregano. The strong spiced scent told Kane that the management, no matter what the name of the restaurant, was probably Greek.

Kane sat at a back booth. He'd ordered a small steak and a salad and he'd eaten with almost no appetite. Now he was on his third cup of coffee. Throughout his meal and afterwards he'd watched the waitress who worked the forward section of the restaurant. At first, from a distance he'd believed she was younger. Even close up, when she moved to the set-up area, he saw that the skin seemed to hold together well. It was the hip joints that gave her away. The hip joints were at least forty years old.

He waited. By the time he'd finished the third cup of coffee the last customer left the forward area. The waitress bussed that table and gave the table top a brief sweep with a damp cloth. It was dead still in the restaurant and Kane heard her, after she moved to the cash register, say, "It all right if I go off, Al?"

The man behind the counter nodded.

Kane got up and carried his check to the register. While Al made change, Kane turned and watched the woman go to a coat rack and take down a light weight sweater. Kane hesitated just long enough to reach the door a step ahead of her. He held the door open for her and followed her outside. She angled across the parking lot, as if headed for the bus stop. Kane lengthened his stride to stay even with her.

"Mrs. Franklin, do you have a minute?"

Janice Franklin's shoulders jerked and she stiffened. He could understand that. Atlanta was a rape and murder town. When she faced him, he gave her his best warm smile.

"I don't know you, do I?"

"Not yet," he said. He gave her the business card that Jackson Carter had furnished him. "It's a matter of business."

She looked him up and down before she lifted the business card and turned slightly to place the light over her shoulder. "Which one are you? Carter or Callan?"

"John Callan," he said.

"What kind of business is it, Mr. Callan?"

"We can go back in and have some coffee," he said.

Janice shook her head. "I've done a split shift. That's enough time in there."

"A drink then?"

A moment of hesitation before she nodded. He took her elbow and led her to his Duster. He put her in the passenger side and walked around and got behind the wheel. "Any suggestion about a bar?"

"The Clairmont is just down the street." She looked down at her waitress uniform and pulled it down over her knees. "It's a place I won't feel funny being dressed this way."

"You look fine," he said.

She smiled. It was a beginning.

The Clairmont Lounge had gone through a lot of changes. It had been a go-go place at one time. Now it was a kind of burlesque theater but the show wouldn't begin for a bit over an hour. Kane and Janice were at a table in the far back of the room. Kane sipped his cognac with the water chaser he'd been furnished without asking for it. She sipped her vodka and tonic and made a small face over it.

"How's the drink?" he asked.

"It would be if they'd put some vodka in it," Janice said. "No, I guess it's fine." She took a cigarette and he lit it for her. "You haven't said what your business was."

"It's about Ben Carpenter."

The cigarette quivered in her hand. It fell and she caught at it. Her finger touched the coal and she said, "Damn."

Kane said, "I'm sorry."

"I'm not going to talk about that man." She reached into the breast pocket of her uniform and took out the business card. "If this is phony and you're really a newspaper reporter ...."

"I'm not," Kane said. Slowly, convincingly, he went through the story that he and Jackson Carter had fabricated. The matter of the small inheritance. The provision that the bequest would not go to Carpenter unless there was some reasonable doubt that Carpenter had committed the crime.

"That's a funny job for a C.P.A.," she said.

"You'd be surprised what clients expect of us." He shook his head, slowly, wonderingly. "Of course, in this particular case, we're working closely with the lawyer handling the estate. If you like, I can furnish you the name of the lawyer and you can…"

She'd bought it. He could tell by the way she placed the card on the table and lifted her vodka and tonic. After a long drink she said, "I guess I'm just surprised. I thought you were picking me up."

Kane laughed. "It occurred to me."

"That's nice." The old hurt was in her and the flirting didn't quite come across. "I'm the last one you ought to talk to. I believe he's guilty as sin. I believed it then and I still do."

"I'm sorry to bring all this up again."

"Tim would be about fifteen now," Janice said, "if it wasn't for Ben Carpenter."

"I had trouble finding you."

"I remarried three years ago." Her dark eyes were bright, seeing him, trying him. Maybe the hurt wasn't that deep after all. "It was a mistake. The divorce just came through a couple of months ago."

"I need to ask a few questions. I hope you don't mind."

"Ask your questions." Her drink was almost gone. Kane lifted a hand and ordered another round from the passing waitress. "After ten years I guess I can stand it."

"Are you sure that no one else in the apartment building could have let Tim in that morning?"

"I warned him against strangers," she said. "The only one I allowed him to go around with was Carpenter and look what came of that."

"But the other men at the apartment weren't strangers. Maybe he didn't know them as well as he knew Carpenter, but he did know them. If Tim got to the apartment and couldn't wake Carpenter, could he have rung one of the other apartment bells?"

"That's what Carpenter's lawyer kept asking me."

"And ...?"

"That morning, I remember it like it was yesterday. I told him to ring Carpenter's bell and if he didn't come out that he was to come straight home."

"I thought you said that Carpenter was expecting him."

"He was," Janice said. She stopped when the waitress placed the new drinks on the table.

Kane paid and waved the change away.

"But I knew how those construction workers were," Janice continued. "Always drinking hard on the weekends and chasing some women. For all I knew he might have even had a woman in his apartment that morning. That's why I told Tim to come home if Carpenter didn't answer. I didn't want him around any of Carpenter's slutty women."

Kane could feel the anger and he knew she was backing away from him, freezing him out. He couldn't allow that yet. He shifted the line of questioning. "I went by the apartment building this afternoon. It's empty now and about to be torn down."

"It should have been years ago," she said.

Kane brought out a pad and flipped through it until he found the page on which he'd written the names of the four men who'd lived in the apartment building at the time of the murder. He passed the pad to her and waited while she read it.

"Do you know how I can reach any of these four men?"

"The police questioned them at the time."

"I might have some different questions," Kane said.

"I don't know why I should be helping you." Her finger had stopped on the bottom name on the list. *Arnold Bashear.* He waited. He finished off the first cognac and sipped at the second.

"Maybe I'm just soft-headed."

"It would be a big help," Kane said. "And no matter what you think we're not trying to white wash Ben Carpenter. Facts are facts and we're not trying to change them."

"The others I don't know about," she said. "Arnold Bashear, I saw him a couple of months ago. I wasn't sure it was him at first. He'd lost some hair."

"Where'd you see him?"

"He's working for Marta now, driving a bus."

"You know which line?"

"I think it was a 27, the one that runs from Hapeville out past Ansley Mall to the Red Cross."

"And you don't know about any of the others?"

She shook her head. "The only reason I remember Arnold is that he was interested in me at one time. He wanted to take me out."

He waited. She didn't add any more.

"I get a feeling," Kane said. "It's nothing you say, but I feel you liked Ben Carpenter."

"I did. He didn't seem like the rest of the people he ran around with. You know, better. He seemed to be a better person. That was why I let Tim spend so much time with him." She shook her head and he could see a misting in her eyes when the light struck them. "Maybe he wasn't better, just different. And that difference I thought I saw, maybe that was because he was a pervert."

Kane turned the pad toward him and flipped over until he found a blank page. He had her write down her name, address and phone number. She did the writing with a flair but the handwriting was blocky, like a child's printing run together into a strange kind of script.

"If you do anything to get him off," she said.

Kane shook his head. "He won't get off. No way." He lifted the cognac and tossed back the rest of it. "You see, he's dying now."

"Ben's dying?"

"Yes."

"He deserves it," she said. The hardness was back in her. "He deserved it ten years ago."

Kane looked at her. "I've got to leave. Another appointment. Can I drop you somewhere on my way?"

She touched her drink, lifting it and putting it back down. "You've ruined my evening. There's no reason to go home now."

Kane said that he was sorry and left. At the doorway he looked back at her. A young man with dark greasy hair, wearing a loud sport coat, left the bar and headed toward her table. Kane remained in the doorway long enough to see that she'd nodded when the man spoke to her. The young man was easing into the chair across from her when Kane stepped out into the parking lot.

CHAPTER THIRTY

Kane sat right behind the bus driver's seat. It was the next morning and he'd had to do some talking to the supervisor at the information booth at the corner of Baker and Peachtree to find out which run Bashear had. He'd had to kill an hour before he caught the bus at the stop in front of the Ashley Art Theater on Peachtree.

After he boarded the bus, Kane gave Arnold Bashear his card. The driver didn't read it until he caught a red light. He turned and looked at Kane. "What's it about?"

"Ben Carpenter."

"Him? I thought all that was water under the bridge by now."

"It is."

"It's hard to talk now," Bashear said. "I've got six or seven minutes at the end of the line, when we reach the loop at the Red Cross headquarters."

Kane nodded and found a seat. He closed his eyes, resting. It was twenty minutes before the bus passed Ansley Mall, continued on for a few more blocks, and pulled into the parking lot at the Red Cross. The bus looped through the lot and parked on the curb. The bus was empty.

Bashear cut the engine, opened the front and unlocked the side doors. He got a bent pack of cigarettes from his dark driver's uniform coat that hung behind the driver's seat. He stood up and stretched. After a look at the open-faced leather watch case on his belt he said, "I've got six or seven minutes. A bit more if I cheat on the speed on the way back." He moved down the aisle and sat on a seat across from Kane. "What is it you want to know?"

"You know where I can reach these three?" Kane passed him the tenants list.

Bashear read it and said, "Not really. After the thing with the boy and Ben's arrest and conviction I got married and moved out. My wife didn't want to live there." He puffed at his cigarette and narrowed his eyes. "The last I heard, all three of them were working for Arnold Construction out in Marietta. That was about eight years ago."

Kane took the list and made the Arnold notation next to the names.

"One more thing," Bashear said. "A couple of weeks ago ... it must have been about seven in the morning ... I stopped for a light down near where they're putting up that new hotel, the Park, and I saw this guy in a hard hat crossing the street right in front of me. I just got a quick glimpse of him but I thought it was Bill."

Kane looked down at the list. *Bill Dunn.*

"That help?" Bashear asked. Kane nodded. "That all you need?"

Kane folded the list and put it away. He shook his head. "When that happened back then, did you really believe Ben Carpenter was guilty?"

"Not for a minute," Bashear said. "I drank with him and he was one of the guys. He has the right number of balls and he chased tail with the rest of us."

"You were drinking with him that Friday night, the night before it happened?"

"Just for a couple of beers." Bashear walked to the front door of the bus and flipped his cigarette out. He returned and stood in the aisle. "You see, we got off work that day and cleaned up and headed for the Driftwood. The other guys settled in for the night but I had to see Betty." His mouth twisted, sour and dry. "Betty's the one I married."

"How'd Ben seem that night?"

"The same as usual. It was the weekend and he was blowing it all out."

Kane nodded. "The boy, Tim Goddard, how well did you know him?"

"What kind of question is that?" Bashear's face tightened and his chunky hands balled into fists. "That's some shitty question."

"It wasn't meant that way. Just … what kind of kid was he?"

"A good boy," Bashear said. "He had some problems, of course, the way his mother was. But he seemed to be handling all that pretty well."

"You see Ben with the boy?"

"That Saturday? Bashear shook his head.

"No, I meant other times."

"Sure."

"How were they together."

"Ben was a damned good guy. All the things a guy ought to be. I think he felt something for the kid. Maybe he'd had the same kind of childhood or he just felt it more than the rest of us. Let me tell you, I still don't believe it was him that did it. He was like a father to that kid."

"That Saturday morning, you were in the building when they found the body of the boy?"

"You coming back to that, huh?" Bashear sounded tired. "Look, I told it then, just like it was and Betty didn't speak to me for two weeks." Bashear smiled and shook his head slowly. "Maybe I should have let it go at that. You see, I was at Betty's place all night and when the police asked where I'd been there wasn't anything else I could say. I had to tell the truth or put myself in hot water. The only thing was that when the police checked my story with Betty, you'd have thought I'd called her a whore or something." Bashear looked at his watch. He turned and walked to the driver's seat. He got behind the wheel and started the bus engine. "If I'd had any sense, I'd have let her stay mad at me."

Kane held onto the bar that formed part of the enclosure behind the driver. "One more question. The other three…you think one of them might have been capable of doing that kind of thing to the boy?"

Bashear turned the bus out onto Monroe and headed back toward Ansley Mall. "Them? Not a chance. Not a boy. But any girl sixteen and over, they had to be locked up at night."

Kane rode with Bashear as far as the stop on Baker and Peachtree. He thanked Bashear on the way out. He crossed the street and got his Duster from the parking lot next to the Kopy Kat Club.

It was a few minutes before two in the afternoon.

The black Capri had been parked in the lot that fronted the small shopping center since a few minutes before twelve. The albino, Freddie, was behind the wheel. The tall, lean-faced Cuban, James, sat next to him but as far away as the seat would allow.

When Zack and Carl had made their agreement, it was established that they would work in teams of two, one Cuban and one of Zack's men. Zack had put forward a pairing of James and the albino. James had been frightened of the albino but he'd had too much pride to admit it. In the two hours he'd been with Freddie, the fear and the superstition hadn't lessened much. It was as real as a quiver in his stomach. Still, the albino hadn't tried to make conversation. He was moody and quiet. He spent the first two hours reading a stack of comic books he had stashed in the back seat.

At two, a black Continental pulled into the lot and passed the Capri. It parked in a space in a row that was closest to the buildings. A short man in a gray suit with the glint of silk in it got out of the Continental. While he locked the car, he looked around the lot. James saw the bulging eyes and the thin, hard mouth.

Freddie closed a Spiderman comic book and said, "That's Jackson Carter."

James reached for the door handle, ready to step out of the Capri. The albino reached out a hand and grabbed his shoulder. The chill ran down James in a shiver-like fever.

"No, that's the one we can't touch," Freddie said. "At least, not yet."

Freddie released James' shoulder and moved away. James dropped his hand from the door handle and tensed himself, using all his strength to fight the chill. "It is a stupid thing."

"Might be. Right now, we watch. That's all."

Carter left the Continental and walked through the entrance-way of the low, two-storied building. The glass door closed behind him but he stopped for a few more seconds and stared out at the parking lot.

"I think he sees us," James said.

"It doesn't matter." The albino picked up his Spiderman comic from the seat between them and flipped through until he found his place. He placed the open book on the wheel and began reading. "It might make him sweat some."

Jackson Carter looked down at the parking lot from the upstairs window. He couldn't read the license plate from that distance. He went to his office and opened the bottom left drawer of his desk. It was the drawer that contained a pack rat's accumulation of junk and plunder. He dug around in it until he found the small pair of Japanese folding opera glasses. He cleaned the lens in the bathroom and dried them with toilet tissue.

At the front window again, he peered down at the Capri through the opera glasses. Because of the angle he could not see the faces of the two men in the car. But he could read the license plate. It was a Missouri tag and he repeated it to himself several times until he had it memorized.

He returned to his office and wrote the tag letters and numbers down on a memo pad.

Then he made two phone calls.

Charlie O's was a working man's bar. There wasn't a suit or a tie or a jacket in sight. Kane saw only sweat-stained work clothing and the hands and faces with dirt and oil and grease grained in.

The three men seated at one of the center booths stopped talking when Kane approached them. It wasn't a guilty kind of silence. Not that at all. It had an angry quality, like he'd walked into a conversation where he was an outsider.

Kane put down the three bottles of Bud and the tall can of Country Club. He returned to the bar for the glasses.

It was the bar they'd suggested when he'd found them on the job at the new Park Hotel on Peachtree. They'd been thirty minutes late getting to the bar and now they looked at him with a sullen anger. Kane felt a little angry himself. He'd have preferred to talk to the three of them one at a time. He'd tried to set it up that way but the three of them had insisted they didn't have time for all that foolishness.

Bill Dunn was the man he'd sought out first on the job. He was a slim, in his late thirties or early forties. He needed a shave and he'd needed one for several days. He'd probably been a strong and healthy man ten years ago. Now a kind of softness ate away at him. His eyes had what seemed to be a permanent red rim to them and there were purplish broken blood vessels on his nose and chin. Kane decided he had, among other things, a drinking problem.

Next to Bill Dunn, on the inside seat on that side of the booth was Pete Batten. Pete was thin, wiry, with the sort of baby face that would stay with him for another ten years or so. Then, all of a sudden, age would catch up with him and he'd be an old man overnight.

Inside, against the wall and at Kane's left shoulder was the third man. This was Curly Gibson. There was a fleshy look to him and a monk's wreath of hair edged around the bald top of his head.

Bill Dunn poured off a glass of beer and looked at it. Next to him Pete Batten drank his Country Club straight from the can. Bill lifted his glass and had a long swallow.

"We've talked about this," Bill said. "On the way over here and while you were at the bar."

Kane waited. There wasn't anything he wanted to say.

"We don't see any reason to open this up again. After what happened you couldn't imagine the kind of kidding we took on the job."

To Kane's left, Curley shifted his weight and cleared his throat. "Things like, I hear you guys like tight little boys."

Pete Batten dipped his head. "And a hell of a lot worse, all because we ran around with Ben Carpenter."

Bill said, "It took us a year or so to live all that down. None of us want to go through that again."

"I don't think you understand," Kane said. "I'm not a newspaperman. Everything you tell me is confidential. And think of it this way: this is the last look at it. After that, it all gets buried with Ben Carpenter. Three, four, five months and it's all over." He looked at Curly and Pete and saw the puzzled expressions on their faces. "You did tell them that Ben's dying, didn't you?" he said to Bill.

"How?" Pete asked.

"Cancer," Kane said.

"It's not our problem," Curly said.

"You're right about that." Kane pushed his glass away. He got out a pack of cigarettes and lit one, taking his time, letting it drag out while the three men waited. "You don't owe Carpenter anything, right? All those bridges got burned years ago. Still, I wonder why you came all the way over here to tell me this."

"If we didn't show," Curly said, "you're the type who'd come sniffing back around."

"Curly's all for climbing your ass," Pete said.

Kane placed his cigarette in the ash tray and turned slowly and looked at Curly. "You climb that high?"

Curly didn't answer. His puffy face flushed.

Pete said, "Curly's also chicken and he expected help."

Bill said, "Shit" and went to the bar. He came back a few seconds later with a shot glass with what looked like a double shot in it. "What is it you want to know?"

"I'm weeding out," Kane said. "I talked to Bashear this afternoon. All I want to know is what you three did that night and where you were the morning the boy was killed."

"The first part's easy," Bill said. "We got drunk that night. We get drunk every Friday night."

"The four of you together?"

"Five," Bill said, "until Bashear went off to shack up for the night."

"And you stayed together the whole time?"

"Sure, until about midnight. That was when the bars closed then. We'd put some beer in the car and after the Driftwood closed we rode around for an hour or an hour and a half and drank beer." Bill Dunn looked at Pete Batten. "Pete went off with some new girl he ran into at the bar. That was about ten. I don't remember how long he was gone."

Curly laughed. "It usually takes Pete about one stroke. This time he was gone about an hour. Must have had trouble getting it up."

Pete gave Curly the high finger while he looked in Kane's direction. "It was about an hour."

"And then, after you rode around?"

"We went back to the place on Saint Charles."

"We split," Pete said. "Ben had a place on the ground floor. Bill and Curly and me, we all lived on the second floor."

"And all of you slept in the next morning?"

Bill and Pete nodded. Curly said, "The next thing we knew the place was full of cops."

"Where did Bashear live?"

"On the ground floor ... when he was there. That thing with Betty made a stranger out of him." Bill lifted the shot glass and poured back half of it in one swallow.

"Carpenter's lighter, there was a lot made of that at the trial. Ben thinks he had that lighter with him that night at the Driftwood. Any of you remember it?"

Bill shook his head. "That was ten years ago."

Curly said, "He always had it with him. Like he was proud of it. You know, right there on the table on top of his smokes."

"And that Friday night."

Curly shrugged his shoulders. "No way of knowing. Not then and not now either."

Kane went to the bar and got another round. After the beers were passed around, he said, "If Carpenter had the lighter with him that night, the only people who'd have had access to it would have been the three of you and Bashear."

"The hell you say." Bill stopped in the middle of pouring a beer and tapped the Bud bottle on the table top. "I don't like what you're trying to suggest. Anyway, people kept dropping by. You know, they'd stop for a few words or to have a beer. Maybe they'd pull up a chair and visit for a few minutes before they moved on."

"How many people dropped by that night?"

"Might have been six or it might have been a dozen."

Kane pushed away his glass and drank out of the bottle. "Any of them people who did any visiting to the place on Saint Charles?"

"A couple of girls," Bill looked at Pete. "Who was that girl…Amy…the one Ben did a few times?"

Kane said, "I think we can leave women out of it."

"Hey…" Curly blurted out.

Kane swung around to his left.

"That guy," Curly said, "…what's his name?"

"Which guy?" Bill said.

"You know, the one who had the apartment there for more than a year."

"That one…sure." Bill jerked his head at Pete. "The nut."

Kane leaned in. "Who?"

"He was some kind of genius or something. He thought he was whether he was one or not. His mail box was always filled with stuff from some correspondence school, from courses he was taking."

Kane lit a cigarette and pushed the pack into the center of the table. Curly took one. "Which apartment did he have in the house?"

"Well…" Curly puffed on his cigarette and looked down at his beer. "I think it was the one where the kid was found."

"You sure?"

"It was a long time ago." Curly said.

Across the table Pete Batten had his eyes closed. Now he opened his eyes he nodded. "I'm sure. The empty apartment had been his."

"Know his name?"

"Him? He was such a nothing I couldn't even remember his name then."

"When did he move out?" Kane asked.

"Must not have been too long before the boy was killed," Curly said. "Two or three weeks."

"Why?"

"The apartments never stayed empty very long. Most I ever remembered was a month while I lived there. They were ratholes but the rent was cheap enough."

Kane looked from face-to-face. "Nobody remembers his name?"

All three shook their heads.

Kane had the second beer with them and thanked them. He left before they could offer to buy a round.

CHAPTER THIRTY ONE

Kane parked in the lot outside Jackson Carter's office building, and entered through the front door, and climbed the steps to the second floor. In the outer office the secretary's desk was neat, cleared away for the day.

Carter heard his footsteps and came to the doorway of his office carrying a Colt Commander. "It's you."

Carter flipped on the safety and waved Kane into the office. He placed the Commander on the desk and faced Kane. "You got something?"

"I'm not sure. But there's a chance. You'll have to make another visit to Ben Carpenter." Kane told him about the former tenant at the apartment building on Saint Charles.

"It's thin," Jackson Carter said.

"And, just in case, I'll need to know who handled the rentals."

"Carpenter might know that," Carter said.

"The name's the important thing."

"You think this'll take us somewhere?"

"I hope so," Kane said. "Otherwise we're down a deep hole. I can't see any of these four as a child molester."

"That's your guess. It's hard to know what a person's capable of."

Kane turned and walked through the doorway.

Carter followed him into the outer office. "You notice anything odd outside?"

Kane shook his head.

"A couple of guys have been sitting out there all day in a black Capri. It's got a Missouri tag. I've got a call in now to see who it's registered to." Carter looked at his watch. "Ought to hear something in the next hour or so."

"You see them?"

"Not at first. Just saw their bodies. But I spent an hour at the window. One got out to go to the john or something a while ago. He looks Cuban."

"Harley Wynn's pigeons?"

"Might be."

Kane held out his empty right hand. "I'm not carrying. You got an extra here?"

"A spare." Carter went into the office and returned a minute later with Smith & Wesson Centennial. He dropped it in Kane's hand. "It's clean as far as I know. Bought it off a fence who said some kid sold it to him. Stole it off his dad so he could buy an ounce of grass."

"Loads?"

"Fresh ones," Carter said.

Kane shoved the Centennial into his waist band and buttoned his coat over it. "What are you going to do?"

"Me?" Carter laughed. "I'm not dumb. I'm going to sit here and hope they follow you."

"And if they don't?"

"It gets rough. I've got a call in. Four studs who'll come over and beat the crap out of those two."

"It just puts off the inevitable."

"I know that." Carter let his breath out in a short burst. "First thing in the morning, I'm going to make a couple of calls to New Orleans. Maybe somebody there can still the waters."

"My guess is they want the money back."

"A contract is a fucking contract," Carter said. "As far as I know that money didn't have a return address on it."

Kane sat in the Duster and opened his jacket. He placed the Centennial on the seat, flat against his leg, barrel forward, the gun held there by the weight of his thigh.

He kicked the engine over and backed the Duster around. He headed for the Capri. There was still a bit of light left. There was a chance he'd get his look at the men in the car. It might be his edge if he ever met them on a dark street or in a parking lot. It could be the difference between hurting and getting hurt.

He was still some distance away from the Capri when the door on the passenger side swung open. A tall dark-skinned man dressed in tight black pants and a blue windbreaker got out and rounded the front of the Capri. He ran toward Kane's Duster, one hand held up like a traffic cop, the other hang digging into his waistband.

Kane pumped the accelerator and the Duster jumped forward. He swung the wheel and directed the left headlight at the tall Cuban. At the last moment he saw the twisted face of the man as the headlight and the left fender brushed him and spun him away.

Kane kept going. In the rearview mirror, he saw the man get to his feet and limp toward the Capri.

That would mark him. He'd be limping for a week or so.

Kane drove downtown and parked the Duster in a parking deck on Marietta. He caught a cruising cab and registered in a motel on West Peachtree. He'd decided to go to ground until he knew exactly what the situation was.

James limped out of the bathroom. He was dressed in white shorts and a ragged green t-shirt. He stopped at the foot of the bed and rubbed his left hip. The spreading bruise there felt warm, feverish, to his touch.

Carl watched him from the chair on the far side of the motel room. "Is it bothering you?"

James straightened up and flexed the hip joint. "It will be better in a day or two."

Carl looked at his wrist watch. Five minutes before ten. Even after he'd read the time he continued to stare at the watch. It was a PX military watch with a sweat-stained leather band. The watch had been given to Carl a few months before by a crippled Bay of Pigs survivor. It was about the time when Carl began to move up in the Organization. The man had thumped the stump of his right leg and said, "The watch was given me during the training. It seemed a friendly gesture at the time. Now I want you to wear it so that you will remember that you cannot trust them." The man had said more. There was a rank bitterness because there'd been no air support. Now, pulling his sleeve over the watch, Carl remembered the part about not trusting them. With Harley Wynn, looking into those innocent old eyes, he'd forgotten it for a few hours. And that was why there was trouble.

"The man I ride with today..." Carl began.

"Gibbs."

"I am to meet him out front?"

"That's what he said." James sat on the edge of the bed. Using both hands, he lifted the left leg, keeping it straight until he'd turned and stretched out. There was a gritting of teeth and a long sigh from him when he was still and the leg immobile.

Carl stood up and got a tan linen jacket from the closet.

James shifted his head on the pillow and watched him. "You should take the gun."

"No." Carl shook his head. He reached under the bed and drew out the battered bag. He carried the bag to the bed where James was stretched out. He placed it next to James' right side, next to his ribs. "You watch this for me. Think of it as sleeping with a beautiful girl."

James smiled and wrapped an arm around the bag and pulled it close to him. "All girls are safe with me."

"That is not what I heard about you in Miami," Carl said.

❧ ❧ ❧

Jackson Carter placed the first call at ten o'clock in the morning. It went through the switchboard of an old residence hotel not far from the docks in New Orleans. While he listened to the ringing, Carter could almost smell the room and the hotel and the docks. The man who answered the phone had a throat full of phlegm and a cigarette cough. Carter realized that he'd awakened him.

"Yeah?"

"Jack Carter here," he said.

"Jack, is that really you, boy?"

"The one and only," Carter said. "How are you, Buddy?"

Twenty years before, give or take a few months, Buddy Falk had been the wheelman when Carter did his first killing, the one that they called "the bones." He'd done it well. His father had been proud of him.

"I'm getting by," Buddy said.

"I need a favor," Carter said. "My client says it might be worth two bills."

"A friend like you, I'd do it for nothing, but the bills would help out."

"Hell, I know that, but this man is foolish with his money."

"Tell me about it."

It was a long walk-around-the-park talk. At the end of a couple of minutes, Buddy coughed and said, "I think I've got it for you."

"It go through the Big Easy?"

"Heard something. A word I got on the street."

"Who handled it?"

Buddy said, "I think you ought to talk to Ponce."

"Charlie?"

"That's the one. I heard somebody brought the business to him and he forwarded it West."

"K. C.?"

"That's West, ain't it?"

Carter said, "Got to go now. Watch your mailbox. It ought to be there in two days. Three at the most."

As soon as he replaced the receiver, he heard movement in the outer office. He opened the door and found his secretary, Miss Sarah Timmers, settling in at her desk for a morning of answering the phone and turning away any new business.

From the doorway he said, "I think you ought to take a day off, Miss Timmers."

She hesitated. She had a paper cup of coffee in one hand and a sweet roll in the other.

"If you like, take two days," Carter said, "Go to the mountains or the beach."

He smiled as he closed the door between them. The thought of Miss Sarah Timmers in a bathing suit almost brought a roar of a laugh out of him. Prim, plastic lady that she was.

He heard her leave a few minutes later. He looked in the trash can next to her desk and saw the empty coffee cup and the sweet roll with one delicate bite taken out of it.

He waited until eleven o'clock before he made the second call.

Charlie Ponce, with no small talk, said, "I thought I might hear from you."

"Why?"

"I heard you got your foot stuck in something."

"Where'd you hear that?" Carter asked.

"Some people from K. C. say you've got something belongs to them. The way I heard it, it was twenty of the big ones."

"Those clowns have it wrong and you heard wrong. The twenty came from a friend."

"Some friend," Charlie Ponce said.

"And he is a friend who is not around to argue with them about the true ownership."

"With good reason, the way I heard it."

"You in touch with them?"

"I've had a call or two but I don't have a number where I can reach them," Ponce said.

"Run it back through K. C. then and tell them."

"Tell them what?"

"That they're playing on my ground now. Tell them to write it off. Take the loss, if there is one. If they don't, I'll break some bones."

"That's not the way I'd talk to those people."

"Fuck them."

"Here in New Orleans, you still have a few friends. If the shipment came from here, I might have some say. It didn't and they don't want to listen to me. In fact, I might be on the spot myself."

"That's your ass," Carter said. "You've had fifty years to learn how to protect it."

He broke the connection. After he smoked a cigarette, he got out the folding opera glasses and carried them to the front window.

The black Capri with the Missouri tags was parked in front of the building.

Carter watched the Capri for ten minutes. He didn't get a good look at either of the two men seated in it.

Kane had a late breakfast in the coffee shop down the street from his motel. After he paid the check, he dialed Carter's number from the pay phone back near the men's room.

"You have the information I need?"

"Not yet," Carter said. "I'd planned on going over now, but I might be locked in for the day. They're out front again today."

"Follow you last night?"

"No. They left right after you did."

"Well," Kane said, "it's too early to send for the lead pipes."

"That's true, but I'm working on another idea."

Kane turned and looked around the coffee shop. "I'll have to talk to Carpenter myself. I still have the business cards that list me as your associate. Can you make the call and set it up?"

"Call back in ten minutes."

Kane caught a cab outside the coffee shop and directed the driver to the parking deck on Marietta Street. From the lower deck there, while he waited for the Duster to be brought down, he called Carter again from a pay phone. It was set up.

CHAPTER THIRTY TWO

Kane leaned over the hospital bed. Ben Carpenter lifted his right hand and tried to take the business card. He didn't make it. The hand fell against his thigh. Sweat rolled down the creases of his face, just from the effort.

That close, Kane could smell death on him.

"You're not the same man," Carpenter said. His voice was low, a whisper of pain, and Kane had to lean even closer to catch his words.

"I work with him," Kane said.

"Can't be sure of that."

"I knew your friend," Kane said. Briefly, in fifty words or so, he described the little con man.

"Knew?" Carpenter blinked.

"He's dead."

"How?"

"A rough way."

Carpenter's eyelids fluttered. A single tear reached Carpenter's chin and began to dry. There was only so much emotion left in the man. It was that close.

"I need to know one more thing. I've talked to Dunn, Batten, Bashear and Gibson. A question came up. Who was the man who lived in the front apartment on the ground floor, the one where Tim Goddard was found?"

"It was empty," Carpenter said.

"Who lived there right before that?"

"A funny guy. His last name was…" Carpenter's lips moved without sound for a few seconds. "Sanders or Saunders… like that."

"You know the first name?"

"No."

"Who handled the rentals for the apartments?"

"Goodwin and… somebody. On Forsyth."

Kane stepped away from the bed. He looked down at Ben Carpenter. Eyes closed, he was still as death. Kane rounded the bed and reached the door. He heard a sound like a cough behind him. He turned and saw that Ben Carpenter's eyes were open. He returned to the bed and leaned close, his ear only an inch or so from Carpenter's lips.

"The men… who… Harley Wynn."

"That was not part of the deal," Kane said.

"Shit." Carpenter blinked but there were no more tears.

Zack had a half-eaten sub made with meatballs and peppers on a double layer of paper towels in front of him. The sauce had soaked through to the desk blotter. He was drinking a bottle of Stroh's, from one of the cases Freddie had thrown in the truck before they left Kansas City. It was a late lunch and Zack could already feel the indigestion begin to scrape and scratch away at his stomach lining.

"Go on," Zack said.

Gibbs looked at Carl.

Carl said, "One of the policeman who braced us said there had been some complaints that perverts were loitering in the shopping center parking lot."

"They weren't policemen," Gibbs said, "It was one of those private security firms. I didn't get the name, but it wasn't Pinkerton."

"And there were four of them?"

"Four? Yes. Two stood on each side of the car." Carl was puzzled at the importance of that number.

Zack lifted the sub, started to bite into it, but then lowered it. "You know any security outfits that drive around four to the car?"

"No," Gibbs said. "Unless they're riding shotgun on the Queen's jewels."

"But not to hassle two perverts." Zack bit into the sub. A dribble of gravy ran down his chin. "What else?"

"One of them took a picture of us with a Polaroid."

"Two pictures," Carl said.

"The one who did the talking, he said he had our tag numbers and if he saw us in the lot again, he'd arrest us for loitering, indecent exposure, spitting on the ground, littering and anything else they could think to add to it."

The puzzled look remained on Carl's face. "But could they do this?"

"It Jackson Carter's town," Zack said. "In my town I could do most of that and throw in a busted head or two." He drank some of the Stroh's and smeared the gravy across his chin with the back of his hand. "I think we can make our guess that Carter was the one doing the complaining. Hell, more than that. They might not even be security for the shopping center. Just pickup help he hired."

Gibbs walked around the desk. He reached into the metal trash can where the Stroh's was packed in ice and brought out two bottles. While he looked around for the opener he said, "Do we go on with it or back away?"

"We try the back door."

Gibbs found the opener and jerked off the caps. He handed one bottle to Carl and gulped at his. "Which back door is that?"

Zack reached into his shirt pocket and brought out a slip of paper. "I spent part of the morning checking around. The license on the Duster that hit your man." He nodded at Carl. "I found myself a hungry lawyer hanging around the courthouse. For fifty bucks, he made up some crap about a possible hit-and-run and got me a name and address to go with the tag numbers." He passed the slip of paper to Gibbs. There was a perfect thumb print, the color of the sauce, on the side of the paper.

Gibbs read the name and address and passed the paper to Carl.

"We shift the pressure to him," Zack said. "This John Callan, nobody said we couldn't rough him if we needed to."

"How far?" Gibbs asked.

"All the way down the hill," Zack said.

Kane parked in the deck next to Rich's Department Store and walked down Forsyth to Marietta. It was a sunny cool afternoon. The Hare Krishna dancers were on the traffic island near Five Points. He could hear the bells and the chanting over the street sounds.

He crossed Marietta. He walked near the curb on the left side of the street, his head back, reading the signs in the windows on both sides of the street. He was in front of the Forsyth postal branch when he found it: GOODWIN AND FRENCH, REAL ESTATE. It was printed over a three-window expanse on the third floor of the gray stone building across the street.

He found a hole in the traffic and crossed. He entered the building and looked around. No security man in sight. He ran a finger down the registry to the left of the single elevator.

GOODWIN AND FRENCH ...306.

On the third floor, he stopped in front of 306 and lit a cigarette. It was one of the old-style doors, frosted glass on the top half. The door was closed and he leaned close and looked at the face of the old brass lock. The only word on it was: SAFE. That and nothing else. He backed away and returned to the elevator.

He called Jackson Carter a couple of minutes later from the pay phone in the lobby of the post office branch.

"I need a lock fixed," he said.

"Opened?"

"That's it."

"I know a man," Carter said. "He'll need to know what kind of lock."

"A simple looking one. A brass facing with nothing but SAFE on it."

"When do you want him?"

"Tonight at ten," Kane said.

"Where?"

"The Forsyth Street branch of the post office. I'll be the one on the pay phone."

"Done," Carter said.

At nine-thirty the Eastern Whisperjet from Jacksonville, with stops in Atlanta and Raleigh-Durham, landed at the Washington National Airport. In the coach section was a pudgy man with dark close-cropped hair and a spreading bulb of a nose. He wore a gray knit suit and a dark tie. He carried a briefcase. In the briefcase, in a locked pocket, was the terse message that had brought him to Washington.

Report Washington branch April Seven 0900 hours.
Whistler

The pudgy young man was Robert Louis Foster and he'd been with the Agency for four years. He'd been recruited by Dundee out of the criminology program at Harvard. After training at Valley Farm, his first assignment had been London. His career had appeared bright and hopeful then. His first task had been to dig for scandal in the background of an M.P. who opposed S.A.C. planes that flew out of English bases carrying atomic warheads. His blundering attempts to find something rank in the life of the M.P. had brought him to the attention of Scotland Yard. He'd been withdrawn in the nick of time and flown back to the States in a military transport. After that, he'd been assigned to one unimportant post after another, always in the hinderlands. He'd been in Jacksonville for six months and this unexpected summons to Washington led him to believe that there was still one post lower and that he was destined for it.

He'd collected his two pieces of luggage and was on his way to the area where the buses to downtown Washington waited when a tall black man stepped away from the wall next to the doorway and reached for his bags. "Downtown? Yes, sir."

Foster stepped back and shook his head. "The bus."

The black grinned at him from under the flat cabbie's hat. "Look, I just brought out a fare. About to go back empty. I'll take you for half fare. Say three dollars."

Foster hesitated. The black saw that and reached out and took the bags. Foster followed him to a Blue Dot Cab parked off to the side. It was a company that Foster didn't remember from his time in Washington.

The driver put the luggage in the trunk and got behind the wheel. He started the engine before he turned and looked at Foster. "Where to?"

"The Mayflower." It was a bit too expensive but Foster had decided to splurge. It might be his last chance. And it would be, if he argued it well, covered by his expense account.

"That uptown place?" The black shook his head slowly. "Staying in that place'll eat your breakfast. I know this other hotel. Just as good and maybe half the rent."

"You shilling for this hotel?"

"Not me." The driver laughed. "It's just closer to my stand."

On second thought, that might be better. There was always the chance that this recall didn't mean reassignment. It might mean discharge. Discharged, cut adrift, he might have trouble justifying the expense of an evening at the Mayflower.

"All right," he said.

After they reached the expressway, the driver switched on the radio. He gave it a few seconds to warm up before he said, "Number Eight to the Bramblett."

"Bramblett?" Foster put an arm on the seat back in front of him and leaned forward. "I don't know that hotel."

"Great little place," the black said. "You look at it and you don't like it I'll drive you free to the Mayflower."

"I guess I can't beat that offer." Foster leaned back and closed his eyes.

He was half-asleep when he felt the cab ease to a stop. He jerked upright. The street was almost dark on all sides. He blinked and tried to focus his eyes. He pushed forward and gripped the seat back in front of him. "Where's the hotel? I don't see any hotel."

"Right there, man," the driver said, pointing to his left.

Foster turned his head to the left. The last thing he saw was the dark street and the shapes of two men running toward the cab. The driver shifted in the front seat. He was left-handed and it was a simple matter for him to turn and swing the nine-inch length of iron pipe. He swung the pipe twice and Foster collapsed against the door.

One of the men on the sidewalk opened the door next to the curb. Foster fell out. The two black men grabbed him under the arms and dragged him into an alley. Behind them, the driver closed the passenger door and pulled away from the curb.

The two men in the alley with Foster worked as a team. One took the wallet from the breast pocket of his suit coat while the other stripped the watch from his wrist and scooped the change from his trouser pocket.

That done, one stepped away while the other squatted over Foster and struck him in the face with a length of lead pipe. Foster was dead after the second blow but the man continued to swing the pipe until his breath was harsh, rasping, until the other man leaned over him and touched his shoulder.

"That one's a ghost," the man said.

CHAPTER
THIRTY THREE

"What do I call you?" Kane pushed open the door and stepped out of the Forsyth Street postal branch.

"Nothing." The man stepped through after Kane and stood on the sidewalk. He looked in both directions down the street. "I'm going to be in and out of that place so fast you won't even remember what I look like." Dark, seemingly bottomless eyes appraised Kane. "It's the way I want it."

"You've got it," Kane said.

It was a blocky, square face with a deep cleft in the broad chin. The yellowish hair was worn long. He had the wide, out-of-balance shoulders of a weightlifter. The suit was dark and tailormade and he scratched at the pavement with the toe of a soft black leather boot.

"You paid yet?"

"I'll get mine," the man said, "no matter what happens to you." He stepped off the curb and angled across the street toward the lighted entranceway to the building.

The lobby was empty. He'd been right. No security.

Kane started toward the elevator. The man touched his arm and turned him. They climbed the two flights of stairs. At the third floor Kane led the way to 306. The man looked at GOODWIN AND FRENCH lettered on the frosted glass. "Nothing worth stealing in there."

Kane said, "I don't know your name, you don't know my business."

"That's fair." The man reached into his jacket pocket and brought out a thick ring of keys. "Watch the elevator. If there is any security, most of the guys they hire are too old to climb two flights of steps without having a heart attack."

He bent over the brass facing of the lock. Kane moved down the hall and looked up at the strip of numbers above the elevator door. Nothing moved. The elevator was on the first floor. He checked his watch. Two minutes. Three minutes. He heard a low whistle and spun around. The man motioned him back down the hall. When he got there. he saw that the door to 306 was open, pushed in an inch or so.

"That all you need?"

"That's it," Kane said.

"Remember. I wasn't here."

Kane nodded. He stepped into the office and closed the door quietly behind him.

Within twenty minutes Kane found the rental and payment records for the apartment building on Saint Charles. It was a thick file folder in an unlocked cabinet. Kane searched around the office until he found a brown envelope large enough to fit over the file folder. Twenty minutes later, he was in his motel room on West Peachtree.

At the rear of the thick folder, held together by a large rusting paper clip, were the rental application forms. Kane removed the clip and worked his way through the stack page-by-page. The turnover at the apartment house had been small. Perhaps, as Gibson had said at the bar the day before, because of the low rent.

He'd gone three-quarters of the way through the stack when he found the application form he wanted.

Watt Raymond Sanders
Construction, electrical
Age: 31 Unmarried
Employed: Apex Electrical Company
How long: 8 months

Present address: 24 Spence, Apt. 3

Present salary: approx 200/week

Kane skipped through the references: the owner of Apex Electrical Company, the rental agent for the Spence apartment, a downtown bank.

Credit check : ok

Lease signed and deposit made: ok

$2 key deposit: ok

Deposit returned:_____

Key deposit returned:

Kane hesitated. His eyes jumped to the bottom of the form. He found a REMARKS section.

Notice given July 26th. August rent from apartment deposit. Key not returned. Replacement key ordered September 1st.

Kane dropped the Sanders application on the bed and stacked together the rest of the file folder. He jammed the stack into the brown envelope and dropped it on the floor.

He put the call through to Jackson Carter at eleven-thirty. Kane could hear the late news signing off in the background.

"I think I've found the hole in it," he said.

Carter grunted. "Go on."

"It's not enough to build a house on, but I've got a feeling about it."

"The other man?"

"Sanders moved out two weeks or so before the little boy was found in his empty apartment."

"That's not much," Carter said.

"He didn't turn in his key and get his deposit back."

"What?"

"Look at it this way: the four men who were still living in the apartment, the ones I talked to, were checked out pretty well by the police. We've got to assume the check was thorough and they were cleared. The one man who had keys to the apartment building who wasn't checked out was Watt Sanders."

"The police blew it then," Jackson Carter said.

"Hard to blame them. They had a tailor-made suspect."

"Ben Carpenter wouldn't agree."

"No," Kane said, "he wouldn't."

In the night, Kane dreamed.

They were hunting in a field that was thick with a kind of broom straw. It was fall and their breath swirled in front of them like cigarette smoke. There was frost on the straw and a crunch and an icy crackle underfoot.

He couldn't see the man who was on his right. It didn't bother him. He assumed it was Bill Gordon, the man who lived next door to him and hunted with him. Old Bill, the best man on a hunt he'd ever known.

Three doves broke cover about twenty yards ahead of them. All three curled, swung to the right.

Kane tipped the shotgun up, tracking the doves, spinning in that direction on a toe and a heel. He was ready to fire when he realized that the man on his right, a wide canvas hat pulled low over his face, had turned the wrong way and the twin dark eyes of a shotgun lined up on Kane's upper chest.

Kane said, "What...?"

The man said, "Nothing." A class ring, worn almost smooth by time, glinted on his left hand.

Kane awoke. He switched on the lamp beside the bed and found his package of cigarettes. He lit one and thought of the man in the dream. It hadn't been Bill Gordon. The shape of the man wasn't right. No, this man was shorter, thicker in the shoulders and the upper body.

He wasn't anyone that Kane remembered.

He finished the cigarette and turned off the light. He tried to sleep again. It wasn't that easy. He rolled around until dawn.

⚜ ⚜ ⚜

The Friday morning meeting at the Agency always began at ten sharp.

All three of the directors arrived five or six minutes before the hour. The season was about to begin so there was some good-natured kidding about baseball teams between Pryor and Dundee. Whistler did not join in. He spent that time toying with the empty coffee cup in front of him.

At exactly two minutes before ten, Hazel Appleton brought in a tray carrying a carafe of black coffee. She placed the tray on the center of the table and went out.

Whistler filled his cup and stared down at his wrist watch. At ten exactly, he cleared his throat. The conversation between Pryor and Dundee broke off in mid-sentence. Whistler lifted his left hand so that the other two men in the room could see it and leaned forward to press the RECORD button built into the top of the conference table.

"Friday, April 7th," Whistler said.

When he lifted the hand from the RECORD button there was a dull gleam from the Harvard class ring, class of 1943. All the lettering had been worn away during the almost thirty-two years of constant wear. It was as thin as a wedding band.

"Old business," Whistler said.

Forty minutes later they were discussing OPERATION SIDEARM, an ongoing program to discredit Kawabata, a Japanese leftist leader with strong homosexual leanings.

Dundee held up a hand with two fingers only a fraction of an inch apart, in a kind of pinching motion. "We are about a red cunt hair away from having him."

The buzzer sounded at the locked door. Whistler reached out and tapped the STOP button on the table top. He got up and answered the door.

Burden stood in the hall. He shook his head slowly from side-to-side while Whistler stared at him. "Sorry, but I thought this was important enough to break in on you." He handed Whistler a folded sheet of paper and backed away.

Whistler swung the door closed. He seated himself before he unfolded the paper.

<u>Time in:</u> 1034 hours

Foster, Robert Louis (Code name: Ringer) Found dead in alley SW part of Washington approx. 0700 hours by beat policeman. Cause of death: beating with blunt instrument. Watch and wallet missing as well as personal belongings in two suitcases. Check revealed he arrived Washington National 2130 hours with two suitcases checked through from Jacksonville. Police list as possible mugging. Follow-up underway.

<u>Received:</u> Burden

<u>Action:</u> Routed to Whistler

Whistler passed the message to Pryor without comment. While he read it, Dundee left his chair and stood behind him to read it over his shoulder.

Dundee spun away. He lifted his head and said, "Shit, nobody's safe in this town anymore."

Pryor pushed the paper toward the center of the table. "I wonder what he was doing in that part of town."

"That will be under new business," Whistler said. He leaned forward to hit the RECORD button once more. As Dundee put his back to the two of them, returning to his chair, Pryor met Whistler's stare. Neither man blinked.

The tape was running again.

Pryor said, "Sidearm has been in progress for almost two months. If Kawabata isn't going to drop the other shoe on his own, it looks like we might have to shift the emphasis toward entrapment. Who do we have in who can handle it?"

Head down, face averted, Dundee doodled on the pad in front of him for the rest of the meeting.

❧ ❧ ❧

The Friday meeting lasted until twelve-thirty.

Dundee left hurriedly for a lunch appointment in downtown Washington. Pryor and Whistler remained in the building and dined together in the executive dining room.

Over the soup course, French onion with a heavy cheese crust, Pryor said, "It could have been coincidence."

There'd been no mention of Foster since the meeting. During the meeting, under *New Business*, it had been agreed that Agency security should work the area and contact informers. The time spent on Foster at the meeting had been less than two minutes. It didn't speak much for his importance to the Agency or his career.

Whistler stared down at the earthenware bowl and worried the crust with his spoon. "That would be convenient, wouldn't it?"

"It might be interesting to check Dundee's daily logs for the last two or three days," Pryor said.

Whistler shook his head. "Do it, but he's too slick for that. There won't be an arrow pointing anywhere."

They ate the rare prime rib and fresh white asparagus in complete silence.

CHAPTER
THIRTY FOUR

The Atlanta phonebook didn't list a Watt Raymond Sanders. Kane left the phone booth and ordered his breakfast in the motel coffee shop. After sipping his coffee, he left the table and went back to the phone booth. He dialed the number of the Apex Electrical Construction Company.

"I'd like to speak to Watt Sanders," he said.

He was told by a woman who answered that no one named Watt Sanders worked with the company. Kane thanked her and returned to the coffee shop.

After breakfast, Kane fought the work day traffic out Peachtree Road. He'd almost reached Buckhead before he found the low, flat building that housed the company. He parked in back among the fleet of trucks with the coiled wire logo on the door panels and APEX threaded into the sign.

At the reception desk, inside he paused long enough to draw a line under his name on the card Jackson Carter had furnished him. He passed it to the secretary and said, "I'd like to see the president."

"Oh, he's not in yet."

"The personnel director then," Kane said.

She returned a minute later and led him down a long hallway. She stopped in front of an open door and waved him in. "Mr. Hargrove is our personnel director."

A heavy man with liquid-like bulges in all directions heaved himself to his feet and reached across the desk to offer his hand to

Kane. That done, he sank back into his chair with a wheeze and nodded Kane toward a seat. He picked up the card and stared down at it. "I don't think I understand why a Certified Public Accountant..."

"First of all," Kane said, "I can assure you I'm not looking for a job." He smiled. "Business is quite good at the moment."

Hargrove smiled back at him. "I feel better. The building trades aren't hiring much these days."

"I think I can put it to you briefly." Kane lit a cigarette and watched as Hargrove pushed an ash tray toward him. "My company is involved with an audit. You know how Internal Revenue is? Suspicious, to say the least. Some years back a man who worked for you did some electrical work for our client. He may have been moonlighting. Now, with the audit coming up, we can't find the receipt this man signed after he was paid. And it's a matter of several hundred dollars."

"This man...?"

"Watt Sanders."

Hargrove shook his head. "I remember him but I'm not sure I can help you much. He's been gone for quite some time." He eased his chair back and pulled himself to his feet. At the battered green file cabinet, he selected a drawer and jerked it open. He walked his fingers through a thick expanse of files before he tugged one out and brought it back to the desk. He flipped the folder open. After reading for a few seconds, he said, "Yes... he left us in 1966." He looked across the desk at Kane. "That's nine years ago. Wouldn't that put it beyond the time limitations?"

"In some cases," Kane said, "but this is a special circumstance."

"Well, it's your business," Hargrove said.

"If it was that simple, I'm sure we'd be glad to use that argument."

"I bet you would." Hargrove began to close the file folder.

Kane stubbed out his cigarette. "You don't by any chance have his next employer... where he went from here?"

Hargrove opened the file once more. "Usually we don't. But sometimes...." He flipped to the rear and stopped at the final page. He read it slowly before he passed it to Kane.

It was a Xerox of a letter on the Apex letterhead. It contained a glowing reference for Watt Sanders. It was signed by Robert G. Harper and his title, given below his signature, was president.

Kane got out his note pad and wrote down the full address at the top of the letter.

Mr. Andrew Mableton
Central North Carolina Electrical
Post Office Box 2345
Durham, North Carolina

"Good luck with the I.R.S.," Hargrove called after him as he left. "They got me two years ago."

Back in his motel room, Kane packed the dirty shirts and underwear in the Davison's Department Store bag they'd come in. He added the razor and shaving cream. After a final look around the room, he found the brown envelope with the rental information from Goodwin & French and added it to the stack. He was headed out the door when the phone rang.

"Wake you?" Jackson Carter asked.

"Up for hours," Kane said. He told Carter about the new address for Watt Sanders.

"You're headed for Durham?"

"Soon as I drop by the house," Kane said.

"That might be a bad move."

"Why?"

"The Capri, the one that was watching me, it's camped outside your house."

"How do you know?" Kane asked.

There was a pause, a silence. "I got to wondering about them," Carter said finally. "I had a man drive by."

The pause before he answered a question, that usually meant he was lying or hiding something. Kane decided it wasn't worth pushing at now. No matter how Carter had found out about it, he could be sure that the Capri would be there, parked somewhere nearby.

"I need my ready bag. I've been living off what I've been buying in department stores and I don't like it much."

"It's risky," Jackson Carter said.

"There's a back way in. I'll wait until dark."

"Call me from Hartsfield before you fly out."

Kane said he would.

James and Freddie took turns sitting behind the wheel of the Capri. The other one would walk out twenty yards or so into Jenner Park and sit in the glider that faced the house on Harvard. Now and then, when the call of nature was on one of them, that one would drive the Capri to the nearest service station while the other waited in the glider. If these drives were near meal time, the one in the Capri would stop off, on the way back, and buy sandwiches and beer or pop.

It was slow, grind down work. John Callan, the man with the Duster, hadn't shown up and there wasn't much to do. Now and then someone would bring a dog down into the park. And once, early in the afternoon, an attractive young woman had brought a vanload of retarded children and they'd played games all around James without seeming to notice him.

Three or four times-a-day a tall, erect old man with gray hair would come out of the house next to the one they were watching. He'd walk along the trashed-up stream to the end of the park and back. He came and went without any seeming curiosity. Each time the erect old man passed the glider James felt like speaking to him. He seemed harmless and lonely. It was, James thought, the American way to make old people outcasts. It was not the Cuban way. The urge to speak to the old man was so strong that one time James stood up, the words forming in his mind, but the old man looked away. That was probably the American way also. The frightened distrust of strangers.

At eight-fifteen, Kane parked the Duster on Dogwood Drive, one street behind his house. He spent some time watching the old house directly in front of him. The last he'd heard the house was empty, waiting for a buyer, and he satisfied himself there were no lights in the house before he left the Duster and moved quickly and quietly up the driveway.

He skirted the garage and found the backyard, with some children's swings and a slide, sloping away, toward a low fence. When he reached the fence, he could see the dark shape that was the back of his house. The sloping away continued into his yard and he stepped over the low wire and found the curving stone path that led to his basement. He entered through the double-locked door and closed it behind him before he switched on the basement light.

At the top of the basement stairs, there was a moment he didn't like. That was the moment when he swung the door open and stepped into the narrow hall that led straight into the living room. He could have switched off the light but he wanted a brief look into the living room. He had to be certain that the men who'd staked out the house hadn't moved inside to wait for him.

The living room was empty and he closed the basement door, shutting off the light. In the bedroom a few seconds later, Kane closed the black-backed drapes before he switched on a lamp. He changed into a dark gray suit and brought out his "ready" bag. He kept that packed at all times. It held three shirts, three changes of underwear, socks and ties and a shaving kit.

He turned off the lamp and returned to the living room.

James, seated in the glider with a can of Bud on his knee, saw the flash of light in the house. It was so brief, so quickly there and so quickly gone, that he was not sure that he'd seen it at all. Still, maybe, it was something. He left the glider and ran for the Capri.

"A light," he whispered to Freddie.

The albino lifted his head from the wheel. He hit the door handle and spun his way out of the Capri. At the front edge of the driveway, Freddie turned and hissed at him. "Watch the front."

He sprinted ahead, leaving James at the sidewalk. He went out of sight behind the house. James followed slowly. He continued up the driveway until he was at the front corner of the house. He moved in against the brick exterior, trying to blend in with the shape of the building.

There, one hand inside his windbreaker, clutching the butt of the old .38 he'd bought after their arrival in Atlanta, he watched the front door. And once, turning toward the park, he saw the erect old man pass the empty glider, the one James had been sitting in only seconds ago. Now there was a decided limp in his walk, a stiffness in his right leg, and the old man used a cane.

From the store of what he now considered useless knowledge it floated to the surface: *what walks on three legs in the evening?* Not the way it was meant in the play, almost a pun now. And he watched the old man with a massive warmth and understanding before the urgency of the situation forced him to push the old man into the back of his mind.

Dark in the backyard. The albino waited. After the run from the car, his breathing was rough, hoarse, and he stood between the back door and the steps that led down to the basement and took slow, deep breaths until it was back to normal.

Freddie wished that he'd brought iron with him. No matter what Zack had ordered. Screw him. He was sitting back in the warehouse office eating meatball sandwiches. Zack said no shooters just because Gibbs and the other spic had been fronted in the parking lot. Fuck him. Freddie reached into his jacket pocket and brought out the blade. He hit the spring and the five-inch blade jumped out, nested in his palm.

The albino didn't like blades. It was last on his weapons list. Blades were for blacks. They liked to get in close and work at it. The albino didn't. It made his skin crawl.

Below him, down at the bottom of the steps, Freddie saw the thin pencil line of light that leaked from the bottom of the basement door. It had been there the whole time but it had taken his eyes time to adjust. He forgot about the back door to the house and edged over until he blocked the basement exit.

The Capri was there, just as Carter had said it was. Kane dropped the edge of the living room drapes and backed away. He hadn't seen either of the men, but that wasn't unusual. If they did it right, they weren't supposed to be seen.

He reached the door that led down to the basement. A split second flare of light and he was through the doorway, the door pulled shut behind him. Down the stairs and through the basement, his eyes for a time on his shooting range. He regretted the days away, the days and nights he'd had to spend in the motel, the sessions he'd missed that kept his edge. Eye and hand together when he fired.

At the back basement door, he paused long enough to switch out the lights. He opened the door, stepped through and pulled it closed behind him. He heard both locks catch.

The ready bag in his left hand, he went for the first step. The light was wrong, he realized. He couldn't see the sky. Too dark, the sky blocked by something at the head of the stairs. A shoulder, the pale gleam of skin.

On the fourth step Kane turned and edged toward the right of the steps. He swung the ready bag far back, the image of a discus in his mind before he whipped his body around and threw the bag as hard as he could.

He heard the bag strike the man and he heard the surprised grunt from him. The man fell away and suddenly there was the dark light of the sky at the head of the stairs. Kane put down his head and charged up the steps, taking them two and three at a time.

James heard the grunt. After that, something hit the ground with a hollow thump. He pulled away from the corner of the building. He was one step away when he heard a sound from the driveway behind him. Before he could turn, something round and hard was across his throat. He felt himself pushed against the building, the rough texture of the bricks raking his face. His hand was still around the butt of the .38 but he couldn't get the hand free. He lifted his left hand. He clawed at the hand that held whatever it was against his throat. But the hand didn't give and James felt the massive pressure that crushed the bone and the life out of him.

❧ ❧ ❧

The man was down, stunned, when Kane reached the top step and lunged into the backyard. He saw the pale, almost luminous skin, and knew that the man was leaning forward, on all fours, trying to get to his feet. Kane took two steps and kicked him in the throat. The force of the kick spun the little man around. He landed face down. He was choking, gagging, gasping for breath.

Kane picked up the ready bag and trotted up the slope. At the low wire fence, before he stepped over it, he looked back. There was no movement below him.

CHAPTER THIRTY FIVE

Bill Gordon met the hard eyes that stared back at him from the bathroom mirror. When the water was hot enough, the mirror began to steam over and he dropped his eyes to the wash basin. There were deep scratches on the back of his right hand. Bastard, with the pussy fingernails. He worked the soap into a heavy lather and washed the scratches with care.

He patted his hands dry on a clean towel and reached into the medicine cabinet behind the fogged mirror. He carried the tube into the living room. He took his time rubbing a liberal amount of the first aid cream into the scratches. Satisfied, he capped the tube and put it aside. He lifted the phone and placed it on his knee. He dialed a number in Washington. A man answered and said, "Burden here."

Bill said, "Extension four."

After a few seconds, a woman's voice said, "At the tone, recording begins."

The tone sounded and died away. Bill looked down at the fingernail marks and said, "Blue Mole. Subject was being watched and facing from two assailants. I felt it necessary to take one of them out. Hardfisted one Cuban. Cuban-K.C. faction could get rough. Full report follows. Please instruct."

Bill broke the connection.

He replaced the phone on the table beside the sofa and stood up. He put the tube of first aid cream on the mantlepiece above the old-fashioned fireplace. Right behind the tube there was a framed photograph. It was a picture of Kane and him the last

RALPH DENNIS

time they'd hunted. It had been back in the fall. They'd reached their limit early and gone back to the car. Two other hunters had been passing down the road and Bill had got the Minolta from the glove compartment and talked one of the hunters into taking the picture.

Three prints were made. Bill kept one, the second went to Kane and the third he forwarded to the Agency. There, at the Agency, with Bill sliced away, the print became an entry in the Continuing I.D. File on Kane. A month-to-month and year-to-year study of physical changes: weight gained or lost, alterations in hair and hair style or any eccentric manner of dress.

Bill felt an itching, a burning on the back of his right hand. He rubbed at the scratches, working the residue of the first aid cream into the skin. The raw grooves flashed an image at him, a memory that he'd couldn't duck. Other scratches that first time. 1943, the first mission with the O.S.S. Inserted by submarine and rubber boat, moving by night and sleeping during daylight.

That ratty town. He'd forgotten the name years and years ago. The instructions for contact with the underground had been precise. He was to enter the town from the east at exactly nine-thirty p.m. ("Careful, the curfew begins at nine, old man.") A man with a black slouch hat would approach him and ask for a light for his cigarette. The man would say, "It is a fine night, isn't it?" and Bill would answer, "If you're a farmer." The man would laugh and say, "Isn't everyone?"

It happened that way. Each word exact. A rat-faced man with a pale moon scar on his chin. Afterwards, he and Bill had walked toward the center of town. They could see the town square three blocks away. They'd gone about half-a-block when another man, also wearing a black slouch hat, stepped out of a doorway. A stout man with a limp. He approached Bill and held up a cigarette. He asked for a light. After Bill struck a match, cupped it and lit the cigarette, the man said, "It is a fine night, isn't it?" Stunned, going

264

on reflex alone, Bill said, "If you are a farmer" and the stout man had laughed and given the proper response.

The stout man stepped over to Bill's left and the three of them walked toward the town square. Bill bracketed by the two men. The amazement left him and now he was trying to decide which was the real contact. One was and one wasn't. That was for sure.

The German patrol solved it for him. Two blocks away, the patrol appeared out of a side street. The rat-faced man on Gordon's right didn't hesitate. He whirled and made a leap for the nearest doorway. Bill, the warning about curfew fresh with him, reached the same doorway a split second later.

The stout man with the limp didn't think that fast. He continued on for two or three more paces, obviously not concerned about the patrol, until he realized that Bill and the rat-faced man had left him.

When he made his leap into the doorway Bill and the rat-faced man were waiting for him. The rat-faced man pinned his arms to his sides, at the same time turning him so that his back was toward Bill. He nodded at Bill, who wrapped an arm around the fat neck and began to strangle him.

The stout man freed a hand and clawed at Bill's locked hands. Thick nails with dirt under them. The pain was brief pain because the rat-faced man caught the stout man by the scrotum and squeezed. The hand dropped and, in a minute or so, the stout man was dead. Crumpled in the doorway in a pool of urine, in the green stench of excrement.

Bill was on the run for a week, the operation compromised and aborted. All the time watching the scratches, waiting for the infection. It didn't come, the scratches scabbed over, and in two weeks he was back in London.

There hadn't been first aid cream then.

Now Bill retrieved his cane from its position beside the front door. He carried it into the bedroom and placed it out-of-sight in the back of his clothes closet.

❖ ❖ ❖

It was a shallow grave in the country.

Gibbs did most of the digging. Freddie helped out some but he was having trouble swallowing and breathing. He tired in no time at all. Gibbs wanted to stop digging when the grave was only three feet deep and Carl had to curse and argue with him before he picked up the shovel and dug down another foot and a half into the heavy clay.

After Gibbs and Freddie dropped James into the hole, Carl filled in the grave himself. He shook off Gibbs' offer to relieve him. His shirt was stuck to him and his arms and shoulders were numb when he finished.

He stood off to one side, catching his breath, while Gibbs swept the grave top with a piece of uprooted brush. When Gibbs was satisfied the three of them worked together and threw molded leaves, twigs and limbs over the raw dirt.

There was a light rain falling when they drove back to Atlanta.

It is the wrong country for a man like James to die in.

It is the wrong country for his burial. He should be buried in Havana next to his mother and father and his two younger brothers.

And it was not the proper way to die.

In a strange land. Buried like a stray cat or dog. In the dark night. Left to rot. Soaked by rain.

In the front seat, passing a pint of rye back and forth, neither Gibbs nor the albino paid any attention to Carl. It was just a nasty job and it was done.

Dead in a strange land. Carl began to cry. He'd never been sure quite how he felt about James. But someone had to weep for him. A man deserved that.

By the time the Capri reached the city limits, the tears had dried to an invisible salty crust. And anger pumped his blood when pity wouldn't.

❧ ❧ ❧

Kane spent the night at the Air Host motel at Hartsfield and flew to Raleigh-Durham on the 8:24 a.m. flight. It was a short flight. He rented a Mustang at the Avis booth in the concourse. On the way out front, he stopped at the bank of pay phones and checked the Durham yellow pages. The Central Carolina Electric Company had its offices listed on Angier Avenue.

About an hour later, after being lost a time or two, he pulled into the empty parking lot next to a low concrete block building. The building was deserted. Vandals had broken every other window pane down one side of the structure.

Kane found a pay phone a couple of blocks away. Information told him there was no new listing for Central Carolina Electrical. He dialed the residential listing for Andrew Mableton. A woman with a soft southern voice told him that Mr. Mableton was at the Durham Tennis Club.

The old man dozed in the slant of the weak sun. The pool in front of him was filled with green water but there were no swimmers. On the other side of the pool, there were two empty deck chairs. The cabanas, three tiers of them, surrounded the pool and showed the blank faces of closed doors. In the distance, the *thuck-thuck* of tennis balls and rackets flattened out in a chill wind.

Kane stopped beside the old man and waited. When the man didn't move, Kane stepped closer and said, "Mr. Mableton?"

Eyes as green as the pool water stared up at Kane. "That's me."

Kane reached into his jacket pocket and brought out one of Jackson Carter's business cards. "I'd like a few minutes of your time."

Kane explained his business, the same lies he'd told before, and asked if Mableton remembered Watt Sanders.

"Of course, I remember Watt," the old man said. "He was about as close to being a true genius as you'll find in your time."

The blue veined hands bent the business card and scraped it along his thigh.

"Was Sanders with you until you closed your business?"

"Didn't close it exactly," Mableton said. "Sold it out. People who bought it dropped <u>Central</u> from it and moved out on the Raleigh Highway. I don't know why they did that."

"Was Sanders retained?"

The old man shook his head. "He left three years ago. I tried my best to keep him."

"You know what happened to him?"

"Not exactly." The green eyes searched Kane about chest high. "You smoke?"

Kane brought out his Pall Malls. The old man took one. Kane lit it for him.

"I'm trying to give them up. I've been trying for five years."

"Hard to do," Kane said.

"Let's see." Mableton closed his eyes and blew a thin whisp of smoke out of his nostrils. "The last I heard about Watt…it was about six months after he left Durham. That would be two and a half years ago. What I heard wasn't directly from him."

Kane waited. He turned and looked at the wind rippling the pool water.

"An F.B.I. man came to see me at the office. He was doing what you'd call a security check on Watt."

"A government job?"

"Must have been. The F.B.I. man asked questions about Watt's personal life…as far as I knew he didn't have any…and about his loyalty to this country. That kind of thing."

"And that's the last you heard of him?"

"As far as I can remember," Mableton said.

Kane waited. The old man kept his eyes closed. After a couple of minutes, Kane realized that Mableton had gone to sleep. There was a flutter-like snore and a dribble of spit ran down the left side of his chin.

❧ ❧ ❧

Kane checked into a Holiday Inn and called Jackson Carter with a research request. Carter called back two hours later.

"You know the General Weapons Corporation?" Carter asked.

"Nope," Kane said. "Should I?"

"That's where Watt works now. It's a company doing weapons research for the government on contract. From what I could find out, for the last couple of years, it's been working on some top secret design for electronically controlled anti-tank missiles that are fired from helicopters. Like the ones that were used in Vietnam but a bit more sophisticated."

"Then that's how the F.B.I. got into it. The fact that it's top secret."

"That's it," Jackson Carter said. "Watt Sanders, somehow, got to be resident genius over there."

"From electrical construction to top secret research ... that's a big leap."

"Hell, he's not the whole program. Just a big part of it."

"Where is General Weapons located?"

"All over," Carter said. "Sanders is with the Design and Testing Unit in Parker, Virginia."

"That's easy enough."

"Maybe not. It's like a fortress out there. Like a stockade, like an armed camp."

"I'll have to find a way in."

"Good luck," Carter said.

"I'll need some things."

"List them."

"I might need a backup identity. A driver's license, not from Georgia, Social Security card, some charge cards."

"That all?" Carter asked.

"A Sport, shells, some kind of recent map of the General Weapons compound."

"Where'll you be?"

"I'll call you tomorrow and give you an address."

"Done," Carter said.

Kane had an early supper and got directions from the waitress to the public library, where he spent three hours hunched over a microfilm viewer look at the front pages of the *Durham Morning Herald*. He started back four years and he'd flipped through seven months before he found what he was looking for. A first grade student went missing, a boy named Johnny Turner. Two days later, two front pages later, the boy had been found. In a ditch on the Durham-Chapel Hill highway. Abused before he'd been strangled.

Maybe, Kane thought. *Just maybe.*

The Extension Four tapes were transcribed every three hours. The secretary in Room Four hand-carried the single copy of each message to the duty room where she placed them in the Incoming file on Fred Burden's desk. Ten messages had arrived during the 6 p.m. to 9 p.m. time period. It was the slow time anyway.

Burden was on the eighth message when he stopped and went back and pulled out the third one in the sheaf. Holding the third and the eighth ones in one hand, and the file in the other, he rode the elevator to the tenth floor. During the ride he read the messages again, just to be sure. Yes, it meshed.

Whistler read the third message and passed it across the desk to Burden. He read it once more before he returned it to the file.

From: Blue Mole (Atlanta) Subject has deep watered. Likely that hardfist is underway. Advise.

Whistler read the eighth message. He placed it on the desk and stared down at it. "What's the source for this?"

"It's an intercept," Burden said. "Rather the digest of one. The Bureau has been taping one of their clerks. Some doubt about his style of living. It seems that he called Jackson Carter and gave him some information about a Watt Sanders who got security clearance about two and a half years ago. When the Bureau pulled its file on Carter, they saw that we had an ANY INFORMATION tag on it. So they passed on the digest to us."

"General Weapons Corporation in Parker, Virginia. Why is Carter interested?"

"I'd have to go along with Blue Mole," Burden said. "It looks like a hardfist about to go down."

"General Weapons ... that's sensitive." Whistler said. Burden nodded. "I'll need to know more. Blue Mole will have to push and shove."

Whistler passed the eighth message to Burden.

"I'll call him right away." Burden placed the message in the file and turned to leave.

"Check the roster," Whistler said. "See who we have in the area."

After Burden left Whistler, lifted a hand and rubbed his eyes. The days were long enough without this. Without this.

He'd known it might happen sooner or later. Long Rope, that whole operation, was predicated on the assumption that Kane would never be in conflict with national security. Now it looked like he was. And that was shaky ground.

The earth was moving. It was opening up and if Kane moved across that line, that invisible line that had been set for him, then he was only hours away from being a dead man.

CHAPTER THIRTY SIX

Kane flew to Dulles the next morning, rented a car, and drove out Highway 29. It took him a bit over an hour of driving to reach Parker, Virginia. It was bump in the road kind of town. There was a motel, a general store, a service station and two cafes.

Kane passed through Parker and continued for another three or four miles before a newly paved road cut into the highway. The sign beside the road put it bluntly:

G. W. CORPORATION
NO ADMITTANCE
OFFICIAL BUSINESS ONLY

Beyond a stand of woods, the new leaves curling open, he could see the dull glint of a high fence. Past the fence, in the green haze that was April, he could see the sprawling conglomeration of buildings. It looked like a military base.

Kane turned and drove back to Parker. He registered at the Virginia Home Motel and placed a call to Carter in Atlanta.

In the early evening, about twilight, Kane was about ready to leave his motel room for Miss Fay's Cafe to try the supper special when there was a knock at the door. A little gray man stood in the doorway holding a cardboard box that was about half as big as he was. Behind him an old black Buick coughed and rattled.

"You Callan?" The man asked.

Kane nodded.

"This is for you then." He passed the box to Kane and stepped back a pace or two. "The rest of it is being mailed."

The little man walked to the Buick and got in. Kane closed the door and placed the cardboard box on the bed.

There was more packed in the box than he'd asked for. The Sport was there and the box of shells. But there was also a tan twill shirt and trousers, a worn hunting jacket, a pair of hiking boots and canvas pouch packed with foil bags of dried food. Carter was thinking ahead.

At the bottom of the box, Kane found a rough map of the General Weapons Corporation compound. It wasn't to scale but it would be good enough. He studied the map for a few minutes and then packed the box again, placed it under the bed and crossed the road to Miss Fay's Cafe.

"He's in Parker," Burden said.

Whistler looked at the file that Fred Burden held in his hand but didn't reach for it. "Where?"

"Registered in the motel."

"That from Rachel Carson?"

Burden nodded and waved the folder. "Kane went to visit an inmate the other day, a guy named Ben Carpenter, in prison for life for molesting and murdering a kid. Jackson Carter has also been in to see Carpenter."

"How does Sanders tie in?"

"Sanders once lived in the same apartment building as Carpenter and the dead kid." Burden gave Whistler the folder.

"So that's the hardfist job," Whistler said. "I wish we had somebody there other than Rachel. Kane will eat her breakfast."

"Harry Bender is in Richmond."

"I don't want to pull him off Blackball," Whistler said. "Rachel will have to do. How long has she been in the compound?"

"A month. She's working as a typist."

"She know Watt Sanders?"

Burden shook his head. "She will by this evening. What will Kane do?"

"What I would," Whistler said. "Go over the fence and play fox."

After supper at Miss Fay's Café, Kane returned to the motel room and dressed in the tan twill, the hiking shoes and the hunting jacket. He slung the pouch over his shoulder, now with the Sport and the map packed inside. He carried his suitcase out to the car and locked it away in the trunk.

He made his arrangements with the motel owner. He'd leave the car in the motel lot and the front desk would hold any mail that arrived for him in the next couple of days.

The owner folded the twenty and stuffed it in his pocket. "You do much of this?"

"Every spring," Kane said. "It feels good to get the city out of my system."

By full dark, Kane was in the woods across the highway from the General Weapons Corporation compound.

Rachel Carson left Building A at four-thirty in the afternoon. Building A was Administrative and there was a typing pool of six girls in the basement. Rachel had lived and worked with the five other girls for a month. All they talked about was drinking and men. Rachel liked drinking and men, too, but she didn't like to talk about them.

Rachel was a tall girl, a bit less than five-ten, and she wore her dark hair in a boyish cut. There was nothing else boyish about her. In her month with General Weapons, she'd knocked down more passes than a defensive back with the New York Jets. She did it well, with the ease of practice, and with such good natured charm that none of the men got their feelings hurt.

For six years, Rachel had been with the New York Police Department. She'd been working undercover with narcotics when Pryor met her and recruited her for the Agency. During her year at Valley Farm, in a group with four other women, she'd spent more than half her time learning to type and take shorthand. She struggled with ASDF while the other four women sweated and groaned in hand-to-hand and fired their quotas on the outdoor range.

At the end of the year, she was assigned to the Agency in Washington. She was loaned out to the Design and Testing Unit two months later. It was fairly routine work. The security man at General Weapons put out a call for a trained operative with secretarial skills. It went out to all Federal agencies. Since Rachel was still waiting for assignment, Pryor had offered her. It was a two months' loan, a watch-and-listen operation. Locked away in her suitcase at Dorm #3, the women's living quarters, was a ledger. At the end of each day she spent an hour or so going back over the events of the day. Who said what to her, who was drinking too much, who was jumping in and out of which beds.

There were no rules that you couldn't leave the compound if you wanted to, but the top secret nature of the research meant that security was a major concern. Management went to a lot of expense to make the Design and Testing Unit a world of its own. The food at the dining hall was better than it was at many restaurants and the booze at the Club was inexpensive. At first, many of the new contract employees drove into Washington on the weekends. That was usually only during the first month or so. There was as much or more to do right on the compound.

And, as if it had been planned that way, there was nothing at all to do in Parker, Virginia.

That changed for Rachel during lunch. It wasn't routine any more. The call from Fred Burden took care of that. It was now a high-risk, bodyguard assignment. Burden told her to get close, and stay close, to Watt Sanders. Any way she could.

Rachel entered the security office upstairs in Building A just before the end of the lunch hour. The secretary was still out. Joe Blaustein was at his desk. He was eating a sandwich from the mobile canteen. He waved Rachel into his office and closed the door behind her.

"I've got a request from town," she said.

Blaustein nodded.

"I need to know if a certain man is in Parker. And I need a picture of him." Her instructions from Burden had been exact. Tell only as much as you need to. Just enough to get cooperation.

Blaustein listened to her brief description of Kane. He chewed slowly and swallowed. "If he's in Parker, he'll stick out among the rednecks."

"Let me know as soon as you can," she said.

He followed her to the door. There was a questioning look on his face. "This have anything to do with us?"

"It's just a trace," Rachel said. "He's probably headed for Charlottesville and points west."

Blaustein called the typing pool a bit over an hour later. He confirmed that Kane was in Parker. The photo was being processed and would be sent down to her as soon as it was ready.

Blaustein was waiting for her in the hallway at the afternoon break. He passed her a 3 by 5 photo. She carried the picture into the ladies room, went into a stall, and closed the door.

The man in the picture stood in front of a motel door. He was dressed in a dark gray suit. His hair was dark and there was the suggestion of graying at the temples. The face was lean and hard, the mouth a thin, harsh line.

Mid-thirties, she guessed. Give or take a year or two.

It was, she decided, the face of a man you could either love very much or hate with all your soul.

Zack said, "This is stupid shit. We've traced him to Hartsfield. The Duster is there. It looks like he flew out. If this was my town, I could find out a few things. It's not and I feel boxed."

Gibbs got a Stroh's from the metal waste can and popped the cap off. "You can bet Carter knows where he is."

"Let's assume that Carter has to stay in touch with him. How?"

"Phone," Gibbs said. "or the mail."

"Mail is a long shot," Zack said.

"What the hell else have we got?" Gibbs tipped the bottle up and poured about half of it down.

"The secretary at Carter's... any pattern to that?"

"Leaves about four-thirty. Takes the mail and drops it at the Highland branch on her way to her apartment on Briarcliff."

Zack looked at his watch. "You've got time."

Carl, who'd been leaning against the wall listening, pushed away from it. "I'll go with you."

"Why not? You might learn something."

Miss Sara Timmers stayed away from the office two days. On the morning of the third day, she returned to work. She'd seen but hadn't understood the smile that passed over Jackson Carter's face when he saw her.

"Back from the beach already?"

She blinked. "I didn't go."

After the door closed to the inner office, she thought she heard Jackson Carter laughing.

At four-fifteen, while she was straightening up her desk, he brought out a thick brown envelope and dropped it on her desk.

"This one is important," he said. "I want you to go to the main post office downtown. It stays open until eight or so. " He peeled off a five dollar bill and dropped it on top on the brown envelope. "I want it sent air mail special delivery or anything else that will get it there in the next day or two."

"Yes, sir."

He dropped five or six other envelopes next to the brown one. "These aren't important. Send them regular mail."

At four-thirty, Miss Sara Timmers left the office and walked down the single flight of steps. She passed through the empty lobby and stepped outside. Her gray Opel was parked in the front row of the spaces, two cars over from Jackson Carter's black Continental.

She was only steps away from the Opal when two men, one heavy and short and the other dark and thin moved toward her. One, the heavy one, had his back toward her, arguing with the other man. He was laughing and saying, "Not a chance, buddy." At the last minute, a step away from her, the heavy man whirled around and bumped into her.

It was a hard push and she felt herself falling. Going over backwards, she dropped her purse. The other hand, the one holding the letters, jarred open when she hit the pavement. The letters spilled out of her hand.

"Jesus, Lady," the heavy man said. "I'm sorry."

She'd landed on her rump. He reached down and pulled her to her feet. "I hope I didn't hurt you."

"I think I'm okay."

The dark skinned man reached down and lifted her purse and handed it to her.

The heavy man, after he'd pulled her to her feet, leaned over and collected the letters, gathering them one by one. He seemed to be dusting them off. While he continued to apologize, he brushed the letters off and handed them to her, one by one.

She was so stunned that she didn't realize that the heavy man was reading the addresses.

Rachel carried the leather shoulder bag with her when she left Dorm #3 and walked the four blocks or so to the Dining Hall. In the bag was the Agency-issued Python that Blaustein had allowed her to bring into the compound.

She had dinner with two of the girls from the typing pool, left them and crossed the patio to the Club.

The Club was the main exception to the bare functional architecture of the Design and Testing Unit. It was as if a New York nightclub had been dismantled and transported into the backwoods. The polished wooden bar was about half the length of a football field and there were tables and booths dotted about the large room. It was barely dark outside but it was dim as midnight in the Club.

Rachel paused in the doorway. She remained there until her eyes became accustomed to the smoky darkness. She found Watt Sanders seated alone at a small table near the back of the bar. She knew him from his picture. That went back to an early briefing session with Blaustein when he'd gone through the ten critical and important people on the project.

Rachel walked in, past the bar, and sat down at a table near the one where Watt Sanders was.

He was drinking beer. There were five empties on the table, lined up. His head was down, straining in the dim light while he doodled on a legal pad.

He seemed bigger than he really was. That was the effect of the wide shoulders and the big arms. Standing, he was only about five-eight and his legs appeared dwarf-like. As if the rest of his body, his trunk, had continued to grow after his legs had stopped.

His face was lean and pale. The green eyes almost hidden under the heavy bushy eyebrows. The hair, blond and graying now, was cut so close that his scalp gleamed under the stubble.

Rachel ordered a whiskey sour from the waitress and waited. He didn't lift his head.

After ten minutes, she knew that she'd have to make the approach without any encouragement from him. She stood up and carried her drink to his table.

"Mr. Sanders?"

He lifted his head and stared at her.

She smiled. "Run me away if you don't want company," she said, "but I'm tired of talking to myself."

There was a hesitation, a catch, before he nodded. "Sure," he said, "but I don't know your name."

When she was seated, she saw that he'd taped the morning crossword puzzle to the legal pad. He was about three-quarters of the way done with it. She leaned in and said, "Oh, you do the puzzle, too."

In ten minutes, with her help, they completed the puzzle.

It was the apartment of a monk.

The walls were bare. Everything seemed to have its place. Nothing had the mark of the man who lived there. With one exception: in one corner there was about a four-foot stack of dusty scientific journals.

The bedroom was as monastic as the living room. Sanders and Rachel were naked in the bed, lying side-by-side.

Watt Sanders said, "I'm sorry ... I just can't ... not right now."

"It happens to all men now and then," Rachel said, though no man had ever been soft with her before. *Ever.* They might shoot their load too soon, but they never had a problem getting hard. Not that she was complaining tonight. She was glad that he couldn't perform. "Don't worry about it. Worrying is what makes it bad."

Her hands rubbed his shoulders. His skin was as hairless as a woman. Low on his back, near his left hip, there was a black crusty birthmark about the size of her hand.

His eyes were almost luminous in the darkness. "I've been under a lot of stress on the project and maybe I've been drinking too much. I can't seem to relax."

Rachel shushed him. "It's okay. Just being with a man, sharing his warmth and his strength, is enough for me tonight. The rest will happen another time."

She held him close, relieved that she didn't have to finish what she'd started. He curled against her like a child, burying his face in her breasts.

CHAPTER
THIRTY SEVEN

By one a.m. Kane had the security pattern figured out.

For three hours, Kane sat with his back to an old oak, one that was about four feet from the nine foot high perimeter fence. A jeep with two armed guards passed that point in the fence every half hour. Every fifteen minutes, a low flying helicopter swooped over, following the line of the fence. The helicopter crew used no light so Kane assumed that they had some kind of night sight device.

Kane decided that he had at least fifteen minutes. At the high end, between the passing of the jeep and the arrival of the helicopter, because once there'd been an interval of seventeen minutes between the two. At the low end, the interval had been thirteen minutes.

At one-thirty-two the jeep passed. Fourteen minutes later, at about one-forty-six, the helicopter swung overhead and moved away. Kane stood up. He'd chosen the old oak for two good reasons. It was close to the fence and he could reach the bottom limbs. About half of the tree had been sheared away; all the limbs that might have reached toward the fence.

Kane pulled himself up into the tree. He climbed quickly. There wasn't much time and he could feel the clock ticking inside him. Five minutes and he was level with the nine-foot fence. Another two minutes and he was four feet beyond it. He hugged the trunk and swung himself around, his feet reaching out for the nub of a thick limb that had been sawed away. He found it and edged around until he faced the fence. First he tossed the pouch over the fence. That committed him. His feet dug at the limb nub. He braced his back against the trunk and pushed away, uncoiling.

It was like a dive into a swimming pool. He cleared the fence by inches, losing height as he fell. Once past the fence he went into a tumble. At the last moment he brought his feet over and landed on them. The shock of impact numbed his legs to the hips. He took the rest of the impact on his elbows and rested for a minute, waiting for the feeling to return to his legs. It was another minute before he crawled forward and found the pouch.

His legs didn't want to work but he forced them. He struggled to his feet and limped away from the fence. He could hear the approaching jeep in the distance.

It was slow going. Other security men, in patrol cars, circled through the dark streets of the compound. He passed the inner city of buildings and looped past the helicopter landing pads and the hanger area. Twenty minutes, later he was deep in a wooded band that ran between the landing pads and hanger area and the back length of the perimeter fence. He found a hiding place in the brush.

It was cold. The temperature had been dropping all night.

He curled himself into a ball, and, shutting the cold out, tried to sleep. It was a twilight sleep. He heard each circle of the helicopter, each passage of the security jeep.

Kane awoke at six shivering. It was still an hour or so before full light. While he chewed on a package of beef jerky he walked toward the hanger and landing pad area. He was almost a hundred yards from the first hanger when he heard the *pop-pop* of the rotor blades of one of the copters warming up. He swung away and made a wide loop that would bypass the hangers.

The sky was graying by the time he stumbled upon a small fleet of garbage trucks parked in a strict row in front of a low wood frame building. The trucks had *G.W.C. Maintenance* on the door panels. The building beyond the trucks was dark, not showing any lights. Kane shirted the trucks and tried the door to the dark building. It was unlocked and Kane went in.

He found himself in a rank smelling room. It was long and narrow, both sides covered by narrow metal lockers. Two low benches ran the length of the center space between the lockers. At the back of the room, Kane found the bathrooms and off to one side a large shower. The bathroom was part of the rank smell. The rest, he realized, was the smell of old dried sweat.

Kane worked his way down the right side of the row of lockers, looking inside, until he found a clean white pair of coveralls that fitted him. There was an identification badge over the left breast pocket. The face that looked out, chin to forehead, was of a black man. Kane unpinned the badge and dropped it in the locker. He looked in several more lockers until he found another badge. This time it was of a white man but the face was too blocky, too full. But when he couldn't find another badge, Kane took that badge, placed it face down on the rough concrete floor and rubbed it back and forth under his shoe.

He spent ten minutes in the bathroom. There was an old razor on the side of one of the wash basins. He soaped up his face with hand soap and shaved quickly. Then he undressed and stood under one of the showers for a few minutes. The hot water cleaned him and warmed him after the cold night in the woods.

After he dressed in the coveralls, he rolled up the twill trousers, the shirt and the hunting jacket and stuffed this roll, along with the pouch that contained the Sport and the food, into the space between the back of the lockers and the wall. It lodged there.

Smoking a cigarette, he sat on the bench and studied the rough map. It took him a minute or two to locate the Dining Room.

Ready. He stood up. He stuffed the map in his pocket. It was time for a hot meal.

⚜ ⚜ ⚜

It was early at the Dining Room. Two of the dining room employees sipped coffee at one of the back tables. Kane pushed the door open and walked in. He was halfway across the dining room before he heard a man's voice behind him. He turned.

"You."

The man was dressed in a blue security man's uniform. There was a brass badge on his shirt and he wore a blue .357 Dan Wesson butt forward on his left hip. The man's face was red and scaly, wind roughened.

"Yeah?"

"You know the rules," the security guard said.

"Huh?"

The guard walked a couple of paces closer and stopped and propped his left hand on the butt of the Dan Wesson. "No work clothes in the Dining Room."

"Hell," Kane said, "you know how it is."

"How what is?"

"Shit work," Kane said. "I got to get over there and change plugs on number two before we can start pickups for the day." He swung an arm at the empty room. "I can be out of here before any of the fancy dudes and ladies get in here." He let a bit of a whine slip into his voice. "Come on, buddy, just this one time."

"All right." The guard stepped away. "But not again."

"That's a promise," Kane said. "And thanks a lot."

The security guard turned away and walked back outside.

The waitress brought his order. Two eggs over easy, bacon, toast, orange juice and coffee. He ate slowly, watching the entrance.

Within minutes, the other works began drifting in and he marked them off. *Too young, too young, too old.*

He was on his second cup of coffee when the couple entered. The girl was tall, about thirty, with short dark hair. The man was at least two inches shorter than she was, broad shoulders and with his hair cut close to his scalp. The man's hand was on her elbow, possessively. They passed in front of Kane's table. Kane tried to read the identification badge on the man's jacket. At the last moment, the man turned toward the woman and said something.

The man was about the right age, but coming in with a woman that early in the morning, probably after spending the night together, meant it probably wasn't Sanders. She was the wrong sex, and the wrong age, for the man.

Kane reached into the breast pocket of his coveralls and got out a Pall Mall. He carried it over to the table where the couple was seated. The man was saying, "…the poached eggs, I think…" and then broke off and looked up at Kane.

Kane held up the unlit cigarette. "Got a match?"

While the man fumbled in his pocket for a lighter, Kane stared down at the identification badge. Right the first time. Watt Raymond Sanders. Pure, dumb luck. Maybe he'd underestimated Sanders. Maybe he wasn't past using a woman as a cover for his real desires.

Sanders found the lighter, flipped it until it flamed and lit Kane's cigarette. Sanders didn't look directly at him. Kane said, "Thanks a lot," and backed away. As he turned he saw the widening eyes of the dark-haired girl.

Kane puffed on the cigarette and walked straight out of the Dining Hall.

It was bright and cool outside. The sun was just beginning to warm the air. Kane found a wooden bench across the street and sat down. He smoked his cigarette and then another one.

Starting at eight, the traffic in and out of the Dining Hall became thick.

Watt Sanders came out at eight fifteen. He still had his hand on the dark-haired girl's elbow. At the sidewalk, he stopped and said a few words and they separated. She turned right and he turned left.

Kane waited until Sanders had about a fifty-yard head start and then he got up from the bench and headed in the same direction. The sun burned in his eyes.

Zack made his call first.

Carl stood at a distance and waited.

The man in K.C. said, "The week's about up."

"It's sour," Zack said. "We can't touch Carter and the other guy, the one we could put a glove on, is out of town. We've got an address up in Virginia."

"That's a waste of time. It's time to cut our losses."

"That's the way I feel. The other party here, the buyer, doesn't feel that way. One of his people got hurt. It's more than the money now with him."

"Fuck him," the man in K.C. said.

"What deal do I make with him?" Zack turned and looked at Carl, who was puffing at a cigarette and looking away.

"Give him a day to scratch up the twelve thou. If he can't we can settle for ten. That's bottom."

"If he can't…?"

"See if he'll go for part of the shipment. We've got too much time and money invested to come out with a zero. Hell, Zack, do the best deal you can."

"I'll get back to you," Zack said.

The man in K. C. broke the connection. Now it was Carl's turn to make a phone call.

Zack left Carl at the phone booth and returned to the warehouse. He sat behind the desk and took the .45 automatic out of the center desk. He placed it on his thigh and waited for Carl.

⚜ ⚜ ⚜

Julio answered the phone at the candy store. Carl asked to speak to the old man.

"We have come up with eleven thousand more," the old man said. "It is as much as we can collect in such a short time and it will be a hardship on some."

"It is much more than I expected," Carl said.

"It is being changed into one hundred dollar bills as soon as the banks are open." The old man paused. "That's in half-an-hour."

"When can it be up here?" Carl turned and looked across the street at the warehouse. "I think the sellers are getting impatient."

"By early afternoon. Julio will bring it."

"Julio has the address?"

"He has it," the old man said.

"Tell him to take a cab in from the airport. I will pay for it when he gets here."

"The other business ...?"

"After we have bought the ... tools ... I will leave Julio with them and make a trip up north."

"Do you think it is worth the trouble?"

"Is James worth the trouble?"

"The tools are the first business," the old man said.

"I will rent a truck," Carl said. "We will load it before I leave. If anything happens to me Julio can bring the tools alone."

"If that is what you believe."

"It is," Carl said. "A man has to be worth that much."

The old man said goodbye and hung up.

    ❧   ❧   ❧

In the warehouse office Zack placed the .45 on the desk top and said, "It is time we had another serious talk."

"You do not need a weapon to talk to me," Carl said.

Zack shook his head slowly. "Maybe not. Maybe so. My boss in K. C. says we have fucked around too long. We're sorry about your man but..."

Carl said, "I will have another ten thousand early this afternoon. It is being flown up to me. That will make it seventy thousand. It is not what we agreed upon, but it is as much as I can collect."

"And there is a matter of the time we wasted here," Zack said.

"I can do nothing about that. My hands are tied."

"My ass is in a sling," Zack said. "But I guess it is the best deal we can do."

Carl let out his breath slowly. "I would like to rent a truck and load it."

"On one condition," Zack said.

"Yes?"

"I hold the keys to that truck until I see the other ten thousand."

Carl nodded. He placed the scuffed leather bag on the desk top. "This is the first part of the payment."

Zack was counting the money when Carl left and went looking for a U-Haul truck.

❧   ❧   ❧

Kane kept his pace measured, maintained his distance, while across the street Sanders walked on without looking back. After two blocks Sanders turned up a walkway toward a white frame building. Above the door was a sign STAFF QUARTERS. Kane stopped and squatted to retie his shoelaces. His head was down when he heard the woman's voice. It was the dark-haired women who'd been with Sanders in the Dining Hall. She was running up the walk after Sanders.

"Watt … Watt …"

Kane could hear the rest of it, it was that quiet on the street.

"Left my gloves …." she said.

"Come on in," Sanders put an arm around her shoulders and turned to go up the steps with her. At the top of the steps, just before he opened the door for her and she passed inside, the girl looked over her shoulder at Kane.

Kane stood up and walked away.

He knew enough. He'd found Sanders and where he lived. Now he needed to go to ground for another twelve hours or so. Until it was dark. Then there was a question or two he'd have to ask Sanders.

And he'd ask him down the barrel of the Sport. The answers were always better that way. Truth came with the sweat.

CHAPTER
THIRTY EIGHT

Whistler arrived at the Agency exactly at ten a.m.

When he stepped out of the elevator on the top floor May Baker, the receptionist said, "Mr. Pryor has been asking about you."

Whistler looked at his watch. 10:03. He nodded, in passing, and turned to the left in the direction of Pryor's office. The door was open. Behind his cluttered desk, Pryor had just lit his first Cuban cigar of the day. The delicate aroma drifted across the desk toward Whistler.

Pryor said, "The situation in Parker is out of hand."

Whistler put out a hand for the message.

Pryor shook his head. "It didn't go through taping. It was a hurry call. I took it."

"From Rachel?"

"Yes."

"Kane is over the wall?"

"And he's tracking right now," Pryor said.

"The security man at General Weapons …?"

"Joe Blaustein."

"We could involve him," Whistler said. "It's his ballpark."

"It would have to be a good story. A class A lie. Otherwise there are a few too many questions I'd rather not answer."

"That's true enough." Whistler closed his eyes for a moment. When he opened them he said, "Where's Dundee?"

"On a flight to Japan to coordinate Operation Sidearm."

That was fortunate, Whistler thought. "Where's Burden?"

Pryor looked at the wall clock. "In bed in the duty room for the last four hours."

Whistler turned for the door.

Pryor stood up. "Do you have any ideas?"

"I'll think about it for the next couple of hours. There is a chance that Burden and I might take the scenic route to Parker."

"It's a nice time of the year for it."

"Isn't it, though?"

Whistler pulled the door closed behind him. Going down the hall toward his office he could smell the smoke from the Cuban tobacco in his jacket. It warred with the harsher scent of the John Cotton that he smoked in his pipe.

At noon, with a morning's work behind him and no clear decision made, Whistler called Joe Blaustein at General Weapons.

Kane passed the morning in aimless circling.

At noon, he found himself near the mobile canteen and bought two hamburgers and a shake. He ate in the shade of a nearby tree and returned to the canteen. He bought a ham and cheese to go and buttoned it away in his huge hip pocket. That was for later, for supper. If nothing else was available.

Later in the afternoon, he passed an unattended mainte-nance truck. In the back, he found a number of canvas trash bags with shoulder straps and short poles with spikes at one end. The rest of the afternoon, head down, oblivious to other movement around him, Kane worked his way around the compound. By five, he'd filled the canvas trash bag with cigarette packs, candy wrappers and other scraps of paper.

No one paid the least bit of attention to him. It was the way he wanted it. Exactly the way he wanted it.

❧   ❧   ❧

Whistler and Burden checked into the Virginia Home Motel a bit after four. Whistler's first call was to Rachel Carson.

"Can you talk?" he asked.

"Yes," she said.

"Stay close to Sanders. I'm working something out."

"I'm nearly as close as a woman can get," Rachel said and laughed.

Her laugh had the scrape of a knife on bone in it.

His second call was to Joe Blaustein. Fifteen minutes after the call, Blaustein knocked at their motel room door.

Burden let him in and Whistler pointed toward the bottle of Chivas Regal. "Too early for you, Joe?"

"Not for a taste," Blaustein said.

Burden mixed him a drink.

Blaustein sipped at it. "So that's what good scotch tastes like?"

Whistler smiled. "So I hear."

Blaustein lowered his glass. "When you called you said you were just passing through."

"That wasn't quite honest of me," Whistler said.

"I didn't believe you anyway." Blaustein sat in the spare chair and placed the glass on his right knee. "It didn't smell right to me. And there was the matter of your girl, Rachel. She ended up in a strange bed last night."

"You know everything," Whistler said. He sighed helplessly.

"Just enough to be curious."

"You've guessed enough. It's Watt Sanders. There's a bit of a security problem."

Blaustein stood up and carried his unfinished drink to the table where the bottle was. He put the glass down and whirled to face Whistler. "Maybe you'd better tell me about it," he said.

"As much as I can," Whistler said.

❖ ❖ ❖

At eight, with the darkness almost full, Kane returned to the locker room. It was empty. He retrieved the bundle of his clothes and the pouch from behind the lockers. He dressed in the twill shirt and trousers. He rolled the pouch inside the hunting jacket. That done, he searched the lockers until he found a larger pair of coveralls. After he drew the coveralls on over his clothing, he seemed to be a stouter, heavier man.

Ten minutes later, with the rolled up jacket under his arm, he walked up the stairs and entered the STAFF QUARTERS building where he'd seen Watt Sanders earlier that day.

Sanders' apartment was on the second floor, the back corner one on the west side of the building. Kane tried the door and found it locked. He moved a short distance down the hall to a door marked by a red exit light. He pushed the door open and found that he was on the fire escape landing. The landing dog-legged left before it turned into a straight and narrow stairwell. There was a window above the stairwell. It was about chest high. A lamp burned in the room beyond and enough light spilled into the room so that Kane could see the shape of it. It was the kitchen to Watt Sanders' apartment.

No screens. That was a break. Kane tried the window and found it unlocked. It slid up easily, without a catch. Kane gripped the ledge and pulled himself up. He turned and sat on the ledge. He drew his legs up and swung them into the room. One push and he was past the built-in kitchen sink.

He stood in the center of the kitchen for a long time, listening. No sound in the apartment. He placed the rolled up jacket on the kitchen counter and unwrapped the canvas pouch. He drew out the Sport. Still no sound. He crossed to the doorway and stopped. The door was ajar and he could see that the lighted living room was empty. Beyond that, the bedroom was empty and dark.

He returned to the kitchen table and drew back a chair. He sat down and placed the Sport on the table in front of him. It might be a long night. The waiting had begun. The waiting was a big part of any job. Particularly a hardfist job.

After half an hour, Kane looked in the refrigerator. There was nothing in it except a quart bottle of soda and a half gallon of sour milk.

The Club was packed by nine. In the far corner of the room, on a low bandstand, a three-man combo played old favorites from the 1940's and 1950's.

Watt Sanders paid for his beer and Rachel's whiskey sour. He waited until the waitress moved away before he put his hand under the table and fumbled until it covered Rachel's knee.

"You know," he said, "this is usually my chess night."

"You can play chess *any* night."

"Perhaps tomorrow," he said.

"And perhaps not," she said.

The hand tightened on her knee. Two tables away, Sally Hart and Brenda Temble, girls from the typing pool, looked up from their drinks and waved.

There goes my reputation, Rachel thought. *What I had left.*

At ten-fifteen, Joe Blaustein met Whistler and Burden at the man gate and guided them past the security check. He got into the back of the Agency LTD.

Whistler turned and placed an arm on the back of the seat. "Where is he now?"

"Still at the club ten minutes ago," Blaustein said.

"With Rachel?"

"Yes." There was a sour twist to Blaustein's mouth. "That girl of yours is really earning her money this month."

Whistler didn't comment. He dropped the arm from the seat back and looked out of the side window.

"Straight ahead," Blaustein said to Burden. "Right."

A few minutes of driving and Blaustein reached over the seat and touched Burden on the shoulder. "Pull up here. This is the Club." Burden edged toward the curb and stopped. In the back seat Blaustein moved toward the curbside door and put his hand on the handle. "I have a feeling this isn't kosher."

"It's kosher," Whistler said without turning. "And the buck stops with me, if that's your question."

"It was. I'll see if they're still in the Club."

Burden and Whistler watched him cross the street at a fast walk.

"Odd scruples," Burden said.

Whistler shook his head. "He's ass-saving."

Blaustein returned a couple of minutes later. He got into the back seat. "They left a couple of minutes ago. If it's like last night, they'll be at his apartment."

Burden pulled away from the curb.

Whistler said, "It would have been better if we could have taken him off the street."

"Best laid plans," Blaustein said.

Whistler's mouth tightened into a hard line. It was not a joking matter. Blaustein, for all his good reputation, was a bit of a wise-ass. A bit too much of one.

The key scratched at the lock. Kane stood up and reached the doorway in four long steps. He pivoted when he reached the door frame and let the kitchen wall shield him from the sight-lines in the living room. The lock clicked and the door swung open.

A girl giggled. "Watt, I don't know what you must think of a girl who invites herself to a man's apartment this time of night."

"It's still early." Sanders closed the door behind them. "And as far as the rest of it goes, I can guess."

"Have you got anything to drink? I need another drink."

"Later," Sanders said. "Much later."

Kane heard the click of a switch and the light that beamed toward the kitchen was stronger. The overhead light in the bedroom, Kane guessed.

"You know the way," Sanders said.

"Can't we have one drink before ...?"

"Afterwards."

Still pressed against the wall Kane moved his head just far enough so that one eye cleared the doorway. He watched as Sanders turned the girl and gave her a push toward the bedroom. Legs wide apart, dress hiked up, she sprawled across the bed.

"Don't be so rough," she said, turning.

"I think you like it rough."

Sanders blocked the doorway to the bedroom. Kane watched while he stripped off his jacket and dropped it on the floor. His tie followed and then his shirt. He wore the old-style undershirt. He kicked off black loafers, unbuckled his belt, and dropped his trousers.

"Did anybody ever tell you," Sanders said, "that you've got an ass like a fat boy?"

"Don't talk that way, Watt."

Sanders moved out of the doorway. "How am I supposed to talk."

The girl stood up and reached behind her to find the zipper at the back of her dress.

"That's a girl." Sanders pulled the undershirt over his head and tossed it aside.

The doorbell rang. It was a long, insistent ring.

Sanders said, "Oh, shit, who's that?"

There was another, long ring. Sanders walked in socks and jockey shorts to the door. "Who is it?"

"Blaustein ... security ... I've got to talk to you."

"Tomorrow," Sanders said. "See me tomorrow."

"Tonight," the man beyond the door said.

The girl dropped her hands, the zipper forgotten, and stood in the bedroom doorway. Kane moved his hand down the Sport and flipped the safety off. He turned his head and looked at the kitchen window. It was closed. No way out and even if there was, if this security problem had anything to do with him, there would be other men outside. That was the way it worked.

"God damn." Sanders unlocked the door and jerked it open. Two men stepped through the doorway. One was lean and tanned, with dark hair and a nervous, jerky walk. The other was taller and he held himself erect, with a kind of military carriage.

The man with the dark hair said, "This is Mr. Burden from Washington."

"What's this about, Blaustein?"

Blaustein put an arm on Sanders' shoulder and turned him. "You'd better get dressed."

The girl left the doorway and walked to the center of the living room. Blaustein guided Sanders past her and into the bedroom. He closed the door behind him.

The girl grinned at the tall, erect man, Burden, and said in a low whisper, "Saved from a fate worse than death."

"Didn't want to spoil your fun," Burden said.

"Fun?" The girl laughed. "What now?"

"Whistler's outside. We're taking him to the safe house in Rockville."

"2120 Bridger Road?"

"That's the one," Burden said.

"You need me?"

Burden shook his head. "You stay here for a few minutes after we leave. Then it's back to the routine."

"I never thought that would sound so good."

"All in a day's work," Burden said.

The door to the bedroom opened. Watt Sanders, dressed now and carrying his jacket and tie, stalked into the living room and stopped in front of the girl. "Rachel, I don't know what this is all about. If I'm not back first thing in the morning you…."

Burden said, "Nothing to worry about. You'll be back in time to get a night's sleep."

"Rachel…?"

"Whatever you say, Watt."

That seemed to satisfy Sanders. He nodded and the three of them left, pulling the door closed behind them. The girl returned to the bedroom. She picked up a leather shoulder bag from beside the bed. On the way out of the bedroom, she switched off the overhead light. Back in the living room she placed the shoulder bag on the coffee table and got out a pack of cigarettes and a lighter. While she lit the cigarette, she stared down at her wrist watch.

Kane stepped through the doorway.

One look at him and the girl turned and lunged for the shoulder bag.

Kane lifted the Sport. "You won't make it, Rachel."

Rachel turned slowly to face him. Her smile was shaky. "This has really been my day."

CHAPTER THIRTY NINE

Carl didn't fly North after all.

With one thousand of the eleven thousand dollars that Julio brought from Miami tucked away in his pocket, Carl watched while Zack dropped the money packet in the scuffed bag without counting it.

"Good to do business with you," Zack said.

"You have been patient," Carl said.

"A bit against our will." Zack reached into his pocket and took out the key to the U-Haul truck. He placed it on the desk in front of Carl. "You think your man would like a beer?"

Carl put the key in his pocket. "He might."

Zack nodded at Gibbs. Gibbs left his position beside the door and leaned over the trash can to lift out two Stroh's. After he closed the door behind him, Zack seated himself and leaned back.

"Look," Zack said, "it's none of my business and you can tell me to shove it if you want to. It won't hurt my feelings. It's what I'd say to anybody who messed in my business."

"I don't know what you're talking about."

"The trip north," Zack said, "is a bad move."

"If it was your man instead of mine ..."

"That's not the point."

"What is the point?"

Zack put his elbows on the desk top and ticked them off on his fingers. "You've never seen this guy, Callan. That's one strike against you. You can bet that he's seen you. That's one for him and zero for you. Once you get to Virginia, you'll need a piece.

No way you can carry one up there on the plane. You've got an empty hand unless you know somebody who'll meet you at one of the airports and pass iron to you in the parking lot. I'd make book that Callan's not empty-handed. That's two for him and zero for you."

"You make a good argument," Carl said.

"I'm not done yet. There's a better way, the way I'd do it. My way, it's even up at the worst and at the best you'd have the edge."

"Why tell me this?" Carl asked.

"It's the economic slump." Zack smiled. "You handle yourself right and you might be a customer again."

Zack and his men left in the moving van within the next twenty minutes. It was a long drive back to K. C.

Carl gave Julio two hundred dollars for expenses and started him down the road to Miami.

As soon as the U-Haul was out of sight, he caught a cab to his motel. After a shower and a change of clothes, he packed a gym bag with underwear and shirts. At the bottom of the bag was the battered .38 that had belonged to James. He slept for four hours. The cab he caught in front of the motel dropped him on Harvard next to Jenner Park.

At eleven, Carl entered Kane's house through a window in back. It was the way Zack said he'd handle it and Zack probably knew his business.

He settled in for a wait. A week or a month, it didn't matter.

The security guard at the General Weapons main gate was a young man. That shifted the balance toward Kane. While the flashlight beam was on him, Kane sat up straight and blinked. He was wearing a white sweater he'd taken from Watt Sanders' closet. The scuffed identification badge was pinned to the sweater.

A brief probe at Kane and the light shifted over and lingered on Rachel. It remained on her for a long time, a mark of the man's interest. "A late trip, huh?"

"Just out for a short drive," Rachel said.

The guard swung the light away. "Take care."

Rachel waved and pushed the battered tan VW through the gate. As soon as they were on the road she said, "That was easy."

"It was supposed to be." Kane lifted the Sport from the seat next to his right thigh. "There's one more thing. We can do it the hard way or the easy way."

"What?"

"Change cars."

"By all means," she said, "let's do it the easy way."

Kane stripped off the sweater and tossed it in the back seat. He put on the hunting jacket and closed it over the Sport. Kane directed her into a parking spot at the Virginia Home Motel and took her arm and walked her into the office. He motioned her to a chair. She sat there stiff and pale while he checked with the desk clerk. The letter from Jackson Carter hadn't arrived. Leaning on a hip, turned so that he could watch her, Kane left an address where the letter could be forwarded. It was the P.O. box at the Peachtree Center substation.

A couple of minutes later, they were on the highway headed for Washington.

"You've created a bit of a problem," Kane said.

"I'll get out and walk."

Kane laughed. "I guess you would."

"Gladly," she said.

Kane shook out a cigarette and lit it. "The men who took Sanders away, who were they?"

"Security."

"You too, I guess."

"I suppose you could call me a sleeper."

"Why did they pick up Sanders?"

She hesitated and covered it with a yawn. "We got word there was some background of perversion, something in his past. I can't say I'm surprised."

"And that makes him a risk."

"In a top secret project like this? Of course."

"So why the safe house ...?"

He could feel the shock pass over her. "What?"

"2120 Bridger Road. Don't play dumb with me, Rachel."

"Oh, God." She put her head back and closed her eyes. "You'd better get out the whip and the pliers. Either that or you're talking to yourself from now on."

Kane turned on the radio. He drove the rest of the way to the loud beat of a late night rock and roll station.

Whistler took the cup of coffee Burden brought him from the kitchen. It was harsh and bitter, brewed earlier in the day. Sanders sipped at his and made a face. He put the cup aside.

"I want to know what this is all about."

"It's a security matter," Whistler said. "You've just become high risk."

"Blaustein said ..."

"You see Blaustein around anywhere? You've been passed into other hands."

Sanders looked past Whistler. Burden leaned a shoulder against the open doorway. "You said I'd be back on the compound in time for a good night's sleep."

"Sometimes I lie," Burden said.

"I know my rights," Sanders said, "and I demand ...."

"Tell us how much you like little boys," Whistler said.

The bluster poured out of Sanders. He faltered and looked down at his hands. "I don't know anything about any boys."

"Start with the one in Atlanta," Burden said.

"What was his name?" Whistler looked over his shoulder at Burden. "Timmy, wasn't it?"

"Look, you know so much, you know I was around at the time. That's true. But you also know somebody else did that. He's in prison right now."

"That was a bad rap on him," Whistler said.

"You like fat boys or skinny ones?" Burden said.

Sanders got up from the chair. There was a narrow cot against the wall. He fell back across the cot and stretched out. His hands covered his eyes.

Whistler lifted an eyebrow toward Burden. Burden shrugged. Whistler carried his coffee cup past Burden, into the hallway. He called down the hall. "Eddie."

Edward Mason came out of the kitchen with a half-eaten sandwich in one hand. He was a local operative. He didn't have a lot of experience, but he was big and he was tough. Right for a job like this, keeping a pervert locked down. "Yes, sir?"

Whistler looked at his wrist watch. He nodded at the open door. Burden reached back and drew it closed. There was a slide lock on the outside. Burden slipped it into place.

Whistler walked down the hall until he reached Mason. He dropped his voice. "I'll get you some relief by morning. Until then he's yours."

"He's not going anywhere," Mason said.

"We've put a scare into him. I don't think he'll be any trouble."

"No reason he should be," Mason said.

"I'll be back at noon. Maybe a bit after that."

Mason nodded and bit into his sandwich.

On the drive into Washington, Burden said, "If it's true, and Sanders molested and killed a child, I don't know why we're protecting him from Kane."

"Sanders has unique skills, a special intelligence, that's needed by the government on this crucial project," Whistler said. "That might buy Sanders his life, at least for a time. It's not our decision to make. It's the Pentagon's."

"What about Kane? What will he do now?"

"He'll find Sanders is gone. That ought to be sometime this morning. He'll come back over the wall. He can look all he wants to. I don't think Sanders will be going back to General Weapons to finish out his work."

"So Kane will have to turn the contract back?"

Whistler nodded. "It'll be a first for him."

"The teacher outsmarts the pupil," Burden said.

"It won't be the first time."

※　※　※

The house at 2120 Bridger Road sat alone near the end of the road. There were vacant lots on both sides. It was a two-story Tudor house painted white with gingerbread trim. A flagstone walk curved through the well-kept lawn. Off to the right, in the driveway, was a two year old blue Rambler.

Kane drove past the house twice before he stopped across the street. He turned and studied the house for a time. There was no movement outside and the only lights burning were on the ground floor. The porch was dark.

"I don't like this." he said finally.

"You can drive away."

"No, I can't." He took a deep breath and let it out slowly. "You're going to have to get that door open for me."

"No."

"The hard way or the easy way. I can't leave you here at my back."

"You don't give a person much choice, do you?" she said.

"The same ones I have." He waited.

"I might not know whoever's in there."

"In that case, you've having car trouble." Kane got out. He walked around and opened the door on the passenger side. She got out slowly. He took her arm and turned her.

"What is he to you … this Watt Sanders?"

"Nothing," Kane tightened his hand on her elbow. "No more talking."

They crossed the road and turned up the walkway. He walked on his toes, his footsteps buried under the click of her high heels. They reached the porch. He pushed her forward until she was directly in front of the door.

Kane had the Sport out when he leaned close and whispered, "No games."

He moved to the left of the door and put his back against the wall. A few seconds to still his breath and he pressed the doorbell. Thirty seconds or so passed before the porch light went on. Kane watched her face. He wanted some warning if she decided to signal the man inside.

The inside door swung open. The man said, "Hey, Rachel, I knew I was getting relief, but I didn't know it was going to be this kind of relief." He was laughing when he pushed open the screen door and reached out for her.

Kane leaned out and hit the man in the side of the neck. The man grunted and fell forward. Rachel stepped in to him, her arms up, as if trying to keep him from falling. Kane moved in and pushed her away when he realized that her hands were fumbling for the belly gun in the man's clip holster.

"Stop it, Rachel."

Falling away she aimed a kick for his groin. Kane saw it coming and turned to make most of it on his thigh. The shock ran all the way up to his shoulder. His left hand caught the doorframe. That steadied him. He pointed the Sport at the fallen man.

"Stop it, Rachel."

She stopped. Her breath was loud and rasping against the stillness of the street.

CHAPTER FORTY

After Burden dropped Whistler at his apartment, he circled the nearby area until he found a pay phone. He dialed the Agency number and when the girl answered he said, "This is a hurry call."

Wilson was on the duty desk.

"Burden here. We need a man at the 2120 house by morning."

"I've got Turbeville and Jacobs." Wilson sounded like he'd been sleeping.

Burden thought back over what he knew about the two men. Stan Turbeville was a tall lean southerner from North Carolina. Nate Jacobs was a New York hustler, small, dark and sly. Both men were new to the Agency. "Send Turbeville." It wasn't, after all, a job that called for a lot of quick thinking. Turbeville would be just fine.

It was a gray twilight sleep for Carl. He didn't feel comfortable in this man's house.

Around four a.m., he awoke to the April morning chill in the living room. He found a blanket in the bedroom and brought it back to the sofa. He sat there for a time with the blanket wrapped around his shoulders. The afternoon nap and the time he'd slept on the sofa had spoiled it.

Carl gave up on sleep and prowled the rest of the house. He found the firing range in the basement. There were two loaded

Sports on the counter at the head of the range. He fumbled with them until he flipped the safeties off. He emptied first one pistol and then the other at the full face and profile targets.

His hand shook. He didn't bother to walk down the range to inspect the targets.

He'd never fired at a man. He wasn't even sure that he could.

Kane came out of the bathroom. He had one hand firmly on Rachel's shoulder. In the other hand he carried a wide roll of adhesive tape he'd taken from the medicine cabinet.

The man that Kane knocked down was stirring on the rug. Kane released Rachel and motioned her to a chair across the room. He squatted over the man and turned him so that his head pointed toward Rachel. That way Kane could watch her while he taped the man's hands behind him and ran a few loops around his ankles.

Finished, Kane stood up. "You want this, too, or are you through with the high kicks for the day?"

"I'm through."

He smiled. "Girl Scout's honor?"

"Who was a Girl Scout?"

Kane pointed toward the hallway. "Show me where they're keeping him."

Rachel shook her head. "That's not the deal."

"Then we'll check until we find him."

In the hall, at the foot of the flight of stairs that led to the second floor, she pushed past him and reached the second step before he caught her arm and pulled her back.

"No reason to waste time." He grinned at her. "You've just cut the house in half for me." He pushed her down the hallway ahead of him. He tried two rooms before he found Watt Sanders. The door on the right led to a kitchen. The one past that, on the left, was a book-lined study.

Sanders sat up and swung his short, dwarfed legs over the side of the cot. He'd aged ten years in the last few hours. His eyes were red-rimmed from trying to sleep in the constant light, a light that could only be turned on and off from a switch in the hallway.

"Rachel, what are you doing here?"

Kane arranged two chairs behind the small round table. He motioned Rachel into one of the chairs, the one on his right. He sat in the other one and placed the belly gun and the Sport on the table top. "That's your last question, Watt. The rest of the questions are mine."

"Look," Sanders said, "I've already told those other people that I know my rights and I know…."

"I'm not with them," Kane said.

Confusion marked Sanders' face. "If he's not with them," he said to Rachel, "then who is he?"

"I don't know his name." Rachel looked at Kane. "I think he's here to kill you."

Kane lifted the belly gun and flipped the safety. "I came for some answers."

"I don't have anything to say."

Kane turned the belly gun in his hand. He lifted it, swung it toward Sanders, and squeezed off a round,.

The sound was deafening. Plaster showered the cot from the wall behind Sanders. The acrid smell of burnt powder was strong in the room.

Kane waited. When the shock to his own ear drums had passed he said, "I still want those answers."

Sanders nodded, his head bobbing. "Okay, okay."

Kane placed the belly gun on the table. "Tell me about Tim Goddard."

"I didn't know him that well. He was Ben Carpenter's friend."

"How do you mean, friend?"

"Anyway you want to take it." Sanders spread his hands. "I know how I meant it."

"How was that?"

Sanders shook his head.

"Where were you that Saturday morning?"

"At the library. I spent every Saturday morning at the library."

"Which one?" Kane asked.

A hesitation. "The downtown one."

"Not the one at Highland and Saint Charles?"

Sanders didn't answer.

"I'll tell you how it was. You were on the way to the library on Highland and you stopped by the apartment house. Why? To see if any mail hadn't been forwarded? To return Ben Carpenter's lighter, the one you'd picked up from the table at the Driftwood? Which one, Watt?"

"Neither. Look, you know as well as I do. It came out at the trial. It had to be somebody who had a key to get into the apartment house. I didn't live there anymore."

Kane waited. He stared at Watt Sanders while he dug a cigarette out of his hunting jacket and lit it.

"That's what led me to you," Kane said.

"What?"

"The keys. You still had the keys."

"No, I didn't. I turned them in."

"And there was another boy in Durham, five months or so before you left there. You dumped that one on the Durham-Chapel Hill highway. How many others were there, Watt?"

"None."

"How many altogether, Watt?"

Sanders lowered his head and shook it slowly from side-to-side.

"Only those two, Watt? Or were there three or four or five?" Kane lifted the belly gun and banged the butt on the table top. "Answer me now, or I will start putting bullets in you. I can put in a lot before you die.

Sanders lifted his head. "I ... couldn't help it. It was ... like someone else ... did it."

Kane placed the belly gun on the table and looked at Rachel. There was a pale, sick look on her face.

Down the hall, at the front of the house, a door slammed shut. A man with a hoarse southern voice called out. "Hey, Eddie, where the hell are you?"

Kane turned and reached for the Sport. His hand closed over the butt at the same moment Rachel lunged for him. She landed on his back and rammed him against the side of the table. The table tipped over and the belly gun slid across it and bounced and skidded until it ended up at Watt Sanders' feet.

Sanders picked up the gun, a stunned look on his face, and sprinted out of the room. Kane jerked and pulled at the arms Rachel had wrapped around his neck. It took him a few seconds to shake himself free of her. He dumped her on the floor and ran for the hall.

When he turned down the hall he could see Sanders passing the living room entranceway. He got the door open and pushed at the screened one as Kane lifted the Sport.

He was applying pressure to the trigger when a tall man in a dark raincoat stepped out of the living room and into the line of fire. A Colt Commander was in his raised hand. He fired three times into Sanders' back. The force of the rounds or the thrust of his forward motion threw him beyond the doorway.

The man in the dark raincoat approached the open entrance-way slowly, cautiously. He'd almost reached the doorway when Kane, running behind him, barreled into him and slammed him hard against the wall. The Commander dropped out of the man's hand. He slumped to the floor. Kane stopped long enough to kick the Commander down the hallway. He stepped over the man, ducked low and stepped outside.

Sanders had cleared the hedges that bordered the front edge of the porch. Kane walked down the steps and stood over him. There was a gagging, a choking from Sanders.

Kane leaned over him.

Sanders blinked up at him. Blood ran out of Sanders' nose. His lips moved but no sound came out.

Kane straightened up. He stood over Sanders until he was certain he was dead.

He heard a noise on the porch. He looked up.

Rachel Carson stood to the left of the lighted doorway. The Commander was in her right hand and she'd turned to the side in the firing range stance. Her left hand crossed her body and gripped her right wrist.

"Put your hands on your head," she said.

"No."

"I'll burn you. I swear I will."

Kane pivoted and walked down the lawn toward the road. At the curb, just before he stepped into the street, he looked over his shoulder.

Rachel still stood on the porch. Now the lighted doorway was behind her. The Commander was down at her side, flat against her leg.

Two hours later, after he'd disposed of the Sport and changed from the hunting clothing into the dark gray suit, Kane caught a dawn flight from Dulles to Atlanta.

Kane arrived at Hartsfield a few minutes before eight. He drove to the shopping center and parked in the front row facing the building where Jackson Carter's office was. After he ordered breakfast at a Huddle House a few doors down, he placed a call to Carter at home. He ate breakfast and then returned to the Duster and waited until the black Continental pulled into the space on his left.

Twenty minutes, later they were in the prison ward at Grady.

CHAPTER FORTY ONE

The blinds were drawn in the room. Even in the near darkness, Ben Carpenter's skin seemed as transparent as wrapping plastic. The veins in his face were pale blue, like fresh milk.

Carpenter opened his eyes and blinked at them. "Is it over?"

"It's over," Jackson Carter said. "Early this morning."

"It was Saunders or Sanders or ... whatever his name was?"

"Watt Sanders," Kane said.

"A short man, wide shoulders?"

"That's the one," Kane said.

"How?"

"Shot three times at close range," Kane said.

"Before that ...?" Beads of sweat ran down Carpenter's face and pooled at his neck.

"He admitted it." Kane repeated the exact words Watt Sanders had used.

"Now ..." Ben Carpenter said.

Kane looked toward Jackson Carter. Both men had heard the failing breath, the flutter in his voice.

Carter leaned closer, one hand on the side of the bed. "Yes?"

Carpenter said something to Carter that Kane didn't hear.

Carter leaned away. "I guess that's true."

Out in the parking lot, with all the smells of death behind them, blown away by the warm April wind, Kane asked what it was that Ben Carpenter had said.

"He said he could die now."

The cover-up at 2120 Bridger Road was completed by sunrise. Even protesting, not liking it, Joe Blaustein drove Watt Sanders' Impala from the General Weapons compound. At an agreed upon site, an abandoned service station about halfway between Parker and Washington, Blaustein met the Rambler driven by Edward Mason. As soon as the Impala pulled off the road the Rambler switched on its headlights and pulled away. Blaustein followed the Rambler down a dirt road for two or three miles. It was a deserted road. The two men struggled with Sanders' plastic-wrapped corpse. They carried it around the Impala and dumped it into a ditch.

Mason placed the bloody plastic in the trunk of the Rambler and dropped Blaustein at the main gate of General Weapons.

The search for Watt Sanders would begin later in the day. Blaustein would make sure the body was found. After that, it would be a matter of a state-wide search for the hitchhiker Sanders must have picked up on his way back from Washington.

It was a crime without a solution. Most of the random ones were.

Starting a bit after nine in the morning, two Rockville policemen worked the whole length of Bridger Road. They said they'd had complaints that someone had been exploding some kind of fireworks early in the morning. Two or three people said they vaguely remembered the noises but that they hadn't lasted very long.

Whistler and Burden arrived at 2120 Bridger Road at noon. Rachel Carson and Stan Turbeville were waiting for him in the living room. Edward Mason, who hadn't slept most of the night, was in one of the bedrooms upstairs.

Whistler sat in the stuffed chair across from the sofa. He packed a leather-covered pipe with John Cotton's Mixture. His eyes were level and hard behind the flare of the match as he touched it to the tobacco and formed a small coal in the center of the bowl. Past his right shoulder Fred Burden blocked the doorway.

"Rachel," Whistler finally said, "Burden will talk to you in the study." After the footsteps faded and the study door closed, he took the pipe from his mouth. "Tell me about it, Stan."

"I was sent here by Wilson at Mr. Burden's orders."

Whistler nodded.

"I let myself in with my key."

Whistler looked down at the white ash that topped his pipe.

"I called Eddie. He didn't answer and I looked in the living room. He was face down on the rug, his hands taped behind him, and tape was wrapped around his ankles." Stan Turbeville lifted his right hand and ran it over his forehead. It came away greasy wet. He rubbed it against the thigh of his trousers. "I was checking to see if he was all right. I couldn't tell because he was unconscious. About then, I heard a noise down the hall. I got out my piece and charged it. I was heading for the hall when a man ran by. He was carrying a piece in his right hand. I could see that."

"You call out to him?"

Turbeville hesitated. A long breath hissed between his teeth. "No, I didn't call out."

"Why not?"

"He was armed."

"I see." There was a dry tone in Whistler's voice.

"So I knocked him down."

"How many rounds?"

"Three," Turbeville said.

"And then?"

"Somebody ran up my back and knocked me down."

"And you were out?"

Turbeviile nodded, "Rachel says for about twenty minutes."

Whistler stood up. "Wait here."

"One bad step you made," Burden said. "You brought him here."

"He brought me here," Rachel said. Realization touched her. "I see what you're thinking. Well, you're wrong. Remember the conversation you and I had while Blaustein was in the bedroom with Watt Sanders?"

"I remember."

"That man, whoever he was, heard us from the kitchen."

"But you helped him."

"The hell I did." In short and slashing words she told him about the two times she'd tried to jump the man. "And I've got the lumps and bruises to prove it."

Whistler entered and closed the door behind him. Burden waited until he was seated before he continued.

"And what happened after Turbeviile shot Watt Sanders?"

"Nothing."

"Nothing?"

"I was half-knocked out. By the time I was over that and got to the front door, after I'd stopped to be sure Stan was okay, the man was gone. He'd driven away and there was a body to be taken care of on the front lawn."

Whistler leaned forward and tapped the dottle out of his pipe. "You were in the room when he questioned Sanders?"

"Yes."

"And...?"

"What he admitted, it made me want to throw up. I wanted to blow Sanders away myself."

Whistler nodded and stood up. "Eddie will give you a ride back to the Agency later today. You won't be going back to General Weapons. You'll be given another assignment."

Rachel couldn't help asking. "Who was the man...?"

"The masked man?" Burden laughed. "The one with the silver bullet?"

Whistler didn't smile. "It wouldn't do you any good to know. It might even be dangerous for you."

Burden drove. Whistler sat in the passenger seat next to him.

Burden said, "Anyway we try to cut it, it was our mistake."

"Our fuck-up," Whistler said.

"How do we handle it?"

Whistler stared out at the road. "We ship Stan Turbeville to Jacksonville to replace Foster. We have a few words with Rachel before we assign her to Madrid. She's to forget that Kane had any part in this. Eddie Mason's a dependable type. He'll go along with our story that Watt Sanders overpowered him."

"That's possible."

"It's our afterbirth," Whistler said, "and we've got to eat it."

"Afterbirth?" Burden was puzzled.

"Never had a mama cat?"

"No," Burden said.

"Too bad," Whistler said. "It gives a person a number of good metaphors to play with."

As soon as he entered the house Kane caught the scents. There was a smell of closed-in sweat and the fading scent of burnt gunpowder. He looked straight ahead and saw that the basement door was open.

A Cuban with a webbing of acne scars on his face stood in front of the sofa with a .38 in his outstretched hand. "Close the door behind you, Mr. Callan."

Kane closed the door and waited.

"Bring the bag over here." The Cuban pointed with his other hand at a spot about three feet from the sofa. Kane rounded the end of the sofa and put the ready bag on the rug. "Take off your coat."

Kane slipped off his jacket and dropped it.

"Turn around."

Kane turned and the man patted him down from his armpits to the tops of his shoes. The man grunted and stood up. "Walk away two paces."

Kane took two short paces and pivoted.

The Cuban drew the ready bag toward him and sat on the sofa. He opened the bag with his free hand and, with his eyes still on Kane, dug around in the clothing. After a minute or so, he leaned back and kicked the open bag away from him. The bag stopped about three feet away from him.

"Where is the twenty thousand?"

"I don't have it," Kane said.

"Then you are all I have."

"That's true." Kane stared at the man. "There was Harley a few days ago. You got your pound of bloodmeat there."

"The old man?" A quiver of distaste moved across his face, "It was not a thing I liked."

"Perhaps your man did, the tall one."

"He was a hard man," the Cuban said. "He did not have enough imagination to know what someone else's pain feels like."

"Was?"

"That's why I am here. To take your life for his."

"It's not a good exchange," Kane said. "I roughed your man with a fender or a headlight. I didn't kill him."

"A man lies when he has to."

"Under the gun?" Kane shook his head.

"It was the night they watched your house. Perhaps you forget killings that easily."

"There was a man at the top of the basement steps. He wasn't as tall as your man. I got past him."

"That was the albino."

"I didn't see your man that night."

"If not you ...?" The Cuban looked down at the .38 in his tightened hand. "That would leave only the albino."

"Any reason he'd kill your man?"

"It is a political fact that you isolate a man before you deal with him."

"I don't understand."

"It does not matter." The Cuban stood up. "Step closer. I want to see your face. I want to see if you are lying."

Kane flicked his eyes down toward the ready bag. He wanted it directly in his path. He lifted his head and met the Cuban's eyes. He stepped out firmly. He didn't look down. He meant to kick the bag toward the Cuban. Three steps and he thought he'd missed it completely. Instead he stepped into the bag and tripped and fell into the Cuban.

The Cuban shouted something and tried to lift the .38. Kane slammed an elbow into his throat and felt him fall back onto the sofa. Kane fell on top of him. His left hand grabbed the Cuban's right forearm and slid down it until he gripped the wrist. The Cuban lifted a knee toward him. Kane took it on his thigh. He drew the hand that held the .38 toward him and then slammed it against the front of the sofa armrest. Once, twice, a third time. The hand opened and the .38 fell to the rug.

Kane gave the Cuban a final shove backward and pulled away. He jumped for the .38 and scooped it up and whirled, expecting the Cuban to follow him. The Cuban sat still, eyes very big, one hand clutched at his throat.

It was a few seconds before the man could speak. "Now you can kill me," he said. "That is only fair."

"There's no percentage in that."

"You did not kill James?"

"He was the tall one?" Kane shook his head. "Who are you?"

"It does not matter."

"There's the door."

"I can leave?"

"When you're ready," Kane said.

"I need my bag."

"Get it." Kane followed him to the bedroom. The Cuban picked up the gym bag from beside the bed. Kane followed him to the front door. The man went out without looking back.

From the doorway Kane watched him cross the park. He climbed the steps on the other side and went out of sight down the street that sliced toward the park.

It was early evening, with all the doors and windows open, before the house was fully aired out. A thunderstorm hit around eight. Kane slept to the harsh surge of rain on his windows.

ABOUT THE AUTHOR
AND THIS BOOK

Ralph Dennis was born in 1931 in Sumter, South Carolina, and received a Masters degree from University of North Carolina, where he later taught film and television writing after serving a stint in the Navy. He is best known for his legendary Hardman series of twelve crime novels, which were published in mid-to-late 1970s.

But seven books into Hardman, Ralph walked away from the series to try other things. He wrote a standalone novel called *Atlanta*, intended as an Arthur Hailey-esque potboiler, and *Kane #1* and *Kane #2*, the first two books in what he hoped would become a new series about an assassin.

Kane #1 was released in paperback under the title *Deadman's Game* by Berkley Medallion in 1976. At about the same time, according to Ralph, the editor who championed the book left the company, leaving the *Deadman's Game* without a champion in-house and without the editorial support for a robust marketing campaign. The new editor, eager to make his own mark, rejected the sequel and any hope of a Kane series.

So Ralph went back to Hardman, writing five more books in the series before walking away from it for good. His final published novel, *MacTaggart's War*, was released in 1979 (and has been re-released, with substantial changes, by Brash Books as *The War Heist*)

Ralph died in 1988. In the decades that followed, the Hardman series gained cult status among crime-fiction lovers and *Deadman's Game* became a rare, highly-coveted, and expensive paperback collectible.

In 2018, Lee Goldberg, a #1 *New York Times* bestselling author, acquired the rights to Ralph Dennis' published and unpublished work from the author's estate.

Among Ralph's papers were the original, typewritten manuscripts for *Kane #1* and *Kane #2*, which Lee combined, interweaved, and substantially edited to create this new book.

Made in the USA
Lexington, KY
26 November 2019